Build A Man

Talli Roland

RECENT REVIEWS FOR *BUILD A MAN*

There was nothing I didn't like about *Build A Man*. It had characters I really, really cared for, it had an inspired plot (Talli is a plot genius!), it had warmth and humour and it wasn't all sweetness and light, either . . . I can't recommend it enough.
Chick Lit News and Reviews

Talli's writing is fresh, lively and different. Her words carry you along and her characters make you care what happens to them. . . If you want a book that will make you laugh and make you cry, then this one comes highly recommended.
Bookersatz

Build A Man is fast-paced, well-written chick lit that I can't recommend highly enough. Talli Roland has a sequel to this one coming out titled *Construct A Couple* and I've already added it to my wish list.
The Book Chick

All of Talli's books are funny, romantic and easy to read, and you find yourself constantly turning the pages, becoming involved in the story and wanting to find out more. *Build A Man* is just the same . . . This is a hugely entertaining book, light-hearted yet with hidden messages of self belief, hope and about following dreams.
Kim the Bookworm

Talli Roland is extremely witty as a writer . . . If you have read any of Talli's other books then you already know that you're in for a treat. If not then I recommend that you give *Build A Man* a go. I don't think you will be disappointed!
Dot Scribbles

To all the women who inspired this story — thank you for being you. Or, at least, a surgically enhanced you.

CHAPTER ONE

If I see another set of boobs, I'm going to lose it.

Wrinkled or saggy, those insanely pert fake ones, I don't care – I'm sick of the sight of them. In my six months as receptionist here, I've seen more booty than Russell Brand . . . or maybe even that old Playboy man with the mansion. And that's just in the waiting room! What *is* it about cosmetic surgery clinics that makes women think it's okay to show off body parts normally buttoned under prim little cardigans or swathed in silk scarves?

Even as I think it, old Mrs Lipenstein is lifting her shirt and flashing another patient I call Lizard Lady (she looks like she's moulting), who makes admiring noises then reaches out and–

Oh, God. I grimace and glance away before contact is made. As posh as this seating area is – all leather chairs and low lighting designed to make even shrivelled Lizard Lady look youthful – it should come with an X-rating.

"Mrs Lipenstein?" Peter strides into the room, and Mrs Lipenstein's face tries to smile. Which, with all its Botox, means the corners lift a fraction of an inch.

"What do you think, Doctor?" she asks as she swivels in his direction, practically knocking him off his feet with her chest. "They've come out nicely, haven't they?"

Peter nods, his face carefully neutral. Honestly, I don't know how he does it when he has women shoving their tits in his face day and night. And not just tits – he's worked on butts and he's even performed vaginoplasties, which are . . . well, you don't really want to know, believe me. I've always wondered what doctors are thinking when they're faced with people's nether-regions. I know what I'd be thinking: *gross*.

It should bother me, having my boyfriend examine other women's goods on a regular basis, right? But somehow, it doesn't. Peter's so respectable, so responsible. I can't imagine him going behind my back with someone, let alone a patient.

Mrs Lipenstein trots down the hall behind Peter and the door to the consulting room closes. With Lizard Lady's perfectly sculpted nose jammed in a magazine, I grab the opportunity to creep into the bathroom – loo, whatever. Collapsing on the toilet seat, I jab a limp strand of sandy hair back into my ponytail and slip off my high heels.

God, it's tiring, this receptionist gig. It's not the actual work so much, but having to be nice to snooty women who treat me like a piece of fat squished out of their thigh is beyond draining.

The job was only supposed to be for a month or two, until I found my feet in London and made it big as a reporter in the tabloid world with a job at, I don't know, *Metro* or something. I want to see my byline on the thousands of discarded newspapers each day. I *live* for that moment.

Doesn't seem like much to aspire to, being face down on the floor of the Tube, right? But half a year, thousands of résumés, and several zillion article pitches later, and I'm still working at Transforma Harley Street Clinic, which isn't even on the famous Harley Street, for God's sake – it's on a little mews just off it.

"Hello." A loud knock at the bathroom door interrupts my thoughts. "Hello!"

Rap, rap, rap.

"Hello! Girl!"

Rap! Rap!

It's Lizard Lady; I can tell by her Russian accent. Peering in the mirror, I wipe away an errant trace of make-up underneath my lashes. In the dim light, my grey eyes are black and my round face looks like a luminous moon. Sighing, I slip on my high heels – Peter insists I dress up – then yank open the door.

"Yes?" Jesus, I can't even go to the bathroom in peace around here.

"I need *vat-er*," Lizard Lady says, feigning a pathetic cough.

"Sorry?" I understand her perfectly but I want to make her suffer. Silly idiot, she actually passed the water cooler on her way to the bathroom.

Lizard Lady puts a hand to her throat. "I need VA-TER!" she shouts, her hot lizardy breath hitting my face.

Peter walks by with Mrs Lipenstein in tow. "I think Mrs Markova would like some water, Serenity." He shoots me a look that says he's less than impressed by my attitude. We've been having a lot of those 'attitude' talks lately at home.

"Oh, wa-der!" I say, jacking up my American accent a notch. Smiling sweetly, I trot to the cooler and pour some liquid in a plastic cup, dribbling a bit down the side so Lizard Lady will get her claws wet.

"Here you go." I pass her the water, fascinated by the speckled, crinkly skin on her hands. Maybe she *is* moulting.

Lizard Lady mutters something in Russian that sounds like a sneeze. I scurry behind the reception desk and climb up on the rickety stool. I'd love Peter to buy me a padded one, but I had to beg him just to let me sit down, so I don't see that happening anytime soon. He has this nineteen-fifties notion that a receptionist should always be standing at the ready for an emergency, like administering a shot of Botox to a saggy eyelid or something.

Mrs Lipenstein goes out, still buttoning up her shirt – I'm surprised she's not going to flash her driver – and Peter ushers Lizard Lady into his room.

Alone at last. I click onto my Word document and re-read my latest tabloid pitch.

```
First there were pop-up shops.
Then pop-up restaurants. Now,
there's pop-up Botox, the latest
trend in cosmetic surgery. Forget
running to the doctor's office.
Why not get topped up on the
street corner?
```

Pretty good, right? And true. On Portobello Road last Saturday, I saw a stall with two doctors injecting a line of women with Botox. Street-market surgery: a great story for a tabloid.

"All finished here." Peter's fake jovial-doctor voice drifts down the corridor, and I close the Word window. He's a bit paranoid about me writing anything to do with cosmetic surgery. Apparently having a girlfriend who wants to be a tabloid journalist is bad enough (I keep telling him, though, *Metro* has standards). But when that wannabe journalist works at a clinic where confidentiality is uber-important, well . . . It's ridiculous, I think. All the famous people go to the real Harley Street clinics. We just get the leftover Euro trash and D-list celebs only tabloid-junkies like me recognise.

I glance at the bill Peter's handed me, momentarily stunned by all the zeros. And when I think what that is in dollars!

"That will be two thousand pounds, please," I say, scanning Lizard Lady's face. That's my new game: 'Guess the Procedure', because these women usually don't look much different than when they first came in. Sometimes I wonder how Peter can–

"Girl!" Lizard Lady shoves a fistful of bills at me.

"Thank you," I say calmly, reaching out my arm as far as it will go to grab the money from her hand, which she's barely bothered to extend an inch. I'm tempted to knock her arm so the bills go flying and I'll get to watch her scrabble around on the floor, but Peter's right there so I manage to restrain myself. Barely.

We both watch Lizard Lady leave, then Peter hoists himself onto the reception desk. "Who's next?"

I glance at the schedule, my eyebrows flying up when I see it's a man. I can count on my fingers the number of times a man has walked through that door – so much for equal Botox opportunity.

"A new patient. Jeremy Ritchie."

"Don't forget to have him complete the consultation form," Peter says, sliding off the desk. I bite back a reply that I *always* remember, even though technically, that's not true. But honestly, after being knocked off my feet in the rush to see Mrs George's new knee lift, it's a wonder I even recalled my name that day, let alone silly paperwork.

I settle back onto my stool, just about to check out *Gawker* when the clinic door opens again.

"Hello, welcome to Transforma Harley Street Clinic." I try to 'put a smile in my voice' like Peter insists, but with my half-assed effort it sounds more like I need to burp.

But the guy doesn't seem to notice the burp in my voice. He lumbers into the clinic and bashes his leg on the door, nearly knocking over a phallic-looking bamboo shoot. His face sags, his eyes are red, and sadness hangs off him – along with about twenty extra pounds.

Immediately, I start playing 'Guess the Procedure'. A little liposuction? A little – I lower my eyes to his crotch – *extra endowment*? Looks pretty sizeable already, but men never think they're big enough, do they? And they say women have body issues.

"Hello. I'm here for a consultation," he mumbles.

"For?" I'm not supposed to ask patients, but I'm super curious.

The man lifts his hands and looks at me. "I don't know. For everything, I guess."

"Everything?" Without meaning to, my gaze drops to his crotch again.

His round face colours and he smiles. He isn't bad-looking – late twenties, I'd say, with a decent crop of dark hair and bright green eyes against lovely tanned skin.

"Well." His smile widens to a grin. "Not everything." His voice has a soft lilt to it, different from Peter's crisp accent.

"Come sit down." I motion to the leather chairs. "We'll go through the consultation form together."

It's not normal practice – usually I just give the Botox Wannabes the paperwork, then watch to see if they can actually grip a pen with their talon-like nails. But this guy couldn't be further from our usual clientele if he tried, and there's something about him that makes me want to help.

"So." I give him my best competent-receptionist smile and position the pen over the first question. "Name?"

"Jeremy Ritchie."

I scribble it down with my big, loopy letters that never seem to stay on the line. "Age?"

"Twenty-eight."

"Kind of young for cosmetic surgery, isn't it?" I ask, before I can stop myself. I should know better – we've had women as young as twenty in here for their first bout of Botox. Purely preventative, of course, as Peter would say.

Jeremy shakes his head. "Look at me. I'm a fucking mess." He glances my way. "Sorry, but it's true."

"You're hardly a mess." I have to say that, but honestly he *is* a bit of a mess. Still, he doesn't need surgery to fix that. A new haircut over at the Aveda on Marylebone High Street, some clothes that fit properly, and he'd be fine. And – if he lost that extra twenty pounds or so – quite cute.

Jeremy sighs. "If that's really true, why can't I find a girlfriend? Someone who wants to stick around; who likes *me*?"

I reach out and touch his arm, feeling sorry for the guy. "Maybe if you just exercise?" I bite my lip, hoping I haven't gone too far. Peter's always telling me

Americans are way too direct.

"It's not enough." He shakes his head determinedly. "No. This is it. I mean, I've got the money. I just need the looks. So why not use my money to buy them?"

It's hard to refute his logic, but it just seems . . . wrong. I don't know quite what to say, though, so I carry on with the consultation. "Let's start from the top. Rhinoplasty?"

"Is that the nose?"

I nod.

"Oh, yes. Definitely."

"Blepharoplasty? That's eye bag removal," I explain quickly. No one ever knows that one.

"Yeah."

Half an hour later, we've only made it as far as the neck. My sheet is full of checkmarks, and Jeremy's perking up more and more as we go through it. I can't help noticing the gleam in his gorgeous green eyes.

I've seen this so many times I can almost predict it. It's like when you go to IKEA, and suddenly you realise how much you've been missing; how many wonderful possibilities exist for your home. Before you know it, that horrible blue shopping bag they give you is cutting into your shoulder, filled to the brim with ten thousand tea-lights you'll never use and muffin tins you don't need. This consultation form is IKEA for the face, and women who start off wanting just a squirt of Botox end up like a pin cushion.

"All finished?" Someone clears their throat and we both swing around to see Peter standing in the corridor.

"This is a new patient, Jeremy Ritchie," I say. "Give me five minutes and I'll have his consultation form completed for you, Doctor."

Peter peers over my shoulder at the paperwork, his eyes lighting up when he sees all the checks.

"No, no, that's okay, Serenity." He shakes Jeremy's hand. "Nice to meet you, Jeremy. Come on through. We'll finish your form together."

Jeremy smiles back at me and the pair heads into the consulting room. The door closes behind them and silence descends. I climb up on the stool, kicking off my high heels. Evil things! Nine-thirty and already I can feel a blister forming on my heel.

I click back to *Gawker* and try to focus on Lady Gaga's latest crazy outfit, but Jeremy's face keeps floating through my mind. By the looks of his consultation form, he really *does* want to be a new man. All to make himself more attractive to women? I shake my head. Then again, look what women do to attract men. I've seen it first-hand, courtesy of Mrs Lipenstein's new rack. Talk about turning a cliché on its head. Men, going to extremes to get with women, rather than the other way around. Hmm, might make a good pitch – even better than the Portobello one.

I tap my bare foot against the cold metal rungs of the stool. How many other men out there have had cosmetic surgery? Of course male celebs certainly have. But what about normal men? Men like Jeremy?

My foot taps faster. Jeremy could be a source. I could do an exclusive interview!

I click open a new Word document and start typing.

```
Every day, hundreds of women in
Britain go under the knife,
looking for transformation through
cosmetic surgery. Now, men across
the nation are flocking to
clinics, too.
```

I'm not exactly sure men are 'flocking' to clinics, but it needs to sound dramatic. If the impossible happens and I do get this commission, I'll just throw in some stats from Google. You can find anything on there if you look hard enough.

```
In my article Man Up, I'll
interview a man about to undergo
multiple surgical procedures,
desperate to make himself more
attractive to women.
```

I'm sure Jeremy won't mind if I ask him a couple questions. I quickly type a few more lines, add that I'm a receptionist in a cosmetic surgery clinic for that 'inside scoop' intrigue, then skim it for typos. (I learned the importance of proofreading the hard way: just last month I sent out a pitch on how I could infiltrate Britain's biggest *pubic* relations firm to see if that world really was as sleazy as everyone suspected. It was the one time I actually got a response – the editor at *Snap!* was interested in learning more about *pubic* relations. Was it a new trend? D'oh.)

I scan my email contacts list. Who should I send this to? *The Sun*? Maybe even *Metro*? My heart jumps as I spot the name Leza Larke, the health and beauty editor at *The Daily Planet*, Britain's biggest tabloid.

Do I dare? I've never pitched *The Daily Planet* before – it seemed too far up there, way beyond even my *Metro* aspirations. But I know Leza's interested in cosmetic surgery. Earlier this year she was a judge on *Botox or Bust*, the hit TV show where contestants had to choose between boob jobs or Botox injections, then parade topless in a beauty pageant. This is right up her alley.

Worst she can say is no, right? And even then, my *Metro* dream is still intact. I double-click on her name and hit 'Send', watching as the email flies off.

"Serenity will set you up with an appointment for the injections." Peter's voice drifts toward me as the door to the consulting room opens.

I sit up on the stool and hastily switch the Word window back to the appointment screen. I wonder what Jeremy's decided on? I don't want him to do *too* much, of course; he doesn't really need it. But the more procedures he has, the stronger my article will be. Already I'm picturing Jeremy's dramatic before and after shots, along with a little photo of reporter Serenity Holland inset . . .

"Serenity." Peter's voice jerks me back to reality.

My head snaps up. "Yes?"

"Book Jeremy an appointment for Botox next week, please." Peter turns to Jeremy and claps him on the back. "We'll discuss the other procedures and set a schedule when you're in next. In the meantime, have a look through the patient leaflets and give us a call if you have any questions, all right?"

Jeremy nods. "Thanks, Doctor." He puts a stack of papers on the desk and smiles at me. Already his face looks brighter and more hopeful – and he hasn't even had the Botox yet.

"So what did you decide?" I nod toward the brochures.

"Botox next week, to start off," he says.

I hold my breath. I need more than that to make my story good.

"And then" – he jabs at the bags under his eyes – "I'll get rid of these, have a new nose, and maybe some chin liposuction."

Good, good. "And?" I don't mean to prompt him, but if he really wants to transform himself, he should go all the way, right?

Jeremy looks at me uncertainly.

"I don't know," he says, thumbing through the leaflets. "There's so much information here. Maybe a bit of liposuction on my stomach, too?" He pats his belly. "I've always wanted one of those six-packs. Women like that, don't they?"

"Of course." I mean, not me *personally* – I prefer a bit of a cushion when I rest my head on a man's tummy – but most women love it.

"So definitely that, then." We smile at each other over the desk. "I need to have a think about the other stuff."

I book him into an appointment for Botox next week and say goodbye as he walks out of the clinic. Taking a deep breath, I flash a look at my inbox. Nothing from Leza – yet. But inside, my heart is pumping. I have a good feeling about this. Watch out, tabloid world. I'm on my way.

CHAPTER TWO

"Crikey, what a day. I'm exhausted." Peter comes into the reception area a few hours later, loosening his tie. "Ready to go?"

I nod and shut down the computer after checking my inbox for the millionth time. Still nothing. It's only been three hours, I tell myself. Leza's probably busy getting the lowdown on aging rocker Zip Johnson's hip replacement, this week's hottest story.

"Kirsty and Tim invited us out for a drink. The Prince Regent." I lock the cash drawer and slide down off the stool, looking forward to seeing my best friend from back home in Maine. We'd been joined at the hip since primary school, so when she got a swanky job in London, I was determined to go, too. It was the perfect place for someone with my tabloid ambitions. Along with soccer and cricket, humiliating celebrities is a national sport.

Peter shakes his head. "I'm knackered, Smitty needs to be fed and have his meds, and you know I like to eat promptly at seven. You go on, though."

"Okay, I think I will. Just for a quick one." With all the nerves and excitement juddering around inside me right now, if I don't do something to take my mind off Leza Larke, I'm going to scream. And that something is *not* cooking plain chicken fillet and green leaves for dinner, while our anxiety-prone kitten dines on a trillion-dollar combo of organic pet food and the feline equivalent of Prozac.

My mind drifts back to the first time I met Peter, a few weeks after landing in London. I'd sent out hundreds of résumés to everyone and their dog, desperate for a job to get me started on my new life here; a temporary post before revving up for tabloid stardom. After spotting Peter's advert in *Metro* (where else?), I'd emailed over my rather sparse CV. Shockingly, Peter had rung a few minutes later, and since the clinic was so close to where I'd been crashing at Kirsty's, I'd rushed over for an interview during his lunch break. His receptionist had resigned without notice, he'd said, and he needed someone immediately.

I remember sitting across from Peter, in awe of the perfectly fitting suit and expensive-looking tie. He'd been so pulled together, so efficient and ambitious . . . so different from the bumbling boys back home who smelled of fertiliser, not Hugo Boss. This is the kind of man I want to be with, I'd thought. Funny, I'd never imagined that man actually would be Peter.

We leave the office and head into the little mews, me struggling to keep pace with Peter's giant steps. The shrieking sirens and rumbling buses are music to my ears after the tomb-like quiet of the clinic. God, it's good to be out of there.

"Any news on your writing lark today?" Peter asks as we turn onto New Cavendish Street. I clamp down on the irritation inside. He asks me the same question every day, and he always calls it 'your writing lark', as if he can't seriously believe an English Literature graduate would strive for publication in *Metro*.

"No, no news today," I chirp, trying to sound as upbeat as possible. I learned the hard way not to let Peter know about my pitches: whenever one ended in rejection, he'd pounce with his 'maybe you should think about' speech. As in, maybe you should think about giving up on tabloids and getting a real job, at something respectable like *Rheumatics R Us* or *Beer Matt Collectors of the UK*.

I shudder now just thinking about it. That would be like dying a slow death, and I didn't endure four years of analysing the crap out of Milton *and* travel across the ocean to waste away in a smelly beige office.

We turn onto Marylebone High Street, following our usual route. I love that we can go from office to home in ten minutes, and Marylebone is such a gorgeous place to live, all red-bricked buildings, chi-chi shops, and organic grocers where even the bananas look like they've been polished. Back home in Harris, the veggies are covered with dirt and resemble country bumpkins next to these crown jewels.

Peter bends down to kiss me goodbye as we reach the Prince Regent.

"Sure you don't want to come?" I ask, suddenly wanting to spend time with him outside the clinic. He's so exhausted by the end of the day that we rarely venture beyond the confines of our flat.

Peter shakes his head. "No, thanks. Anyway, *Time Team* is on. Say hello to Kirsty and Tim for me." He lifts a hand and starts striding for home like he can't wait to get there. Which I'm sure he can't, given that Tony Robinson and his rag-tag crew will be digging up a copper coin any minute now. I'll never understand the attraction of a bunch of men pretending to be Indiana Jones in the back fields of Britain.

I open the pub door and stand there for a second, absorbing the clatter and chatter and taking in the happy faces of punters swigging beer. There *is* a world with normal-looking, noisy people who eat solids. I'd almost forgotten it exists.

"Ser!" Kirsty waves to me from the corner where she's draped all over Tim, as usual. Five years together and they still can't keep their hands to themselves. She's twice his size and I can just make out his eyes peeping from behind her oversized earrings and waterfall of crazy caramel curls.

Heading through the throng – the place is heaving even on a Monday – I squeeze into a chair across from them.

"Where's the *old* man?" Kirsty's necklaces clank together as she leans forward to gulp her drink.

"Kirsty!" I hate when she calls Peter that. Okay, Peter's in his early thirties, but that doesn't exactly make him ancient . . . just old-ish. "Peter can't make it. He's busy." Busy with *Time Team*. I don't dare tell her that, or I'd never hear the end of it.

"Too bad," Kirsty says, her tone suggesting anything but. Tim gives her a look, the kind where he draws his eyebrows together and frowns. He's going to get wrinkles if he keeps doing that.

"So how are things in the wonderful world of finance?" I ask, reaching deep into the confines of my plasticky Primark purse where I'm sure I saw some pound coins lurking last week. A glass of wine is calling, but I need at least one more pound . . . got it. One giant House Red coming up.

Tim and Kirsty nod together.

"Pretty good. Kirsty just closed a major deal with Centralna." Tim smiles at her proudly. They both work at some investment bank in the City, Grant-Jonas-

Blythe Investment, Jonas-Blythe-Grant Investment, some combination or other. The two of them graduated at the top of University of Maine's Economics class, and were snapped up by headhunters and settled into the bank's corporate London flat before I'd even collected my diploma. If only everything in my world was so easy.

But I'll make it soon. *I will*. If not Leza Larke, then some editor is sure to love my Jeremy pitch. They'll be so blown away, they'll offer me a job on the spot, and I'll get to work in one of those big glass buildings and dress in trendy gear from TopShop, not these nineteen-fifties styles I have to pull off for the clinic.

"Guess what?" I blurt out. "I've got a great idea for a tabloid story. I think this might be it."

"Oh, yeah?" Kirsty takes a sip of her drink and turns toward me, face neutral. I know she's heard it a million times before, but this really *could* be it.

I quickly explain about Jeremy and all the operations he wants.

"Why would someone do that to themselves?" Kirsty asks.

I shrug. "Who knows? He just said he wanted women to like him. It'll make a great feature."

"And he's agreed to be in the article?" Kirsty drains her drink and leans back.

"Well . . ." My voice trails off and nerves shoot through me. "Not *quite* yet. But I'm sure he will. He wants to meet women, after all, and this will be a good way to get his name out there." I try to sound confident but small doubts gnaw my insides. What if Jeremy says no?

"And Peter's okay with this? I thought he was, like, Captain Privacy or something." She raises her eyebrows at me, and I flush. I know she's recalling the time Peter reamed me out after I regaled her with clinic tales one night over dinner.

"Not exactly," I mumble, tracing a watermark on the table. I glance up, meeting her hazel eyes. "But I'm sure he will be." *I hope.* "Anyway, I'll wait until I hear back from the editor and cross those bridges when I come to them."

Kirsty nods, but I can see by her expression she doesn't believe those bridges will ever need crossing. I know she thinks my tabloid dream is just a fantasy – along with Peter and half the western world. But I'll show her. I'll show everyone.

"I'd better make a move," I say, after chatting (and drinking) for another couple hours. I stand up just as Tim returns to the table with more martinis. The room swings around me and I grip onto the table for support. That wine has gone straight to my head. "I've got to be at work early in the morning."

"Aw, come on." Kirsty waves her martini in the air, sloshing it all over the table. "What do you care? It's just standing behind a desk, right? You could show up tomorrow with half a brain and the Botox Bitches wouldn't even notice."

A jolt of annoyance flashes through me. Yes, it's true I could rock up with minimal brainpower, and those women would tell me how clever I am when I correctly spell their surnames (because W-H-I-T-E is really challenging, don't you know). But I hate that my friends think I'm doing a job a monkey could. I've got to make this tabloid thing happen – soon.

"Naw, I should go." I lean over to kiss her and Tim, say goodbye, then head for the street. The air is fresh, bordering on cold, the way only an early October night can be. I turn right and walk by Paddington Gardens, breathing in the smell of crisp leaves to clear my head.

Autumn always reminds me of the beginning of school – new books, new teachers . . . *potential*. I couldn't wait to be done with university; to leave Maine behind and to experience the real world. I smile up into the light-polluted London sky. So far, I love it. And even though I'm not exactly fulfilling my potential, I'll get there. All it takes is just one yes.

I turn onto our street and fit my key into the door of the red-bricked mansion block. It's taken me a while to absorb the fact that I, Serenity Holland, live *here*. The foyer is all chandeliers and mirrors gilded in gold, and although the lift's a rather rickety contraption, it's carpeted in deep-red fabric with little gold paisleys swimming through it. I blink, and the paisleys stop moving then start up again like sperm. God, I'm drunker than I thought.

Turning my key in the lock, I nudge open the door as quietly as I can. The voice of the BBC announcer – the one whose name I can never remember but always looks like she's got haemorrhoids – floats through the darkened lounge, and I can just make out Peter's silhouette on the sofa. Flickering light from the television reflects on the shiny parquet floor and glints off the polished antique furniture. I catch a glimpse of myself in the glass of an oil painting above the sideboard and grimace, pushing my hair behind my ears to try to look more presentable. Peter isn't a fan of my 'bed head' look.

"Hi!" I say, a bit louder than intended. I throw my keys toward the little dish on the sideboard. They miss and fall onto the floor with a sharp clang. Smitty looks up, annoyed, from his prime position in Peter's lap. I swear that animal gets more quality time with my boyfriend than I do.

"Hey, you're home." Peter's tone is slightly sharp.

"Bit late, isn't it? Remember, there's work tomorrow."

I kick off my high heels, trying not to let the flicker of irritation show on my face. These days more than ever, Peter's quiet and tense after work. I don't blame him; I'm stressed too after dealing with the Botox Bitches, and I don't get anywhere as close to them as he does. Easing Smitty away, I lower myself into the crook of Peter's arm. The heat from his body seeps through my thin coat, warming me up from the autumn chill.

Peter pulls me even closer. I flip on my side and we watch as the BBC woman talks her discomfited way through the war in Afghanistan, onto the Middle East and then through to some disturbed weather patterns in the North. As if that's news.

Ah . . . it's so nice lying here. I snuggle even closer, thinking we should move this on to the bedroom. It's been ages.

Peter grunts. A grunt that sounds suspiciously like a snore.

"Peter!" I turn, scanning his face. Yup, he's snoozing. Guess I should have come home earlier; I know what he's like after ten o'clock. Still, I'm not going to let a little sleepiness stop me. I move my hand down to the inside of his thigh, smiling when I feel his body respond. Oh yes, the doctor is definitely in.

Peter lowers his lips to mine and presses against me, and I let out a contented sigh. I've got a successful man who cares about me, and a great new life in London. Now all I need is the job of my dreams, and everything will be perfect.

Tomorrow, I tell myself as Peter scoops me up and carries me into the bedroom. Just wait until tomorrow.

CHAPTER THREE

"Have you seen my blue tie?" Peter yells from the bedroom the next morning as I jam myself full of Jaffa Cakes in the kitchen. I don't care how early it is, there's no way I'm facing the Botox Bitches on an empty stomach. My tummy is rumbly enough just thinking about whether there's a response from Leza Larke.

"No," I grunt through a mouthful of crumbs, noting with fascination how several float out of my mouth and onto the black marble counter. I grab some kitchen roll and carefully wipe them up. Brits don't like crumbs. Or maybe that's just Peter.

"Serenity. Serenity!"

I sigh and stride into the bedroom. "I don't know where your tie is," I say, lodging the Jaffa Cake in the side of my cheek to avoid spewing more bits.

Peter stops rifling through his closet and turns to face me. "Didn't you take a load of shirts to the dry cleaner's last week? Wasn't my tie in with that?"

Staring up at the ceiling, I strain to remember. Every week seems the same around here, the days seamlessly blending into one giant mushy time sponge. But I sort of remember thinking I'd do something nice and take

Peter's shirts and that tie I spilled wine on (in my defence, it was abnormally splashy wine) to the dry cleaner's around the corner. The guy had given me the tag and told me to come back . . . Monday.

Shit. Monday *last week*. Eight days ago.

"Oh, um . . . they needed extra time to get that wine stain out," I fib. "Sorry I didn't tell you."

Peter's face relaxes. "Oh, okay. I thought you'd forgotten, as usual."

"Of course not," I say, coughing as more crumbs make their way down my throat. As usual? When was the last time I forgot to get the dry cleaning? Oh, right. Pretty much always. A geyser of frustration gushes inside me. Why can't I remember all these pesky domestic details? No matter how hard I try, they always slip my mind.

I make a mental note to pick up the shirts and tie on my way home from work tonight. Peter's got his monthly dinner with all the other cosmeticians (he gets so annoyed when I call them that, but 'cosmetic surgeons' just seems too pompous), so I'll be on my own. I'm planning an exciting evening of takeaway curry. Then I'll use lots of dishes and leave them wherever I want. It will be nice to have a breather from Peter's all-dishes-must-be-washed-as-soon-as-they-touch-the-surface regimen.

I feed Smitty his organic cat food and mushed-up meds, then Peter and I head out the door, into the silent corridor, and down to the street. Just like I do when I leave the clinic, I let the sounds of traffic and the noise of people wash over me, taking in a deep breath of that wonderfully sooty London smell. I love this city. If I breathed in too deeply in Harris, I'd probably get a noseful of *eau de manure*.

We walk at Peter's break-neck pace to the clinic. It's

only eight-thirty and we open at nine, but sometimes the women are pacing around out front just waiting for us. They stare daggers at me like it's *my* fault we're late, even though they're the ones who can't tell time.

What makes it worse is that Peter actually apologises, then tells me to get them coffee, tea, Ex-Lax, and any other mushy food they consume. When we first opened, we actually had biscuits in the waiting room – until Mrs Rhinod, a recovering gastric-band patient, binged and had to be rushed to hospital. Now we have yoghurt.

For once, though, I don't mind being rushed – I'm dying to check my inbox. I flick on the computer, nervously tapping my nails on the desk as it boots up. *Please please please*, I chant, clicking on Outlook and holding my breath. This could be it. The pot of gold at the end of my pitch rainbow.

But . . . I let out my breath. There's nothing. *Nothing.* Not even spam. Disappointment floods into me, and I slump onto the stool. I was so sure this was the pitch that would launch me straight to my dream job.

Maybe everyone's right, I sigh, clicking open the patient schedule. Maybe I should give up, focus on a real career. Join the pasty-faced zombies I see every morning on the street lurching toward the Tube.

I give my head a little shake to clear the depressing thought.

"Dream it, live it," I whisper, repeating my mother's favourite mantra. Whenever I was faced with anything I doubted, Mom would smile, throw back her braids, and repeat those words over and over.

Dream it, live it. I'm not going to give up. All I need is just one foot in the door. If Leza doesn't respond by the end of the day, there's always *Metro.* I try to push down the hard knot of disappointment, heart sinking even more as I spot that the first patient today is none other than the hideous Madame Lucien (or Madame Lucifer, as I like to call her). I'm *so* not in the mood for her antics.

If there's a speck of dust that dares settle on a nearby surface, she sputters like she's going to throw up a lung, rolling her eyes back into her head in a most unattractive way. Peter had to tell her to stop hacking so much or her recent ear-pinning might come loose.

But the funniest thing is, she refuses to acknowledge my existence – even to pay!

She swans in, gets Botoxed to the eyeballs, then walks out without even looking at me. The first time it happened, I chased her into the street, banging on the dark windows of her car. She rolled down the window and – eyes firmly fixed on a spot over my shoulder – told me to take up 'the matter' with her assistant. My jaw nearly hit the ground. Back in Harris, we call that *stealing*.

Still, she can provide a bit of entertainment. I try my best sometimes to hunt down a mega dust-bunny, strategically place it just peeping out from under the sofa, then await the explosion. And I always ask her to pay – loudly, exaggerating my accent – even though she totally blanks me each time. What can I say? It's the little things that get me through the day.

After Madame Lucien, I'll have a bit of a breather, perfect for reading my favourite websites: *Gawker*, *Heat*, *The Daily Planet*, and, of course, *Metro*. If I'm feeling more upmarket I might hit *Hello!* and maybe click onto the *Guardian* and *The New York Times* so I can feel my university degree wasn't in vain.

The door opens and in sweeps Madame Lucien, wearing her ridiculously large dark glasses. She walks right by me and sinks into a chair at the far end of the waiting room. Of course she can't breathe the same air as me.

"Hello, Madame Lucien!" I say, smiling like I've just devoured a whole packet of Jaffa Cakes. The bigger the Botox Bitch, the sweeter I try to be. It's my passive-aggressive way of showing they won't break me.

Madame Lucien lifts her head a fraction of an inch and gives it a little shake, like she's not quite sure where that strange noise is coming from.

I'M OVER HERE! I want to yell.

"I trust you had a pleasant journey?" I say instead, like she's come from Siberia not Mayfair.

No response. God, I do wish I'd tracked down that dust bunny.

"Oh, *bonjour*, Doctor," Madame Lucien says as Peter comes into the reception area. She raises her sunglasses and stands, kissing Peter on both cheeks.

I shake my head at the transformation in her behaviour. Of course she's nice to *him*. Who wouldn't be? He's about to inject acids and paralytic bacteria into her face. I'd be nice to Hannibal Lecter if he was going to do that to me.

"Come, Madame Lucien." Peter takes her arm, escorting her into his room as if she's the Queen. I snort. The Queen of the Botox Bitches, more like.

As I plonk back down on the stool, my eyes flick to my email and I nearly fall over. There's a response. From Leza Larke! My heart almost pounds itself right out of my chest, and the Jaffa Cakes I've eaten for breakfast shift uncomfortably. Part of me wants to let the email sit there, bolded black, and hang on to the possibility that it could be a *yes*. The beginning of my tabloid career, right there in my inbox.

When I can bear it no more, I take a breath and double-click the email.

Interesting. Call me.

I stare at the words, grinning like an idiot. Leza
Larke thinks my pitch is interesting. Leza Larke wants
me to call her!

I breathe in a few more times to steady myself then
creep down the corridor. Peter's door is closed and I
can hear him telling Madame Lucien not to worry if she
can still move her forehead; the Botox may take a while
to set. Based on my experience, it'll be a good ten
minutes or so before she's convinced, so I'm safe to
make my call.

Settling back on the stool, I get out my mobile and
punch in the number in Leza's email signature.

"Leza," a voice barks after one ring.

"Hi, Leza? It's Serenity Holland?" God, I sound like
I'm ten.

"Who?"

"Um, I just sent you a pitch? About the man and
cosmetic surgery . . ." My voice trails off.

"Oh yes. Sounds interesting. Here's what I'm
thinking."

My heart is beating so fast I can barely take in her
bullet-like phrases.

"We're launching a health and beauty website called
Beauty Bits on Friday, and we still need content. I'd like
you to write a column on this man; follow his progress.
A blow-by-blow account of the whole thing."

"Okay!" I squeak. Breathe. *Breathe*.

"I want you to write about more than the surgery
stuff. This man will undergo an all-round
transformation, courtesy of our readers."

"Courtesy of our readers?" I echo, wondering what
she means.

"Yeah. We'll use polls to have them choose what this bloke does to himself. Dress him up in a tux, design his stubble, cut his hair, whatever. They'll select his new body parts, too. We'll let them think that, anyway – don't worry too much about what he actually does; that doesn't matter. It's all about having the readers *feel* like they're in control. We'll call the column *Build a Man*."

"Wow. Great idea." Now I sound like a bleating goat.

"We don't have a budget for freelancers. So you won't be paid. But if your columns get a lot of hits and you can keep up the pace, we *may* consider you for a junior position on staff."

"That's fine. That's awesome! Thank you." I'm practically panting down the phone.

"I'll send you the details; have our online editor get in touch to talk about word count and technical specs. We'll see how the first column goes and take it from there. Get this man to talk about why he wants a makeover, his background and history. Oh, and make sure to get his measurements, too, so we can do a before and after graph. Can you get me the text by Thursday?"

I gulp. It's Tuesday now, and Jeremy won't be in again until next week. Still, I've got his phone number on the client sheet. I'll get him on-board somehow. I've got to. "Yes, that's fine. No problem."

"Great. Oh, and I think it's best if you don't tell him you'll be writing about him," Leza says. 'To let him fully engage with you."

"Um, what do you mean, don't tell him?" I ask tentatively. How can I interview someone without them knowing?

Leza makes an impatient noise. "You know, go undercover. Just say – well, I don't care what you say;

that's your problem. Look, for this column to work, you need him to let down his guard and give you intimate access."

My cheeks flush at 'intimate access' and I nod before realising she can't see me.

"And sometimes, if people find out you're writing about them, they get greedy and ask for cash. We don't *have* cash. You'll need to write under a different name, of course. Keep the clinic confidential, too. The last thing we want is another lawsuit." She hangs up before I can say anything more.

Oh my God. *Oh my God!* I'm going to be a reporter for *The Daily Planet*. I'll have my own column! Okay, it's not print. It's not paid. And since I'll be undercover, I won't have a byline in my own name. But I could eventually.

A thrill of excitement and nerves hits me as I think about going undercover, and an image of me in a cute fedora and trench coat goes through my mind. Serenity Holland, working incognito, to get the inside scoop on surgery . . . and stuff. *Awesome*.

Thank God I won't need to get Jeremy – or Peter – to agree to this. I'm sure they both would have, of course, but I'll keep everything anonymous. If I'm careful, there's no way anyone will be able to identify Peter, Jeremy or the clinic. And 'careful' will be my new middle name. Anything's better than Joy.

Determination floods through me, and I grip onto the desk to steady myself. This is it – the beginning of my dream.

Bring on *Build a Man*.

CHAPTER FOUR

It's six o'clock, and the clinic is empty and silent. Today has been the longest ever, and when your typical workday feels like you've been forced to endure *Schindler's List* a good twenty times, that's really saying something. I'm desperate for a bit of head space to cook up a scheme to meet Jeremy. Every time a second of quiet descended, though, a Botox Bitch walked in, poking at her face like it was damaged goods and demanding to see the doctor.

One woman even had an anxiety attack as she explained how a freckle on her nose caused her husband's affair. As if. I almost told her it's because she's psycho, but I held my tongue. I need this job now for my column.

I hug myself and shiver with glee. My column. I've got a column! *If* I can construct a plausible story to gain 'intimate access' to Jeremy, that is. My cheeks heat up again at the words.

"Ready to head out?" Peter emerges from the consulting room carrying his suit jacket and wearing a crisp white shirt, all ready to meet up with the other cosmeticians.

"You look great," I say. Between working with him and living together, it's easy to forget how handsome he is, in a dignified, 'I'm-a-doctor' sort of way. With his perfectly cut dark hair and strong, even features, he could step right into one of those sitcoms featuring the perfect husband. The thing is, he really *is* the perfect husband – or partner, anyway. I'm the one who's always messing up, forgetting the milk and leaving things lying all over the place. He's so organised and controlled, whereas I, well, I'm a bit of a walking tornado, no matter how hard I try to be otherwise. You'd think after almost six months together, I'd have got more of a grip on myself by now.

I shake my head. Sometimes, I can't believe we're actually *together*. My mind flips back to our first kiss, right here behind the reception desk. Peter had wanted to get a closer look at the skin by my eyes to see how it was aging (yes, so romantic, I know. You don't see that in the movies). I remember the smoothness of his hand as he cupped my chin; his lemony cologne filling my nostrils . . . the warmth of his lips on mine. I'd almost pulled back in shock – this was my boss, after all. I could hardly believe such an accomplished man would be interested in me, Serenity Holland from Harris. But he was, and our kisses progressed to 'making sweet music with our bodies', as Mom would say. Even though our relationship rarely left the confines of the clinic or Peter's flat, I'd been heady with excitement at a burgeoning romance with a posh, successful British man.

When Peter had noticed me looking at flat listings on the internet a few weeks later (I'd already crashed at Kirsty's far longer than I should have), he suggested I move in with him until I found something suitable. I'd jumped at the chance, of course. Moving in seemed so grown-up, and I couldn't get my stuff there quickly enough. It was a *slight* adjustment at first; I think Peter believed I was the same relatively tidy, efficient person outside the clinic as I was inside. Not wanting to burst his bubble, I tried very hard to put everything in its place and contain my inner slob. Anyway, I wanted to be as organised and controlled as Peter. That was what being a real adult was all about, right? Several months later, and I'm still there. Short-term has morphed into permanent.

Peter comes behind the reception desk and pulls me against him. "So, how's the writing lark today?"

I swallow; I was hoping to get him off to dinner without having to answer that. So much excitement is coursing through me, I feel like I'm about to burst. But as much as I'm dying to tell Peter about my potential professional coup – my shot at the big time – it's definitely better if he's in the dark. What he doesn't know won't hurt him.

Peter's always moaning how he's just as experienced as any of those big-name doctors on *Botox or Bust*, so on the teeny, tiny, miniscule chance someone *did* find out, this could only be good for his reputation as a surgeon.

I smile up at him, picturing his grateful, admiring gaze if the details ever did get revealed.

"Thank you, Serenity," he would croon, leaning down to kiss me in front of a packed waiting room, all filled with royalty and B (no, A) list celebs awaiting his expertise. "Thank you for elevating me and my clinic to such heights. I couldn't have done it without you."

"I'd better push off," Peter says now, thankfully not noticing my lack of response. "Got to be at The Ivy in a half hour."

"Have fun," I say, although fun is the last thing anyone could have at The Ivy.

The food is to die for, but the atmosphere is so stiff and formal. Peter took me there once when we first started going out. I dropped a fork, and from the look on the waiter's face, you'd think I'd castrated Prince William.

While Peter fiddles with the lock on the door, I shove Jeremy's file with his phone number into my bag. Outside on the busy street, Peter flags down a cab then kisses me quickly and climbs in.

I hurry down the pavement. I can't wait to be home, have a look over Jeremy's file, then conjure up a plan to meet and start his transformation. Lucky man!

Smitty comes running when I enter the flat, gives me a foul look when he notices Peter's not with me, and stalks off again. God, you'd think the fact that I rescued him from a filthy life in a London skip would entitle me to *something*. But ever since Peter's taken on the cat as his own personal pedigree project – even naming him after Jurgen Schmidt, a German doctor who pioneered eyelash transplant surgery or whatever – Smitty barely deigns to look in my direction.

I grab Jeremy's file and dump my bag on the floor, then plop down on the sofa. Leafing through his consultation form, my eyes pop when I notice Jeremy's ticked almost everything. I can't help looking to see if there's anything related to the penile area. Nothing. Hmm, must mean he *is* fairly well endowed – guess sex isn't the reason he hasn't found someone. For a second, I can't help picturing him in bed, his green eyes staring down into mine . . .

I flip back to the front of the document, tapping my pen against it as I try to come up with a reason to meet. I could say we need more information, but that could be easily solved over the phone – and there's more than enough personal details in front of me.

Anyway, I need something to start a lasting relationship with my subject. Pride shoots through me and I sit up straight. My *subject*. Finally!

How about a special fashion service from the clinic? New clothes to match your new nose? I glance down at my boring outfit. Um, no. Not exactly believable, given my obvious lack of fashion credentials. But maybe something similar; something that would let me into Jeremy's world and justify a bit of prying – all to help him, of course. Maybe . . . a life advisory service? Transforma Life: creating a new life to match the new you.

Yes – that's it. We could do a little fashion, like Leza suggested, but I'd also get the chance to delve into Jeremy's past, work on his personality, and make him into my ideal man. My *readers'* ideal man, that is. This life advisory thing is inspired, if I do say so myself.

To celebrate, I amble over to the kitchen and grab a handful of Jaffa Cakes. Hastily chomping through their orangey goodness, I clear my throat, pick up my cheapo plastic mobile, and call Jeremy's number. As an official reporter now, I really should get one of those fancy iPhones.

"Hello?" Jeremy's voice interrupts all thoughts of a shiny new gadget.

"Hi, Jeremy. It's Serenity Holland, from the clinic." I try to make my voice smooth and professional, but an errant Jaffa crumb makes me sputter. I hold my hand over the phone and cough to dislodge it.

"Oh, yes. Is something wrong? Do you need more information?"

Suddenly I don't want to launch into my Transforma Life sales pitch over the phone. It would be more convincing in person, right?

"Um, yes, actually," I fib, guilt pinging my gut. "It

would be better to meet up. Are you free this evening?"

"Yes, I'm free." Jeremy's voice is glum. "What time should I come by the clinic?"

Oh, shit. "We're having some work done there tonight," I say, wondering where on earth that lie sprang from, "so we've closed early. Can you meet me at Providores on Marylebone High Street?" Providores is my and Kirsty's favourite haunt. They've got great tapas and lots of good wine. That should help Jeremy relax, settle into the idea. "Say, around eight?"

"Sure." He sounds a bit brighter. "See you there soon."

I hang up and throw on a pair of jeans and a T-shirt, exactly what Jeremy was wearing yesterday. It's a mirroring technique Kirsty taught me, way back when I actually thought at least *one* tabloid would call me for an interview. Dress how you think your interviewer will dress; mimic their actions. If they touch their chin, you touch yours. And so on. I draw the line if Jeremy scratches his groin, though.

After pouring some organic food mixed with meds in a bowl for Smitty, I slip on my favourite trainers. It's seven-thirty, and I want to get to Providores before Jeremy. Claim the space, assert my dominance – another tip from Kirsty, that time in relation to blind dating. I went through a blind-dating phase when I first moved to London, in a desperate bid to widen my social circle beyond Kirsty and Tim. After two weeks and five dates – one with a man who turned up lugging an antique bow and a full set of arrows – I discovered the London blind-dating scene is full of lunatics.

Thank God for Peter, I think, shaking my head. Who would have thought I'd end up with a doctor? My last boyfriend worked in a corner store on Main Street – not that there's anything wrong with that, but when your number one ambition is selling last Easter's Cadbury Creme Eggs, it *might* be time to move on. Last I heard, he'd been promoted to night manager.

I race out of the building and down to Marylebone High Street, past the Waitrose where I once spotted Alan Rickman (so hot, even if he does play an evil teacher) and open the door to the cosy confines of Providores. To my surprise, Jeremy's already there, hunched over a magazine, with an almost-empty bottle of wine on the table. He doesn't waste time, does he?

"Hello." I swing into the chair opposite him, knocking the table by accident. The bottle of wine sways back and forth in slow motion before tipping over and spilling its contents into Jeremy's lap.

"Oh my God! I'm so sorry." I stand and pull some tissue from my bag, pressing it down hard on his thighs to try to absorb as much wine as possible.

Well done, I berate myself. Sneaking a look at Jeremy's face, I almost do a double-take when I realise he's smiling. If it was Peter, he'd be ready to kill me right about now.

"It's okay, it's okay." Jeremy takes the tissue from my hand and gently pushes me away from his crotch area. (That's a first.) "Just relax. It'll dry."

"I'm so sorry," I babble. "Do you want me to grab a cloth for you? You should get as much out as you can."

Jeremy shrugs. "Naw. Don't worry. I live around the corner anyway. I'll just throw them in the washing machine as soon as I get home." He motions to the waiter for another bottle. "Come on, sit down. Relax."

I sink carefully into my seat. "You live nearby? Me, too."

"Yeah, I'm just on Welbeck, down the street." Jeremy waves a hand in the air. "Your clinic was so close, I figured I'd give you a try. I'm happy I did." He smiles. "I was really depressed, and you cheered me up. Well, you and the thought of a new nose." He taps his nose as if it's behaved poorly.

I almost say he doesn't need a new nose, but I snap my mouth closed just in time. Who am I to tell someone what they need and what they don't? That will be up to the women of Great Britain when they vote in the poll.

"So." Jeremy pours me a large glug of wine then fills his own glass. "Why did you want to meet?"

I take a mouthful of liquid, swallow, then breathe in. "Okay. Well." I put on the life-affirming, bushy-tailed expression I imagine every life coach employs. "So here's the thing. For a select group of clients, Transforma offers our life advisory service. And I'm thrilled to report that you've been chosen." God, I sound like I've swallowed a whole pharmacy of happy pills.

Jeremy's brow does a cute crinkly thing. "A life advisory service? What's that, exactly?"

"A new life to match the new you," I chirp. "How to dress, how to date, how to turn yourself into the ideal man, both inside and out." I can feel my face turning red as I hold his eyes.

"Serenity, what are you on about?" he asks with a lovely lopsided grin. "I don't need a new life. I just need a new face." He grimaces, as if an unpleasant memory has come to mind.

"Yes, that's a typical response," I say knowingly. "Many patients don't realise it takes *more* than a new appearance to make one happy with oneself. That's why we, at the Transforma Harley Street Clinic, undertake a global approach, helping our clients become the person they've always wanted by working with them on everything from wardrobe to waistline. Because, you know," – I lower my voice dramatically –

"you can't embrace your future without understanding your past." God! Where the hell is all this spewing from? And is that cheesy infomercial voice mine?

"Well, I *could* use some help with my wardrobe, I guess." Jeremy looks down at his wine-stained jeans. "But I don't know about the rest of it. I'd rather forget the past, to be honest." His face twists, and I can't help wondering what he's so keen to forget. I'll find out soon enough – if I can pull this off.

I nod understandingly. "I know. A lot of people feel that way before they start. But it's a very rewarding process, and when it's over I can guarantee you'll be happy with the results." More than happy, actually.

"Anyway, my methods are very relaxed. Some have even called them ground-breaking," I say in a desperate bid to convince him.

"Ground-breaking, huh? What exactly do you do?"

"Well . . ." My mind works frantically. "We start with a complete clothing analysis. What does your wardrobe say about you, your hopes and your dreams? What do you want it to say?" I risk a glance in his direction, and he's nodding slowly. "Then, we move on to, er," – my gaze falls onto the bottle on the table – "wine therapy."

"Wine therapy?" Jeremy raises his eyebrows.

"Yeah, you know. In *vino veritas*." Or whatever that saying is. "It's a method used to ensure complete relaxation, developed by Ziggy, um, Moyles." Christ. I hold my breath that Jeremy's bought it.

"Well, that doesn't sound *so* bad," he says. "Is there an extra fee involved?"

He's going to go for it! "No, no, of course not," I respond. "If you purchase over five thousand pounds of surgery, the life service is complimentary."

"Give me some time to think about it," Jeremy says.

"I hear what you're saying about the past and all. It's just, well, I'm quite a private person. I'm not sure I'm ready to start sharing it, with wine or without."

My heart starts beating faster. How much time will he need? The first column is due in two days. And what if he doesn't agree? "Don't worry. I'll be gentle with you." For some reason, my cheeks heat up.

"You seem too nice to be otherwise." Jeremy's face is reddening, too.

"Why don't we meet back here tomorrow, around six-thirty? You can tell me then." That won't give me much time to pull together the article, but I'll work at the speed of light if I have to. I grab my wine glass and drain it, trying to wash away the tension. I feel like I'm about to keel over from the stress of it all.

"Sure, okay." Jeremy tilts his head to the side. "Where are you from, anyway?"

If I had a dollar for everyone who's asked me that, I'd be a rich woman.

"Maine. It's right across the Atlantic Ocean, just up the coast from Boston." I launch into my standard answer because few Brits ever seem to have heard of my home state. I'm not surprised – there's not a lot going on there.

Jeremy nods. "I know where it is. I haven't been, but I imagine it's beautiful countryside."

Images of trees and lakes flash through my head and for a split second, I feel homesick. Until I remember how I was about to gnaw off my arm with boredom.

"So you're a life advisor and a receptionist? Busy lady."

I wave a hand. "Oh, receptionist. Well, it's a great way to assess clients right from the get-go, you know? You can learn a lot from how people carry themselves when they first walk in. Plus, since our advisory service is only for select clients at the moment, the receptionist position helps top up my salary."

"I hope Dr Lycett knows how lucky he is to have you," Jeremy says.

"Um, yeah, he does." I think. I hope, anyway. For some reason, I don't feel right telling him Peter's my boyfriend.

"Good. He seems a decent bloke. Really professional; thorough." Jeremy gets to his feet, laughing as he looks down at the red splotches decorating the front of his jeans.

"I'm so sorry," I say again. "If you want, I'll pay for dry cleaning."

"Dry cleaning? For jeans?" He looks at me like I'm crazy. I kind of thought it was crazy, too, but Peter gets all his jeans done, so I figured it must be a London thing. Oh God, I must remember to pick up the dry cleaning tonight!

Thank goodness they're open twenty-four hours, a fact that always makes me laugh. Who's going to need a freshly laundered shirt at three in the morning? I love that some shops stay open around the clock here, though. In Harris, you'd be lucky to see a car on the road past ten.

"No, don't worry. I'm good," Jeremy says. "So I'll see you tomorrow."

"See you." I focus on his back as he leaves, sending 'Do it! Do it!' thoughts into his head with all my might. He *has* to agree – how on earth am I going to get access to his life if he doesn't?

"Miss? Anything else?" A waiter hovers over me.

"No," I say, standing. All I really need is to get Jeremy signed up. If he says no tomorrow . . . I'll come up with something. Somehow.

I push through the narrow tables and head into the

street toward the dry cleaner's. It's quiet and dark now, and a fine drizzle is drifting through the air. I scrabble in my pocket for the dry cleaning ticket, then go inside and collect Peter's tie and shirts. Nothin' says lovin' like starched collars.

When I get home, the flat is silent. I peel off my damp clothes, throw on the silk pyjamas Peter bought me (even though he got them a size too small and the inseam likes to wiggle into places where the sun don't shine) then head out to the lounge. Finally, a night when I can watch whatever TV channel I want without having to feign interest in some obscure History Channel documentary.

"Serenity?" Peter sits up on the sofa, yawning and rubbing his eyes, and I jump. I didn't even see him.

"Hi! How was the dinner?" I walk over to him, surreptitiously tugging down my pyjama bottoms.

Peter shakes his head. "Bloody BlackBerry. I got all the way down there, and then I remembered they'd postponed it this month. I'm sure I keyed it in but it didn't come up as rescheduled."

He looks so disturbed that I snuggle up to him and rub his back. It's rare he does something like this; he's so meticulously organised he even has my periods scheduled in his BlackBerry. And I know how much he looks forward to these dinners. He works hard, and he's so tired that he rarely goes out.

"Cup of tea?" I ask, hoping that might make him feel better. Tea seems to be a cure-all this side of the Atlantic.

Peter smiles and squeezes my leg. "That'd be great. Thanks."

He lumbers into the bedroom, and I head to the kitchen and switch on the electric kettle. I put the teabag in the mug, flat against the bottom, then pour the water so it strikes the centre of the bag. After counting to twenty, I remove the bag and splash in a teaspoon of milk. It's Peter's tried and true tea method, perfected over years of practice to result in the ideal cup. And I have to say, it usually does – for him. I like my tea all milky and weak, more along the lines of tea-flavoured water. Peter always jokes Americans never appreciate good tea: just look what they did at the Boston Tea Party.

"Here you go." I hand him the steaming mug after he emerges from the bedroom, all tucked into his robe. He sits back down on the sofa and sips his drink, and I cuddle in next to him.

"Feeling better?" I ask, soaking in the heat from his body.

"Yes, thanks." Peter takes another sip, then makes a face. "Serenity, did you keep the teabag in for twenty seconds, like I showed you? This is way too weak." Sighing, he strides into the kitchen and I hear the sound of liquid pouring down the drain, then the rattle of a spoon against a mug as he makes a new cup. Oh, for God's sake. I *did* keep the stupid teabag in for twenty seconds.

He's probably annoyed about tonight, I tell myself, forcing a smile onto my face as he comes back into the lounge. I know he doesn't mean to be ungrateful for my tea attempt; he's just a perfectionist.

As Peter drinks in silence, I lean against his shoulder and nestle into him even more. Ah, this is nice. The two of us together, the two of us–

With Tony Robinson? I lift my head as Peter cranks up the volume on a rerun of *Time Team*. Gosh,. I might as well cram a Jaffa into my mouth and blow crumbs. I move away, tugging down the inseam again as Smitty takes my place on Peter's lap.

Still, romance is over-rated, right? What matters is that you and your partner are working toward the same goals; that you complement each other's 'life path', as my mother would say. And right now, I can't imagine a couple more on track than Peter and me. Even though he doesn't know my big news, I feel like we're partners; that he and the clinic are helping me reach my dream. All I need now is to get Jeremy on-board, and I'll start my way down the Yellow Brick Road.

I can – I *will* – make this happen.

CHAPTER FIVE

"Morning."

I lift my head to see Peter beside me on the sofa. He's already dressed and by the light streaming through the window, I can tell it's well past my usual rising time. Sitting up, I try to remember why I'm in the lounge – I must have fallen asleep here. I stayed up until late, trying to figure out something extra to entice Jeremy, along with a back-up plan in case he says no. I even ventured onto Peter's state-of-the-art laptop to Google 'life coaching' for some ideas, but all I could find was some mumbo-jumbo about confidence, setting goals, and getting clarity. Well, duh. I could have figured that out. Still, the fact that it's so nebulous gives me leeway to ask probing questions. Maybe with the help of wine therapy. It *could* be a valid method. And if it isn't, it should be.

"Are you all right?" Peter's impatient voice interrupts my thoughts. "I've got a meeting with one of our suppliers this morning. Come on; we need to be out of here in fifteen minutes."

Even Peter's stressy attitude can't bite into my happy place inside – although that silly inseam definitely can. Ugh! I tug down my pyjama bottoms for the umpteenth time. "Give me ten minutes."

Inside the bedroom, I throw on the one clean pair of black trousers I have left and a polyester paisley nightmare of a blouse resembling a reject from Bozo the Clown's costume. There's no time to change between the clinic and meeting Jeremy tonight, but life coaches are supposed to be bright and cheery, right? This blouse certainly meets that criteria.

"I thought since last night was a dud, we might head out for dinner this evening. I've got a voucher for a new restaurant in Mayfair." Peter's voice floats into the room.

Shit. I've been so busy trying to come up with something to convince Jeremy that I haven't even considered how to give Peter the slip tonight. He often stays at the clinic later than me, and as long as I have the chicken fillet good to go at seven when he returns, he never asks what I've been up to. Tonight of all nights he wants to go out for dinner?

"Um . . . !" I call back, my mind racing as I button the blouse. What to say? "It's just" – what's the one thing Peter has no interest in? – "I've got a special seminar tonight on how to write for tabloids. You know, making it big in the industry and such."

As I await his response, an uncomfortable feeling circles around my empty tummy (no time for Jaffa love today, sadly). I know my column isn't going to hurt the clinic – it might even do great things for it – but it feels strange keeping something so big from my boyfriend.

"Come on, Serenity." I can hear Peter's long-suffering sigh from here. "Not tabloids again. If you're really serious, why don't you focus on a real paper? *The Times* or something? Learn the ropes properly, work your way up. Forget about those silly rags."

Instantly my stomach discomfort morphs into irritation. Peter may think tabloids are silly rags, but millions of people read and love them. And why would I 'work my way up' at the boring *Times* when I've got a big break now – without having to pour someone's coffee for five years first?

"Okay, I'm ready." I skid across the parquet toward the door, grabbing my coat from the hooks by the sideboard on the way.

"You're wearing *that*?" Peter eyes my ensemble as if it's about to attack. Given the vibrant colours, I can't say I blame him. A little appreciation for getting ready so quickly might be nice, though. Before I can open my mouth, he heaves another sigh and helps me into my coat. "Come on, then."

Ten minutes later, we're in front of the clinic. Peter unlocks the door, and I scurry behind the desk and boot up the computer. It's only eight-fifteen – plenty of time to get started on my life-coaching questions for Jeremy. Because once he agrees, I'll need to begin the counselling session straight away. My first undercover interview! Then I'll have all night to craft the column before sending it off to Leza tomorrow morning.

God, I haven't the slightest clue exactly what I need to be an effective undercover reporter. I don't want to blow my cover the first time out. What kind of equipment do undercover reporters use? Visions of me taping a wire to my bits – with Jeremy patting me down to make sure I'm 'clean' – filter through my head. Something flutters in my belly at the thought of his hands on me, and I quickly open the internet, telling myself that's the last time I go without breakfast.

I type 'undercover reporting equipment' into Google then lose myself in the pages and pages of options.

Who knew it was such a big industry? There's a beautiful silk scarf wired for digital sound, and just *look* at the gorgeous stilettos with recorders in the heels. I squint at the number onscreen. For . . . £1,895. Yeah, right. Not with the state of my bank account.

Guess I'll have to settle for a good old regular voice recorder. That makes sense, anyway – as a life advisor, I'd have to tape each session to make notes for my files. I'll nip over to Oxford Street, buy the cheapest one possible, then head to Providores to meet with Jeremy. Done.

My eyes nearly fall out of my head when I realise it's quarter to nine and I haven't even started on my interview questions. I click open a Word document and stare at the empty page. If I was a reader, what would I want to know about Jeremy? I'll definitely need to get the dirt on his past; any gory story of despair. Makes sense to ask, too, given this is our initial life advisory session.

First things first – I'll have to get his measurements. I'll say it's for my records, for comparative purposes. Sounds reasonable. Should I bring a measuring tape? My cheeks flush as I imagine Jeremy facing me while I stretch my arms around his chest . . . no. No way am I getting *that* up close and personal. If he doesn't know his dimensions off by heart, he can always email them to me later.

Okay. Question one.

```
Why do you want to be a new man?
```

Boring, yes, but it's a start. A chance to get him warmed up, drink some wine, and maybe gather some background info.

```
2. Why do you think you haven't
found the right woman?
```

Hopefully there's a terrible tale of heartache in there.
And you never know; he could have a hidden
deformity, like that three-nipple man *The Daily Planet*
featured last month. I live in hope.

```
3.
```

Hmm. I've really got to get in there, get the dirt.

```
3. Will being a new man make you
better in bed?
```

Throwing in a bit of sex always captures people's
attention, right? But can I really ask Jeremy that? Yes. I
can. I'm a reporter now. I need to dig.

```
4. Why aren't you getting
everything done?
```

I'll have to cast a meaningful glance down below to
make sure he gets my drift.

There's a banging at the front of the clinic and I
realise I've forgotten to unlock the door. Still five to
nine, though, so it's not like I'm remiss in my duties. I
stare as the door shakes under the force of whoever's
outside pulling it back and forth.

Bang. BANG! The whole wall shudders.

"Jeez, take a chill pill," I mutter, sliding off the stool
and walking – slowly – over to the entrance. Fitting the
key in the lock, I turn it as quietly as possible, then
tiptoe back behind the desk, awaiting the next round of
bangs.

I've just settled onto the stool when Mrs Lipenstein

throws herself against the door and comes crashing into the reception area, almost landing on the desk.

Ha! That should teach her. She tugs down her cardigan and straightens her scarf, throwing me a look like it's my fault she tried to bust inside before nine.

"Good morning," I say pleasantly. "How can I help you?" I almost smirk as I notice one of her varnish-lacquered curls has dislodged itself and is now sticking out over her ear like a wilted antenna.

"Is Dr Lycett free?" she asks, scanning the room as if he's hiding in the corner just waiting for her to find him.

I glance at his appointment schedule. "No, he's booked up until one. He can see you then."

"But I'm here now!" Mrs Lipenstein cries. "Can't I just duck in? I have this terribly itchy . . ."

She starts unbuttoning her cardigan and I jerk my head away before she can pop her crusty nipple out of her sweater. Honestly, I should get trauma pay working here. When it seems safe to look, I turn toward her. Thankfully her breast is still covered, but she's patting it like it's Smitty.

"Um, well, let me just see." I scurry down the corridor to find Peter, happy to get away from the boob stroking. Peter always squeezes in extra patients when he can – it's money and he keeps everyone content. But that means the reception area gets clogged with crazed women demanding they're next in line, and I'm the one who has to referee. Let me tell you, they don't take kindly to being bossed around by some 'youngster from the Colonies'.

One time a fight broke out, plastic nails went flying everywhere, and someone even lost a hairpiece (we found it a month later, under the sofa, when Madame Lucien was having one of her dust bunny fits).

"Peter?" I call softly into the consulting room. He spins around, wearing those horn-rimmed glasses that make him look so smart. "Mrs Lipenstein wants to know if you can see her now."

"Sure, sure," he says. "Send her in."

"You have Mrs Clarke at nine." Mrs Clarke hates waiting and pretends to faint if it's longer than five minutes.

Peter makes an impatient noise. "That's fine."

I head back to reception. "He says to go on through." Sheesh, she's still touching her breast.

Mrs Lipenstein shoots me a look. "Of course he does," she says as she glides by me, like I'm an idiot for having to check first.

I shouldn't let the Botox Bitches get to me, I remind myself, straightening my spine. I'm a reporter now. This clinic – and Jeremy – is my ticket to a better life.

The day passes in its usual trance-like state, with women traipsing in and out like a Botox beauty parade. The only bit of fun was when Madame Lucien threw a tantrum after spotting a lump of cotton wool I'd done up to look like a dust bunny underneath the water cooler. Might seem like a lot of trouble to go through for ten seconds of entertainment, but when you've got nothing better to do and you're faced with hours of uppity women, fashioning a dust bunny from cotton wool isn't so crazy. Plus, it's a welcome distraction from the 'will he, won't he' stalking my mind whenever I think of Jeremy.

Finally, at six o'clock, Peter emerges from the consulting room. His face is pale and his eyes are red. It's been a crazy day – I've barely seen him.

"You off, then?" he asks, loosening his tie.

"Yup." I pat my bag, making sure I've got the interview questions I printed out earlier. I've even put them on a clipboard so I'll look all official and life-advisor-like.

"Have fun." Peter pecks me distractedly on the cheek before wandering off down the hall to his office.

"I will," I mumble to his retreating back. I know I've lied about where I'm really going tonight, but maybe he could show a little interest in my lie? He hasn't even asked where the session is, or what time I'll be back.

I should be thankful he's not too bothered with my movements, I tell myself as I push out the clinic door and hurry toward Oxford Street. It will make working undercover much easier. Still, I can't help feeling a twinge of disappointment that my boyfriend doesn't care more about my out-of-office activities.

After spending twenty pounds I can't afford on the dinkiest digital voice recorder known to man (or woman), I rush back over to Providores. No chance of asserting my dominance this time, either; I can see Jeremy through the window.

"Hello there." My heart starts beating fast as I approach his table and slide into a chair.

"Hi, Serenity." Jeremy smiles at me and I relax a bit. He wouldn't smile so nicely if he was about to say no, right?

There's a moment of awkward silence. "Would you like some wine?" we both ask at the same time, then laugh.

"I've got this," Jeremy says easily, signalling to the waiter. "Red okay?"

I nod as he orders a bottle. "Thanks. So." I almost don't want to ask him, but I've got to get this over with before my head explodes. "Have you given any more thought to the life advisory service?" I hold my breath.

Jeremy looks straight at me. "Yes. I had a think about what you said last night, Serenity. You're right.

The whole point of doing the surgery is to increase my chances of meeting the right woman. If you have other tips to point me in that direction, then . . ."

"You'll do it?" I'm almost afraid to look at him.

Jeremy nods. "I'll do it."

I let out my breath, a smile spreading across my face. Oh, thank *God*. I mean, I knew I'd get him on-board somehow. But now that he's official, I can finally let myself believe I'm a real live undercover reporter.

"That's awesome," I say loudly, pumping my fist in the air before remembering I'm supposed to be a professional. I lower my voice and clasp my hands in front of me. "On behalf of Transforma, I'd like to thank you for your participation."

Jeremy shoots me a grin. "My pleasure, I'm sure. I can't wait to see what you've got in store for me. So how does this work, anyway?"

"Well, I thought today I'd ask a few background questions. You know, try to understand your motivation for the upcoming surgeries." I lean down and rummage around in my bag for the voice recorder, then try to free it from the packaging.

"Is this a wine therapy session?" Jeremy's voice drifts under the table where I'm still fumbling with the plastic, and I can't help noticing it sounds like he's smiling. That's not good – I need him to take me seriously, to really trust and invest in my role as an advisor. Arranging my face in a solemn expression, I sit up quickly, banging my head on the table.

"Ouch!" Rubbing my head, I stare disapprovingly at Jeremy's twitching mouth. "Wine therapy is recognised by the Institute of Life Advisory Services," I say primly. "Of which I am an accredited member."

Jeremy shrugs. "Okay. Well, I'm all for anything involving wine." He pours us both a large glass. "So how do you and Dr Lycett work together on this? Does what I tell you have any bearing on his decision to operate?"

I gulp – I hadn't even thought of Jeremy talking to Peter about these sessions. "Oh, goodness, no," I say smoothly, toying with the stem of the wine glass. "Peter – er, Dr Lycett – and I have found that our patients respond best when we keep their medical treatment separate from the advisory service. That way, they can be as open as they like without fearing any repercussions." My heart is pounding. If Jeremy utters one word to Peter about our meeting, my tabloid career will be over before it's even begun.

"That's all right, then." Jeremy's face sags in relief, and for a second, I wonder what exactly he might say that could affect a doctor's decision to operate. I've never seen Peter turn down a patient for surgery, but Jeremy's worry means he'll keep his mouth shut about our sessions, thank goodness.

"So!" I finally free the recorder from its packaging and place it on the table. "Hope you don't mind if I record our meetings? I'll need the sound files for future reference."

"No, that's fine." Jeremy sips his wine.

"Great, great." I nod approvingly as he swallows. "That's perfect. You should take another wine injection in" – I glance at my watch – "five minutes."

Jeremy raises his eyebrows but he doesn't question my methods.

"Let's get started." Poising the pen over my clipboard, I cross my legs and lean back. "First of all, I need your measurements for my records."

"Sure, no problem. Which measurements?"

Oh, Lord. I don't know what men like to measure. Well, besides the obvious.

I cringe, remembering one of the questions on my clipboard about getting *everything* done. "Um, just the usual, I guess."

Jeremy rattles off a string of numbers that mean nothing to me and I jot them down quickly, nodding like I appreciate their significance. Right, that part's over and done with. On to the good stuff.

"So, Jeremy. Why do you want to be a new man?" I tilt my head to the side and take a sip of wine as I await his answer, grimacing as liquid dribbles out of the corner of my mouth. Note: do not imbibe with tilted head.

"Aren't you going to press record?" Jeremy asks, pointing to the recorder.

"What?" I wipe my mouth quickly. "Oh, yes. Of course." I squint at the metal contraption on the table. How do you record on this thing? Pressing a few buttons, I pray it's working. God, maybe I should have bought that stiletto-recorder, after all. I gulp more wine to calm my nerves, noticing with surprise that my glass is empty.

"Wine therapy dictates the advisor drinks, too," I say, before Jeremy can comment. "To create a relationship of trust. So, why do you want to be a new man?"

"Well . . ." Jeremy gazes out the window, a faraway look coming into his eyes. "Have you ever dreamed of being someone who just snaps their fingers and they get what they want, straight away?"

I think of Kirsty. Um, yeah. "Go on," I say, nodding.

"Women respect those kinds of men. Men who have it all together, with their appearance and life. Who make things happen and don't just sit back and go with the flow."

I nod again, thinking that's exactly what drew me to

Peter. I love that he's so in control. Granted, he might be a bit *too* controlled sometimes, but still.

"Right, right. And you suspect that's why you haven't found your ideal woman yet?"

Jeremy's face twists. "Is five minutes up? I could really use some more wine."

I look at my watch. "Sure, go ahead." He fills his glass – and mine – and raises it in the air. "Cheers! Aren't you going to join me? Building a relationship of trust and all that."

My head already feels a bit fuzzy, but I lift the glass to my lips and sip. "So?" I prompt him.

"Well, I thought I'd found my ideal woman," he says, shaking his head. "Turns out I wasn't her ideal man."

I make a mental note to probe into that later; I don't want to push too much now. "And you think changing your appearance will help?" I smile quickly to cover the sceptical tone in my voice. His appearance is fine, really. And wouldn't he want someone to love him for *him*? It's not my place to judge, though. I'm here to listen.

"Yes. That, and this whole advisory service." Jeremy's smile is hopeful and a pang of guilt shoots through me. Well, I *could* be a life advisor – based on my internet research, there doesn't seem to be much to it. I can still be helpful, qualified or not.

I glance down at my clipboard. The next question on the list is: Will being a new man make you better in bed?

How on earth did I think I could ask that? It was different when I was back in the clinic, focused only on getting the dirt. Now I have an actual person in front of me.

"Time for more wine therapy!" I chirp, taking

another mouthful of liquid for Dutch courage. I squint at the label. Italian courage, in this case.

I stare down at the question then up into Jeremy's expectant eyes. Come on, Serenity. Come on! I need to do this. I'm a reporter now. I must have professional distance from my subject. Thank goodness that wine is making me feel like I'm floating above my body.

"So, um, will being a new man make you better in bed?" My hand slides over my mouth as if of its own accord, and the latter half of the sentence comes out like I have a Jaffa Cake stuck in my cheek.

"What? Sorry, I didn't get that." Jeremy raises his eyebrows in that cute way of his.

Professional distance, I remind myself. I take my hand away and sit up straight in the chair.

"Will being a new man make you better in bed?" I repeat, louder this time. The couple beside us glances over and starts giggling, and Jeremy's cheeks colour up. For a second, I feel bad for embarrassing him, but I steel myself against it.

"Well . . ." Jeremy looks down at the table, then up at me with a mischievous glint in his eye. "I can't say anyone has ever complained."

I keep the smile off my face and move straight on to the next question before I lose my nerve.

"Is that why you're not getting *everything* done?" The words come out smoothly but when I attempt to do the meaningful look at his crotch, I find I can only drop my eyes to belly level. "You're confident with what you've got?"

Jeremy follows my gaze to his midsection. "What? You know I'm getting my stomach done. What do you mean?"

I force my eyes to crotch level. "No, there." I point for extra emphasis, feeling ridiculous.

"Oh!" He shoots me a look as if he can't believe I've just asked him that. I can barely believe it either, but in a strange sort of way, I'm proud of myself. It doesn't matter that I've sucked back half a bottle of wine in the process.

"Well, yeah. I am pretty confident, I guess," he says.

"Great." I glance down at my clipboard, full of scribbles I hope I can decipher later. Thank God for the recorder. "Those are all my questions. See, that was painless, right?"

Jeremy laughs. "Relatively. I think I like wine therapy! Anyway, if you reckon this will help me find someone for real, I'll do whatever it takes. I'm so bloody tired of getting together with someone, thinking this is it, then having them take off."

He leans forward. "What do you think? How do you know if someone is 'the one'?" His eyes meet mine and for a second – for just a split second – I feel like he can see inside me. Like he actually *knows* me. Sounds dumb, I know.

I jerk my mind back to Peter, sipping the last bit of wine as the question echoes in my head. How did I know I wanted to be with Peter?

Well, he does have everything I ever dreamed of: handsome, good job, stable – none of the hippie, live-and-let-live flakiness I grew up with. On paper, he's 'the one' material, for sure. I'm about to answer when I remember my advisory role.

"No, no, no." I wag a playful finger at Jeremy. "We're supposed to be talking about you, not me. Anyway, we're done for tonight," I say to put an end to any more questions.

"Great. So when will we meet up next?" He actually looks excited at the thought.

"Um, well, I'll let you know. Probably later this

week?" *If* Leza likes my column, I add in my head. God, I hope she does.

"Great." Jeremy shoots me an easy smile and gets to his feet, seemingly unaffected by my alcohol-heavy therapeutic methods. When I stand, however, the restaurant sways before me.

We say goodbye and I watch him walk away, the events of the day running through my mind. Jeremy's signed up to my little scheme, I asked the tough questions without flinching (I may have blushed, but I definitely didn't flinch), and everything is going according to plan.

Even a table-induced knock on the head and the beginnings of a red-wine headache can't drag down my spirits as I head for home.

CHAPTER SIX

The clinic is quiet and deserted this morning, so I have just enough time to put the finishing touches on my column. It's due today, and even though Leza didn't specify exactly when she needs it, I want to send her the copy by lunch at the latest. Not only will that show her I can meet deadlines, I can beat them.

My mouth stretches in a giant yawn. I couldn't start working on my article until Peter went to bed, so I was up until all hours, reviewing the sound files and trying to craft a perfect article of around five hundred words to meet the contributors' guidelines the online editor emailed through.

It's a solid piece of writing, if I do say so myself. I tweak a few words here and there, spell check for the zillionth time, then take a deep breath and email it to Leza.

I drift into a daydream where she emails me back, thanking me for my wonderful contribution and offering me a job at the paper. You deserve to be in print, she says, handing me a juicy contract to sign . . .

My head jerks up as I nearly slide off the stool. I open my eyes wide, trying to stay alert. Honestly, as much as I hate the Botox Bitches, sometimes the dead times here are the worst. I tried to convince Peter to let me play the radio or Hotel Costes; something funky to keep me awake. Instead, he came back from the Pound Shop with wailing whales and chirpy birds. I much prefer silence to the sounds of animals getting it on.

Shaking my head to clear the fog, I glance up at the clock. Thank goodness it's finally eleven – now I can call Mom and Dad and fill them in on the good news. It's only six in the morning in Maine, but my parents get up super early for their 'greet the sun' ritual, or whatever they call it. I swear, the older they get, the more hippie they become.

When I first told them I wanted to move to London to pursue my reporting dreams (I didn't mention the word 'tabloid'; to them it's worse than capitalism), they were behind me one hundred percent, chattering on about all the great socialist papers I could work for.

But as time marched on and no such jobs materialised, their enthusiasm waned. Just last week, Mom asked if I'd think about coming home. But now I can confirm Mom's 'dream it, live it' mantra works in foreign environments, too.

I'll keep the undercover bit to myself, though. There's no need for them to know all the little details, and Mom's always said that if you feel the need to do something in secret, you probably shouldn't be doing it at all.

Obviously that doesn't apply to undercover reporting, but I don't feel like having to explain.

"Hello?" Mom's calm voice comes through the receiver, and I can't help smiling already, just imagining her joyous reaction.

"Hi, Mom." I tap my foot against the chair, bursting with my news.

"Serenity! Hi, honey. Let me get Dad on the line. He's just out back." She puts down the phone and I hear her bellowing for my father.

There's a click as he picks up the extension they installed recently in their hydroponic greenhouse. Since they've only just managed to get the hang of an answering machine, a mobile is a step too far. "Lesley, these plants need more solar power. I thought you turned it up yesterday."

Mom sighs. "Dear, Serenity's on the phone."

"Oh, Serenity. Still saving the world, one cosmetic surgery at a time?" Dad's tone is light, but I know how he really feels about my place of employment: 'a cauldron of all that's wrong with the modern world', or something along those lines.

Good thing I never told them I was shacking up with the head warlock. Not that they'd mind the living together bit – they're all for free love – but in their view of the world, Peter is the living, breathing definition of 'the man'.

"Well, actually, guess what? I'm going to be a reporter. I got a job!" I catch sight of my face in the mirror. I'm grinning like an idiot, but I don't care.

"Oh!" Mom lets out an excited squeak. "I knew it would happen, Serenity. Dream it, live it – that's all you needed to do. What's the name of the paper?'

"Um . . ." I pause, wondering if I should tell them. As happy as they might be about my job, they definitely won't be thrilled it's a tabloid.

My mind flashes to the moment Mom caught me reading *Teen People*, right after Clarissa Dixon teased me mercilessly in front of the whole sixth grade when she discovered I'd never heard of Oprah. (What can I say? We had no TV.) With a look of sorrow and disappointment as if her beloved tomatoes had dry rot,

Mom had sat me down, taken my hand, and explained in her soft voice that today's society is shallow and vacant, and we should look inside ourselves for validation. I had no idea what she was talking about then, and even now I'm not sure.

Mom and Dad won't know *The Daily Planet* is a tabloid, though. They wouldn't recognise one if it walked up to them and introduced itself. Heck, until I saved enough for a TV in my room (no way would anyone accuse me of being a freak ever again), the only bit of pop culture in our house was an ancient, scratched record by John Lennon.

"It's called *The Daily Planet*," I say finally, grateful for once for the distance between us. They'll never be able to find out what it really is.

"*The Daily Planet*," Mom repeats in a reverential tone.

"What's the paper's political leanings?" Dad asks.

"Um . . . socialist." *The Daily Planet* is sort of socialist, isn't it? It's about society and all. "But my column's not going to be in the paper itself," I add, before they ask me to send a thousand copies. "It'll be on a website." Thank goodness my parents don't own a computer.

"That's just groovy," Dad says. I cringe at his use of the word – no matter how many times I tell him it's a cliché, he won't stop saying it. "Your mother and I are so happy you're doing your part for the cause."

"Yeah," I respond weakly, hoping they don't find out exactly what part I'm playing.

Peter walks by the desk, grimacing when he spots me on the phone. My heart starts thumping and I cast a sidelong glance to see if he's overheard anything. His nose is buried in a patient file, and he doesn't even turn my way. God, I've got to remember to be careful.

"I should go," I say, using Peter as an excuse to hang

up before my parents ask for more details. I tell them I'll call later, and say goodbye. Somehow, all my excitement at sharing the big news has faded away.

Sighing, I turn back to the computer. They *will* be proud of me, once I really make it big. And maybe then, I can even write a few articles on homeless people or . . . whatever the burning social issues of the day are here in London. Strange – I can name almost all the members of the British Royal Family and Elton John's pet dogs, but I have no idea what challenges face the nation's citizens.

At least Kirsty knows what a massive break this is for me, landing a column on a tabloid's website – unpaid or not. She'll understand I need to do whatever it takes to make it happen. I'm dying to call her, but this kind of thing demands a face-to-face, and I can't risk Peter walking by again. He wants to watch some TV programme tonight about a king who had eight wives, so instead of hanging around feeling bored and drinking too much wine, I'll head over to her house.

I've just slurped down my tasty lunch of Pot Noodles when my email pings. My heart jumps when I spot Leza Larke's name in the inbox.

I click on the message.

```
Come see me this afternoon. I'm
free at one.
```

Shit. SHIT! What does this mean? She hates my column? I'm through before I've begun? Or she loves it and my dream is about to come true? My eyes flick to the signature of her email. Her office is all the way over in Notting Hill Gate. There's no question – I need to get there. But how can I leave here?

I glance at the appointment schedule. There's a

patient at one for Botox, and another at one-thirty for hyaluronic acid injections, then no one again until three. Peter can handle it, I'm sure. I just need to come up with a plausible excuse. I could say . . . I have cramps? But no, Peter knows I'm nowhere near my period. Stupid BlackBerry.

The only thing I can think of is Smitty. If I say I forgot to feed him – or even worse, I neglected to mix his anti-anxiety medication into his stinky food – Peter *might* let me leave. Then, once I'm free, I can make up something about why it took me so long to get back here. I press my fingers to my temples to try to ease the pounding. All this subterfuge is doing my head in – either that or it's the wine from last night.

Sliding off the stool, I walk down the corridor to Peter's office. "Peter? Can I talk to you?"

"Sure." He points to the chair across from his desk. For a second I almost feel like a patient.

"I'm really sorry. I just remembered I forgot to feed Smitty his medication."

Peter's head snaps up from the computer screen. "You *what*? Serenity, it's almost half past twelve now! You were supposed to give him the meds hours ago. This could have a severe impact on his mental condition and the dosage level in his system."

"I know," I respond gravely, but I can't help wondering what planet Peter's on. Smitty is a *cat*, not a psychiatric patient. Back home, our cats were lucky if they got de-wormed, let alone fed Prozac. "I feel terrible."

"Well, you'd better get back home. I can handle reception until you return." Peter turns to the computer, dismissing me.

"There are only a couple appointments anyway." Relief at my easy getaway floods through me as I back toward the open doorway. "Just check the schedule, and go out to reception to collect the women when it's time."

"Fine, fine." Peter waves one hand in the air and clicks the mouse with the other. "It's hardly rocket science, is it?"

Irritation sweeps over me as I rush out front. I'd love to tell Peter I'm on my way to bigger and better things, but I squash down the desire. Peter wouldn't think a tabloid is a 'better thing', anyway.

I scribble down the address of *The Daily Planet*, then push out of the clinic without a backward glance. Time to meet the maker or breaker of my dreams.

One hot and sweaty Tube ride later – I'm always amazed how many people are on the Tube during the day; don't they have jobs to go to? – I emerge, blinking into the light of Notting Hill Gate. A chip wrapper swirls into the air and smacks into my face. I push it away, hoping I don't have the remains of chips in my hair. I like salt 'n' vinegar as much as the next girl (possibly more), but it's not the kind of look I want when I first meet Leza.

All the way down the Central Line, I rehearsed scenarios in my head. Now that I'm here, though, my brain has gone into fuzzy-TV-screen mode. I wipe my sweaty palms on my skirt, praying the clamminess doesn't have time to seep back again before I shake hands. Or will I even shake hands? Maybe I should kiss; that's what all the media people do, right? One cheek or two? My heart starts pounding again.

Ah, here it is. I stop in front of a modern glass and steel building, exactly what I envisioned in my tabloid dreams. Tugging open the door, I walk into the light and airy reception area. Modern art lines the walls – the kind that makes me feel dumb because I just can't see how it's art – and water cascades silently behind the reception.

"Hi!" I say to a perfectly groomed man, my voice echoing around the foyer. "I'm here to see Leza Larke. I have an appointment at one." Gosh, I sound so official, don't I? A real journalist, meeting with one of London's top editors.

"Here." The man slaps a crimson 'Visitor' sticker on the counter. "Fill this out. Leza's on the fifth floor. I'll tell her you're on the way."

"Great, thanks." I scrawl my name then fix the badge on the waistband of my skirt, attempting to minimise its impact. Striding over to the lift, I do a few deep-breathing exercises to try to 'feel my core', just like I saw on late-night TV. But my core feels kind of queasy and the more in touch with it I am, the worse I feel.

Fifth floor. I wipe my hands on my skirt – again – as the lift doors open.

My jaw drops. In front of me is the office of my dreams, like something out of *Ugly Betty*, only better. In the middle of the floor, lime-green couches form a cosy circle where people sit, chatting and working. Chocolate-coloured bamboo work-pods dot the floor. Inside each, Macs glisten and comfy-looking chairs nestle against steel desks. Off in the corner there's a full-on bar, with hundreds of bottles shining behind backlit glass. Chattering plasma-screen TVs – tuned into the all-news networks, including my favourite from back home, *E!* – fill the space with sound.

I stand there for a moment, watching people dash back and forth between the pods. A rail-thin woman with long red hair swoops by, wearing a leather skirt and a futuristic top straight off the runway. A longing like I've never known sweeps through me, almost taking away my breath with its intensity. I'd give anything to work here. *Anything.*

"Serenity?" A loud voice breaks into my thoughts, and I turn.

"Hi, Leza." I recognise her from *Botox or Bust*, even though she looks like she's sloughed off ten years since then. Instantly I know she's had the new cosmetic procedure Peter's been talking about, using hyaluronic acid to plump up the cheeks. Her blonde hair is even blonder – almost white – and the make-up plastered over her broad features is so heavy it would give Katie Price a run for her money.

I stick out my hand, but Leza turns away before she sees it. I let it drop to my side, feeling my face flame up again. Maybe I should have gone for the cheek, after all.

"Come with me." Leza beckons me to follow as she weaves between the pods. God, I had no idea she was so . . . big. They always had her sitting down on *Botox or Bust*. I'm small, yes, but she'd tower over even Peter, and with her heavy-set frame I'm sure she could take him down, no problem.

We enter a narrow conference room with leopard-print seats and Leza closes the door, fixing me with eyes so blue it can only be down to contacts. She slides into a chair across from me, retrieves a piece of paper from the folder she's carrying, and thumps it on the table.

"What the fuck is this?"

I stare, my mouth dropping open. Is this some kind of tabloid test? Guess the size of the paper? Looks like A4 to me . . . I stretch out my hand and turn it over. Oh.

"It's my column," I say slowly, the words on the page swimming before my eyes. I look up at her thunderous expression. *Shit.*

"Yeah." Leza fishes inside her shirt like she's searching for buried treasure, then hauls up a thick black bra-strap. It snaps against her shoulder but she doesn't even flinch. "It's your column. And most of it is fucking useless. If I wanted a feelgood feature, I'd have hired a fucking Buddhist to write the story!"

Her strident words echo around the small room.

"I want to know the pain this man's feeling. The *agony* that's driving him to get all these operations. You've made him look like a little fluffy bunny all hippity-hoppy happy, off to get surgery for a brand new life." Her mouth twists in disgust.

"Have you ever heard 'if it bleeds, it leads'?" she asks me.

I shake my head.

"It's what we live by here. Put the suffering, the blood and the guts right up front. It's what people really want to see." She stares at me with her flinty eyes. "Now, do I need to get an intern to rewrite this, or can you do it?"

An intern! "No, no, I'll do it," I babble. "If it bleeds, it leads. Got it." I'll bang it into my head if I need to.

"Good. Have it to me in an hour." She pushes back her chair and strides out.

I stare at the paper in front of me. Oh, Jesus. For a second, I feel paralysed. Can I do this? *Can* I be a tabloid journalist?

I take a deep breath. I can. Of course I can. Remember, if it bleeds, it leads. The juicier, the better. I knew that, of course I did. It's just, I thought what I'd written *was* juicy. But I'm in the big leagues now. And if I want to stay here . . .

I take out a pen and make a big red slash across my article. Then I start the task of transforming Jeremy – or James, as I've called him in the column – into a modern-day Heathcliff, all tortured and tormented, and just . . . ugly. I feel weird about that since Jeremy's really not bad-looking, but it's not like people will know it's *him* I'm talking about. Writing about James is almost like writing about a character I'm creating, and for a second I almost forget he actually is Jeremy.

An hour later, I push out of the conference room and over to Leza's pod.

"Here." I hand her the finished copy and my heart starts thumping again. I think I've done it – I've certainly upped the drama and the anguish – but did I go far enough? For a second, I want my article back again, to make Jeremy even more pathetic.

But Leza's blood-red lips are curving into a smile. "Now *this* is what I'm talking about. Good girl."

Relief washes over me. Thank God.

"We'll post it tomorrow for the launch. Have you given any thought to your first poll?" she asks. "I'm thinking the nose."

"Poll?" I echo, before remembering she wants to run a poll alongside my column to have readers choose Jeremy's new bits. "Um, yes. Nose, for sure."

Leza turns toward me, tossing back her platinum hair. "You know, I'm impressed. Most first-time writers here whinge and whine about integrity, blah blah blah. But you got on board, fast. I like your writing; I like how you've gone straight for the jugular after I told you what's what. You could have a future here, after all."

"That's great!" Happiness gushes through me. I knew I could do it. I *knew* this could be the start of my career. I push aside the finger of doubt jabbing my gut – the thing Leza mentioned about integrity. But that doesn't apply to me, right? I'm not hurting anyone.

"If things go well with the column, we might even

consider upping its frequency." She thrusts a pointy red fingernail at me. "Just don't get all wussy. Remember–"

"If it bleeds, it leads," I finish for her, grinning.

Leza grins back, showing off her bleached teeth in all their glory. "Exactly, Serenity. Exactly."

Thirty minutes later, I pull open the door of the clinic, my chest heaving up and down with the effort of sprinting from the Tube. It's almost three-thirty, and I've been gone much longer than the few minutes it would take to medicate Smitty. On the way home, I developed a story: Smitty was distressed, and I couldn't leave again until he calmed down. God knows how a cat in distress behaves, but hopefully it will get me out of trouble.

Thankfully the waiting area is empty, but I hear the low rumble of Peter's voice and a high-pitched squeaky one coming from the consulting room, so I'm assuming Peter's with either a client or a chipmunk. I head behind the desk, eyeing the sharpened pencils and neatly capped pens. Even the envelopes are perfectly piled, edges aligned. Guess it wasn't too busy here, then.

Sinking onto the stool, I let out a big sigh. Every muscle in my body feels like after Kirsty and I did a session on the Power Plate: shaken, stirred, and drained. Thank God I'm on Leza's good side now, that she loved my column in the end, and that it will be posted tomorrow. Determination grips me again as images of the funky lime-green and bamboo office flash through my head. God, I want to work there.

Peter walks into the reception, a haughty woman trotting on stilettos behind him. I can't help smirking at the two stripes of blonde and black dyed into her fringe. She *does* resemble a chipmunk.

"Oh, hello. You're back," he says, with a pointed look at the clock above the desk.

"Sorry, Doctor, it took longer than I thought." I drop my head to hide my annoyance. He's acting like I'm an errant schoolchild returning late from my lunch hour.

"Thank you, Doctor." Chipmunk puts a hand on his arm, smiling as much as her frozen face will allow. "You're a genius. And so lovely, too."

Ugh. I roll my eyes as Peter bids her goodbye and tells her not to worry; that a bit of swelling and tightness is normal post bum-lift. I almost gag just hearing about her butt.

"So." Peter turns to face me once Chipmunk and her swollen bottom have scurried off. "What on earth took you so long?"

"Oh, Smitty was acting weird. I didn't want to leave until he was resting comfortably." Somehow I manage to refrain from rolling my eyes again.

"Is he okay? You know we have that special animal-care hotline you can ring." Peter looks at me anxiously. "Maybe you should go back and make sure he's all right. I can handle the rest of the day here."

"He's fine, Peter," I say, a bit more curtly than intended. Peter wouldn't let me go home last month when I was ready to upchuck my Jaffas, but one hint of something ailing our kitty and he's ready to shove me into the street?

I stretch out my fingers, trying to relax as Peter returns to his office. I'm just stressed after my session with Leza, that's all – no way am I jealous of a *cat*. But even as I think it, I can't help wishing Peter would show an ounce of that same emotion toward me.

CHAPTER SEVEN

Peter and Smitty (now fully recovered from his earlier 'trauma', according to the doctor of the house) are ensconced in front of the *Fat King with Eight Wives* or whatever it's called, so after pillaging Peter's champagne collection, I head over to Kirsty and Tim's to tell them my news. They live in an Edwardian terraced house, just off Baker Street and right next to Regent's Park. On a good day (without high heels), I can be there in ten minutes.

The autumn air is crisp and I turn my face toward the early-evening sun, breathing in the scent of old leaves. The smell reminds me of home, when I used to help Mom rake the leaves from the two massive maple trees in our front yard. Closing my eyes, for just a second I can almost believe I'm back in Maine. But when I open them again, the beautiful buildings neatly lining the street and the red double-decker buses flashing by couldn't be further from the quiet peace of our old clapboard farmhouse.

I smile, shaking my head. I'm actually here, in London. And I'm on my way!

Be there in five, I text Kirsty, half-listening for the

ping of her return text requesting her usual mammoth-sized bag of roasted cashews. But my phone is silent and I quicken my step, bursting to tell her my news. Kirsty's the one person I know will give me a guaranteed thumbs up. I ring the buzzer, smiling already as I hear someone thumping toward the door.

"Ser!" Kirsty's eyebrows fly up when she spots me. Her raspy voice is even raspier than normal, and her face is flushed. "I forgot you were coming by." Flashing me a grin that doesn't quite reach her eyes, she ushers me inside.

"Oh, yeah?" That's surprising. Kirsty's mind is like a Venus Flytrap – nothing ever escapes it. I follow her through to the living room. They've polished the floorboards since I've last been here, and a gorgeous new sofa is positioned in front of the fireplace. Tim's sitting in an armchair, resting his feet on a funky wood and metal table. It always amazes me how they make everything look so fabulous yet cosy and warm at the same time.

"Hey, Serenity." Tim's face is glowing like he's just had an ionic skin scrub.

Sinking onto a comfy leather sofa, I pull the champagne from my bag. I'm just about to open my mouth when Kirsty bursts out: "We've got news!"

I force back my words. I'll tell them after, and then we can have a dual celebration. If their news is good, of course. Judging by the strange look in Kirsty's eyes, I'm not sure what to think.

Has Tim finally got up the nerve to propose? According to Kirsty's Master Life Plan Excel spreadsheet (sad but true), the ideal proposal would take place between the ages of twenty-three and twenty-four, leaving a few years for dedicated marriage time before conceiving a baby at age twenty-six or twenty-seven. Since everything else in Kirsty's life has gone according to schedule, I can't see why this shouldn't, either.

I smile dreamily at the two of them, already picturing Kirsty in a creamy silk wedding gown with Tim handsome in tails, and maybe even a horse-drawn carriage . . . not that Kirsty's the romantic type, really. She'd be happy to do the deed down at City Hall to be more time-efficient.

"Ser?" Kirsty's voice snaps me back to reality.

"So what's the news, then? Don't leave me in suspense." My eyes dart back and forth from Tim to Kirsty.

Tim clears his throat. "Kirsty and I are getting married," he announces, his voice full of pride.

"Oh my God." I stand and pull Kirsty into a hug, leaning back slightly when I notice her lukewarm response. "That's fantastic! Congratulations, you two." I touch Tim's arm and he beams at me.

"Should I crack this open?" Kirsty tries to liberate the champagne from my arms.

"Er, actually, Kirst . . ." Tim's voice trails off. "Are you sure that's a good idea?"

"It's fine, Tim." She narrows her eyes and shoots him a look, then rips the foil from the bottle and deftly pops the cork. "I'll just go get some glasses."

"Whoa!" I grab her arm. "You're not *pregnant*, are you?" I snap my mouth closed, wanting to take back the negative way I've said the word, just in case.

Kirsty turns to face me with an expression I can't read. Before she can reply, Tim slings an arm around her shoulders, his face infused with happiness. "She is. She just did the test this morning. We think she's about seven weeks now."

"Wow. Well," I stammer, trying to think of the right

thing to say. "That's . . . great." At least it explains the strange way she's acting. Things like this don't happen to Kirsty. In fact, I can't remember anything daring to deviate from her life plan.

"Isn't it?" Tim hugs Kirsty to him. "I mean, we would have got married soon anyway. But this just seals the deal, you know?"

"Absolutely." I take Kirsty's arm. "Why don't I come with you to get the glasses?"

I steer her into the gleaming white kitchen, then grab three champagne flutes from the cupboard. Kirsty's face is pale and she's leaning against the counter like it's the only thing keeping her upright. I've never seen my friend look so scared and uncertain.

"So how are you feeling?" I ask tentatively.

"I'm pregnant, not terminally ill," she snaps.

That's more like it, I think, happy to see some of her spirit return. But it goes just as quickly as it came, and her face tightens into an anxious expression.

Tiptoeing over, I touch her back gingerly, as if she's a bomb about to explode. "I meant, how are you feeling about the whole situation?" I rack my brain for a positive spin. "I know it's not how you planned things, but it's not terrible, is it? You and Tim are going to get married. You're going to have a baby!"

Kirsty drops her head for a second and when she lifts it again, I'm stunned by the tears seeping from her eyes. I've never seen her cry, not even when we were ten and Danny O'Brien pulled down her trousers on the playground, then took a photo with his mobile and posted it everywhere.

"For God's sake, I'm only twenty-three. I don't want a baby now." A hollow laugh escapes from her. "This was *not* how it was supposed to happen."

I stare, dismayed to see my strong friend in such a

state. "It's not the end of the world. Sure, it might have happened a few years off schedule, but you and Tim are getting married and everything will go as planned, just a few years sooner. Right?"

Thankfully, Kirsty nods and pushes herself away from the counter. "Right. I just need time for it all to sink in." Wiping the streaks of tears from her cheeks, she grins bravely. "Let's go celebrate." I examine her closely to see if she really means it, but she turns away from me and heads to the lounge.

"Everything okay, ladies?" Tim asks when we join him.

"Fine, just fine," Kirsty says, although the smile nailed to her face looks as fake as Mrs Lipenstein's new boobs. It will be genuine soon, I'm sure: Kirsty can deal with anything. She sloshes some champagne in our glasses, and we raise them in the air.

"Here's to Kirsty and Tim." My eyes well up as the enormity of their news hits me. "Cheers."

"Cheers!" they chorus, clinking their glasses with mine.

Tim leans forward to take Kirsty in his arms again, and a tiny pang of envy mingles with my happiness. It might be a slight deviation from plan, but they're still getting everything they ever wanted – sooner, rather than later.

As the champagne bubbles hit the back of my throat, I cross my fingers that I should be so lucky.

CHAPTER EIGHT

I jerk awake the next morning. My head is heavy from a night of tossing and turning, tormented by dreams featuring screaming babies, a crazed Leza Larke demanding I dye my hair platinum like hers, and, of all things, Jeremy's wide green eyes.

Easing myself upright, my heart starts beating crazily. This is it – finally. The day my first *Build a Man* column comes out; the day I'm a real tabloid journalist. With all the excitement last night (and champagne), I *almost* forgot for a second there.

The *Rocky* theme tune starts playing in my head and even though a glance at the clock shows me it's only five, I carefully crawl out of bed, trying not to disturb Peter who's still snoring softly beside me. Smitty grunts in protest as the bed shakes, shooting me his best 'stupid human' glare.

I jog into the living room, humming *Rocky* out loud now, then grab Peter's laptop and boot it up. It's only seconds but it seems like years before the computer springs into action. I cock my ears in the direction of the bedroom, ready to detect any noise, but all I can hear is Peter's distant rumbling. Fingers shaking, I type the URL into the browser – www.beautybits.co.uk.

I scroll down, my heart in my throat. There it is. Cool! *Build a Man* is written inside one of those triangular construction signs you see on the highways over here, except instead of a person shovelling, there's a man's body with needles and scalpels shot through it.

BUILD A MAN

Ever wanted to transform a dud
into the dude of your dreams? Now
you can! When hideous horror
James* declared his need for
everything from a new nose to
navel, *The Daily Planet* jumped at
the chance to get involved. Follow
James in his quest to become
Britain's new heartthrob, and vote
in our reader polls to help the
nation construct its perfect man.
(* Name changed to protect identity.)

Hmm. I never said Jeremy was a 'hideous horror'; that must be Leza's addition. But it doesn't matter – it's not like he'll ever see this. Somehow, I doubt Jeremy is *Beauty Bits'* target audience.

To the right of the text is the outline of a blank cut-out paper doll shaded in baby blue, just awaiting readers' input. I stare at its blobby shape, an odd feeling sliding over me as I picture that form in the future, with defined features and a brand new wardrobe. Will it even look like Jeremy? Or will it be some kind of Frankenman, cobbled together from thousands of women's desires?

NEW DICK FOR THE RIGHT CHICK

How far would you go to meet the

> woman of your dreams? For James,
> the further he gets from his tired
> old self, the better. From his
> head to his toes – and all the
> bits in between – there isn't
> anything James wouldn't do to meet
> a lady for life.

God, I just love that title. Isn't it clever? I know James – Jeremy – doesn't want his dick done, but I couldn't resist the rhyme with 'chick'. And he might decide to do it, after all.

You Nose Best, the poll header off to the side says, and asks people to help choose Jeremy's new nose from three photo options: Sean Penn, Owen Wilson or Mike Tyson. I stare at the selection. Mike Tyson? Really? What if people actually vote for that?

I click on Sean Penn's nose, by far the best, blinking with surprise when the poll tells me there's already been six hundred votes. What? It's only five in the morning!

Wow. Six hundred people have read my article – at least. For a second, it almost feels unreal. I knew my column would be out there for public consumption, but it hadn't hit me people would *read* it until now. Grinning like an idiot, I sit back and throw a few Rocky-style punches in the air.

There's a noise behind me and I turn to see Peter coming from the bedroom. Flushing, I drop my fists into my lap and snap the laptop closed.

"What on earth are you doing?" he asks, squinting.

"Oh, um, I couldn't sleep." I fake a yawn to cover my excitement. I've never felt more alive in my life.

"Are you using my laptop?" Peter leans toward it, his eagle eyes no doubt catching sight of the flashing lights indicating I haven't shut it down properly. Damn thing. "Serenity, how many times . . ." He reaches out to flip open the lid.

"It's okay," I say shrilly, clutching it onto my lap. "I'll make sure to turn it off right this time. If I don't do it myself, I'll never learn." I parrot his favourite line to me whenever I mess up, desperately hoping he doesn't get his mitts on the computer.

Thankfully Peter just raises an eyebrow and holds up his hands. "Fine. Can we go back to bed now? Still an hour or so before we need to get up."

"You go." I wave him off. "I'm going to stay here." And keep reading my lovely article, relishing my moment of glory – alone. Peter disappears into the bedroom, shutting the door with a thud.

It doesn't matter that I can't share my moment of celebration. What's important is that I'm in, baby! I get to my feet, throwing a final Rocky punch in the air.

Unfortunately, the Botox Bitches don't seem to have got the message that I'm a rising tabloid star. It's a typically crazy Friday afternoon in the clinic, with women near and far coming for their Botox top-ups before heading out to their country chateaux or dinners with Saudi sheikh. I barely have a second to breathe between clients dumping their offspring in my arms as they get pricked, and a ratty Baroness demanding I call her chauffeur to bring forth a special teabag.

Whenever I get a chance, though, I keep refreshing the *Beauty Bits* website to see how many people have voted. At last count, there were two thousand votes! People have started commenting, too, and a minor debate has broken out over the best penile implant.

I've just settled on my stool after heating up Mrs Smythe-Johnson's milk (cold milk gives her colic, she says) when my mobile rings.

I scrabble in my purse to find it. "Hello?"

"Serenity?"

"Hi, Leza," I squeak, recognising the familiar abrupt tone. Beads of sweat immediately gather on my upper lip. I look around quickly to make sure Peter's still locked away with the Page Three girl who, according to her consultation form, wants 'Inglens gr8est nipples'.

"Just calling to say your column has been doing quite well, as you're probably aware." Her voice is wry and I blush, praying she can't see the hundreds of times I've refreshed the page. "We need you to post again on Monday; keep the momentum going. Until the bloke actually has something physical done, focus on wardrobe. Get him to try on different looks for the man he wants to be, or some shit like that, and we'll have our readers choose his new image. We've got to get clothes on our cut-out. Right now, it's more turn-off than turn-on."

"Um, okay." Jeremy was keen to upgrade his wardrobe, anyway, and this will fill the gap between now and his Botox next Tuesday. "But wouldn't it be better to wait until after he has the liposuction?" It seems a bit of a waste to dress the old Jeremy, not the person he'll become.

Leza huffs impatiently. "In an ideal world, yes. But we need to up our site stats, and our most popular columns in the paper have always been women playing dress-up with blokes. Given the response to your first post, our readers are already on-board with this man. Until he starts making physical changes, we need them to get more emotionally involved in his progression."

"Sure. Not a problem," I say, injecting confidence into my voice. This life advisory idea was a stroke of genius, if I do say so myself. It will make almost any intrusion into Jeremy's private life believable.

"Go through his wardrobe Geek Wan style. You know, throw around his rubbish clothes. Bring in a few sample outfits – grab them from the high street; you can return them later. Trendy, sloppy, you get the picture. Do at least three different ensembles, and take some photos from the neck down. I'll have our graphics guy knock up to-scale models of how the outfits look. We'll change a few clothing details so the bloke won't be able to identify himself."

"Okay," I say quickly, wondering who Geek Wan is. Gok Wan's unfashionable twin? "I'm on it."

"Get some more background dirt, too," Leza says. "You know, ex-girlfriend shit. Remember, I don't want any airy-fairy 'we weren't right for each other' rubbish."

"Fine." If it bleeds, it leads, I repeat in my mind.

"Get it to me on Sunday," Leza says, and there's a click in my ear as the line goes dead.

I nod even though she can't see me. Then I hang up and call Jeremy.

"Hi, there," I say when he answers. "It's Serenity, calling from the Transforma Life Advisory Service."

"I know who you are, Serenity," Jeremy laughs. "How are you?"

"I'm very well, thank you," I respond perkily, trying to stay true to my professional role. "Just calling to book our next session. I thought we could do a wardrobe analysis and test drive a few new looks for your future."

"Well sure, that sounds brilliant. I told you before, I could definitely use some help in that department."

"Great! Are you free tomorrow morning?" I hold my breath he is – Leza needs the column by Sunday, so that doesn't leave much time.

"Sorry, I'm away all weekend," Jeremy says. "If you

need to meet up, it'll have to be tonight. Half past six okay? I want to be on the road by eight. No wine therapy this time, I'm afraid." I can hear the smile in his voice.

"Er, that's fine, I don't like to mix therapeutic techniques," I stammer. "And sure, six-thirty works for me." Sort of. I won't get out of here until six. How on earth am I going to gather outfits for him in half an hour? I'll do it. Somehow. Thank God I noted down his measurements.

Jeremy gives me his address and we hang up. I start typing a few random questions.

```
What does your current wardrobe
say about you? Has your wardrobe
ever contributed to a relationship
breakdown? How many relationships
have you had?
```

Tapping my pen against the desk, I can't help smiling and shaking my head. Who would have thought I'd be conducting a wardrobe analysis as an undercover reporter disguised as a life coach – for *The Daily Planet*, no less?

Not in a zillion years would I have imagined I'd be in such a cool position.

CHAPTER NINE

At five past six, I leave Peter to deal with another
surprise visit from Mrs Lipenstein – whose other nipple
has started itching – and rush home to grab my voice
recorder. After dashing into the bedroom to slip off my
high heels and pull on my trainers, I glance into the
wardrobe. Would Peter have anything I could snag for
an hour or so, to save me the trouble of hitting the
shops? Reaching in, I select a dark suit, not unlike the
one Peter's wearing today – or every day, for that
matter.

Assessing the folded trousers, I shake my head.
Without even looking at the measurements, I know
they won't fit. Peter and Jeremy are two completely
different shapes. Peter's long and lean, whereas Jeremy
is slightly stocky and just . . . *solid.* Sure, he's got a bit of
extra weight on him, but I bet underneath that, he's one
of those men that when you hug them, you feel like
they're completely surrounding you; taking you in.
Sometimes when I hug Peter, I can feel his ribs.

I push away the thought of my preferred hugging
experience and jam the suit back in the wardrobe,
trying to arrange it neatly. Then I grab Jeremy's

measurements from my clipboard, scribble down a note that I'm headed to Kirsty's for a few hours, and rush over to Marylebone High Street to do the fastest shop of my life.

Twenty-five minutes later, I've managed to cobble together one trendy outfit (if you call a salmon shirt 'trendy') and unearth a slightly crusty but fully functional tuxedo, complete with cummerbund and bowtie, from the Cancer Research charity shop. The third outfit will be Jeremy's own clothes, his usual uniform of T-shirt and jeans. I've just turned onto his street when my phone rings.

"Hey, Ser," Kirsty says when I answer. I drop my shopping bags to the pavement to take a breather, wondering why she's calling. On Friday nights she's usually out entertaining corporate clients with the bank's limitless resources.

"Hey, engaged mother to be," I joke, thinking how strange that all sounds. If I know my friend, though, she's probably got the whole wedding planned and the nursery set up. I wait for Kirsty to join in with my laughter, but instead there's an odd silence.

"Are you busy tonight? Do you think you can come over? I need to talk." Her voice is tight and I swallow, hoping she's okay. In all the years I've known her, she's never needed to just chat. Usually, it's the other way around. Maybe she wants to sort out bridesmaid stuff? God knows she takes details very seriously.

"Sure, no problem." I do a quick calculation in my head: Jeremy needs to be on the road by eight; I can be at Kirsty's a few minutes later. "Give me a couple hours and I'll see you just after eight."

I hang up and glance at the house numbers. Number nineteen, Jeremy's, has a white stucco facade and lovely columns. Even though I'm running late, I can't help staring for a second at the brickwork covering the upper floors and the bright red geraniums peeping out from the wrought-iron balcony above me. Sometimes I find it hard to believe people actually *live* in houses like this; that it's not a film-set recreation. Hands full of shopping bags, I shove my elbow against the buzzer, and footsteps thump toward me.

"Sorry I'm late," I huff as Jeremy opens the door.

He waves me inside. "That's quite the load you've got there," he says, relieving me of some bags. "Come on in."

Wow, I mouth, walking into the lounge. It's bright and airy, with large sash windows in the front and plenty of skylights. I can see straight through the homey kitchen and out to the back, where lots and lots of greenery gives the impression of being in a forest, not smack in the centre of London. It's cosy and inviting, reminding me of Kirsty and Tim's. Dropping the remainder of my packages with a thud, I sink onto a leather sofa and sigh with pleasure. It feels so good to sit.

"Nice place," I say, trying to sound like I encounter such luxurious abodes on a regular basis.

"Thanks." Jeremy's eyes light up. "It was in a state when I bought it. Rotting walls, no floor . . . rats had chewed through pretty much everything. Took me almost a year to do it up properly."

"You did all this?" I glance around, trying to picture Jeremy pounding nails and sawing boards. Actually, it's not that difficult. He's got those strong, solid hands.

He shrugs. "Yeah. I really enjoy renovating, making something new out of the old. Kind of like me." He gestures toward the kitchen. "How about a bite first, and then we can get started?"

"I thought you had to be on the road by eight?" I

sneak a peek at my watch. Not that I want to cut our session short, but something in Kirsty's tone was unsettling and I need to be sure she's okay. "Maybe we should get started now."

Jeremy's face drops. "But I made us some bruschetta and tomato soup. I thought you might be hungry after work."

How sweet! He builds, he bakes – why on earth can't he find someone? My tummy moans loudly at the thought of food, and Jeremy laughs.

"You might not want to eat, but your stomach does. Come on." He pads into the kitchen. Telling myself it'll be a good chance to get more background info, I follow him and take a seat at an old wooden table. It's large, clunky and scarred, contrasting with the modern surroundings.

"Interesting table," I say to fill the silence that's descended as Jeremy gets the food ready.

"Yeah, it was my grandmother's. She had a proper big kitchen, and it looked just right there. Whenever I visited, I used to climb onto it and watch her cook. She actually taught me how to bake. When she died, I moved the table down here. Every time I sit there, it reminds me of her."

My heart melts and I run my hand along the grooved wood, imagining Jeremy with his gran in an old country kitchen up in . . . where?

"So where did your grandmother live? Are you from London?" I really need to get more detail on him.

"Gran lived in Wales all her life," Jeremy says, placing a tray of bruschetta on the table, then ladling thick tomato soup into a bowl in front of me. God, it smells divine. Mom used to make it all the time, and there's something about the scent that reminds me of feeling all warm and snug on a cold winter's day.

"So what do you do?" I ask, before biting into the bruschetta. It's blunt, I know, but there aren't many ways to frame that question. And I'm super curious now. This house must have cost at least two million, if not more. How does someone as young – and nice and *normal* – as Jeremy come into that kind of money? Maybe he's one of those exiled princes from . . . Wales. Do the Welsh have royalty? Diana was Princess of Wales, right? Prince Jeremy. Has a nice ring to it.

Jeremy smiles. "To be honest, I'm not doing much at the moment. Just puttering around, working on a few property redevelopments, you know."

I nod like I *do* know, but he still hasn't answered my question. Now's not the time to dig, though; I'll get to that later once I've got my hands on his wardrobe. We finish our soup and bread, Jeremy chatting all the while about the house and how he saved it from demolition. When the dishes are cleared, I get out my notepad and pencil, along with the recorder.

"So," I say in a business-like tone, signalling it's time to get started. I look at my watch. God, it's already seven-fifteen and we haven't even begun. I fire off another quick text to Kirsty: *On my way! Be there in 45.* If I go fast, it's possible. Maybe.

"Ready to begin wardrobe therapy?" I paste an I-know-what-I'm-doing look on my face, even though quite honestly, Jeremy would be better off taking fashion advice from Marilyn Manson. At least he has a definite look.

"Let's get this show on the road." Jeremy wipes his hands on a tea towel. "I'm ready for a whole new me."

"Great. To start, I'll need to assess your current wardrobe." I stand and face him, noticing how he's the perfect height for me to stare into those big green eyes without needing a neck brace afterwards.

"Okay. We'll have to go upstairs, to the bedroom." A hint of red tinges his cheeks and I can feel mine colouring up, too.

"Perfect. I can't wait to see it. Your wardrobe, I mean, not your bedroom. Not that I don't want to see your bedroom. I mean, as a life advisor, it offers many key signals to your aspirations." Oh, Jesus. What the *hell* am I saying? My cheeks are flaming now and I duck into the lounge to grab the shopping bags, praying my face returns to normal.

When I no longer resemble an overripe strawberry, I head back to the kitchen. "Lead the way."

I follow Jeremy up a narrow staircase – trying not to focus on the nicely shaped bottom in front of me – and into a spacious room. A puffy, comfy-looking duvet covers a massive bed. The cream walls are bare, and even though the room feels lived in and warm, there's nothing to give any hint about Jeremy's personal life. Guess he really does want to start over fresh.

Settling onto the soft bed (there's nowhere else to sit!), I hit the record button.

"Session two, wardrobe therapy," I say gravely into the recorder, like I've seen all good TV therapists do. "Okay, well, the first thing we'll do is examine your wardrobe in its present condition."

"Sure." Jeremy squeezes past me to a small wardrobe in the corner, then slides open its door. "There's not really that much to see, though." He indicates the rows of T-shirts and jeans, which I'm pleased to note are every bit as jumbled as my own back at Peter's.

I glance down at my pad, thankful I'd written a few questions. For some reason, my head feels a bit fuzzy. "And what do you think your clothing says about you, Jeremy?"

He thumbs through a few T-shirts and shrugs. "Um . . . I like to be comfortable?"

Nothing wrong with that, I almost respond before remembering I'm supposed to be making him over. What is it that Peter always says?

"You need to dress how you want others to perceive you," I state authoritatively, echoes of Peter's voice when he coerced me into wearing high heels at the clinic ringing through my head. I'm not quite sure what impact wearing high heels has on people's perception of me, but at least they can see me over the desk now.

Jeremy raises his eyebrows, shooting my grubby trainers a look. "Okay. So what do those shoes say about you, then?"

I've got bunions from wearing stupid high heels? I respond inside my head.

"We're not here to discuss me," I say primly, tucking my feet under the bed. I glance down at my notepad again. "Has your wardrobe ever contributed to a relationship breakdown?" Trying not to appear too eager for dirt, I stroke my chin to channel my inner Dr Phil.

Jeremy grimaces. "Well, I can't say Julia was too keen on my T-shirts."

"Julia?" I motion for him to keep talking.

"Yeah. I was with her for almost two years. We met at the property development company I was working in at the time. Straight away, I fell for her." A distant look comes into his eyes. "I know that sounds wanky, but it's true. She was gorgeous – tall and blonde, the kind of woman other men stare at on the street. I was so proud to be with her."

Bitch, I think automatically. Tall blonde women just bring out that response.

"She was smart, too. Just . . . together."

Now I really hate her. "So what happened?" I ask.

Jeremy shuts the wardrobe door with force. "About six months ago, we decided it wasn't working any longer. She'd moved on to other interests." His face twists.

There's definitely something he isn't telling me. "Other interests?"

"She wanted to go into a new side of property development. We drifted apart. You know how it is." His face is shuttered and closed now.

I don't know how it is, actually. I've never had a relationship longer than six months (Peter) and you can't really drift apart in six months, can you?

"And has there been anyone since Julia?" Hideous name. Jeremy and Julia – the cutesiness of it makes me want to spew my soup.

"A few here and there." He waves a hand dismissively. "They stay around for a month or so, see that I'm not the type to go out partying or dine in posh restaurants, get bored of me, and go off again."

"And you think redesigning yourself will help?"

"Well, yeah. I need to attract the right women. Right now, I only get those who are interested in this." Jeremy gestures around at the house. "If I look good, too, I'll get women who are interested in *me*." He thumps his chest. "Then I'll have the complete package."

"But Jeremy, you got Julia without cosmetic surgery." I want to hit myself when the words slip out. What am I doing? I shouldn't be planting doubts in his mind.

Jeremy shakes his head. "I didn't look like I do now, Serenity. I was in great shape from all the work I was doing."

"Right, right. I see what you mean." I nod, and a

silence falls between us. I don't know what more to ask, and I feel kind of weird probing him about Julia, even if I do have therapeutic license to be nosy. I'll leave it for now and circle back later.

"Well!" I stand and grab a shopping bag. "New look, new life. Let's see how you can shape your future with clothes. Even if you haven't begun your physical transformation yet, there's nothing stopping you from dressing for the man you want to be." I almost roll my eyes at myself, but Jeremy's just nodding along as if I'm making sense. God, I must be better at this therapy thing than I thought.

I pull out the hideous salmon dress shirt, along with a pair of skinny-fit navy trousers. "Here, try these."

Jeremy looks at me as if I've lost my mind. "That top is *pink*. And you do realise skinny fit is for skinny people, right?"

"No, this style can be worn by anyone, anywhere. All you need is the confidence to pull it off. And salmon is bang on trend right now," I add, throwing in Gok Wan's favourite catchphrase.

Jeremy still looks dubious.

"An important part of wardrobe therapy is being open to trying new things," I say. Plus, I really need a picture for Leza. This outfit will be the Trendy Man look.

"Okay, okay, if you say so." Jeremy starts sliding off his T-shirt, and I catch a glimpse of smooth skin – not nearly as flabby as I'd thought – before he remembers I'm here and lets the shirt drop again.

I lower my eyes and turn toward the door. "I'll wait out there," I mumble, conscious of the heat in my cheeks.

A few minutes later, Jeremy calls me back in.

"I look bloody ridiculous." He grins, pivoting in the

trousers and shirt.

Biting my lip to keep from smiling, I take in the tight trousers (which, in a word, are just *wrong*) and the salmon – okay, pink – shirt that makes his olive complexion appear downright sickly.

"How do you feel?" I ask, struggling to maintain my impartial advisory role.

"I feel ridiculous, too. Honestly, this is not how I want to be perceived." He starts to unbutton the shirt.

"Wait! I need to get a photo. To . . . you know, to help you remember this moment, this *feeling*, for future reference." I grab my mobile, make sure his head is out of the frame, then snap a shot.

"Okay, onto the next one. Why don't you try the tux?" I open the Cancer Research bag, wrinkling my nose at the faint mothball odour rising from the fabric.

"You brought me a tux to try?" Jeremy asks incredulously.

"This is a regular part of our therapy, you know," I blag. "We've got it in several sizes back at the clinic. I'll just step outside again while you get it on, okay?"

I slip into the hallway, eyeing a few open doors down the corridor. My eyes pop as I poke my head into one. It's my dream bathroom come to life, all gleaming white, with a large claw-footed bath and a separate Rainshower installed in the corner. The floor tiles are warm under my feet and even the toilet looks inviting. A giant mirrored medicine cabinet shines above a polished white ceramic sink. Hmm. As an undercover reporter, maybe I should check to see if there's anything interesting in there.

I close the bathroom door then open the cabinet slowly, feeling a bit odd. I mean, I wouldn't like people rooting through my medicine cabinet – not that there's anything of mine in there, anyway. It looked so nice and neat with Peter's toiletries that I couldn't bear putting my plastic BIC razors and drugstore perfume next to his superior stuff.

Jeremy's is cluttered with shampoo bottles, vitamins, and the odd empty package here and there. I'm just about to head back to the bedroom when my eye spots a glimmer of silver. I push aside some hair gel and there, hidden in the corner, is the most beautiful watch I've ever seen. Diamonds almost drip off the face, but there's nothing garish about it. Peering closely, I can make out 'Bvlgari'. It's the kind of watch a woman in *Vogue* would wear; a watch that wouldn't look out of place amidst the twenty thousand pounders that almost made me hyperventilate in Harrods last month – I never dreamed such expensive things existed.

I flip it over. *To Jules, I've had the time of my life. Happy Two Years! Much love, Jer.* Wow. He really must have loved her to write something like that. To *buy* something like that. But what is her super-expensive anniversary gift doing shoved in the corner of his cabinet?

He did say they were together for almost two years. Maybe they split before he could give her the gift. My heart fills with sympathy as I picture him hanging on to her present; unable to bring himself to return it . . .

"I'm ready!"

Jeremy's shout makes me jump and even though I know he's nowhere near me, I shove the watch back in the cabinet and slam the door closed. "Coming!"

I hurry down the corridor and into his room, stopping at the sight of his broad shoulders in the tux. Even from the back, I can tell he's standing straighter, and there's a hint of confidence about him that wasn't there before.

He turns to me and smiles. "Well?"

"You look fantastic." Too late, I remember I'm supposed to be impartial. But he does look great – the tuxedo's classic cut fits like it was made for him. Despite the extra weight, Jeremy has perfect proportions and I can't help admiring how nice he looks all dressed up.

"Can you fix this bowtie?" Jeremy tweaks the strip of fabric around his neck. "I can never get it right."

"Sure, I can try." I move toward him, conscious of his eyes focused on my face. The air between us suddenly feels like it's snapping with energy, and my heart starts thumping. I create a bow as quickly as I can and step back again.

"I must get a photo," I say, eager for something to focus my attention on. What is it about this man that makes me feel so unsettled? It's probably normal for an undercover reporter to feel a connection with their subject, right? That's a good thing, I'm sure – it shows I'm gaining his trust.

Jeremy strikes a Zoolander-style pose and I laugh. "Be serious," I say through my giggles, clicking the photo from the neck down. Thankfully the *Beauty Bits* readers will be saved from his Blue Steel impression.

"If I'd worn something like this more often, maybe Julia would have stayed with me." Jeremy shrugs off the jacket.

"What really happened between you two?" I ask tentatively, sinking onto the bed.

Jeremy sighs and sits down beside me. "Whatever I tell you is completely confidential, right? I know you told me before that it stays between us, but . . . I just want to make sure."

"Of course!" I say quickly, pushing away the pangs of guilt. It's not like I'm lying: whatever he says *will* stay private. I'm certainly not going to reveal his identity. And I was right – I am gaining his trust.

"Well, a friend and I started up a company together. It grew to be pretty big and quite successful. And then I met Julia. We had a couple good years together – or at least I thought they were good."

"What happened?" I ask.

"Turns out for the last few months before we split, she and my business partner David had started seeing each other behind my back. I walked in on them one day in our offices."

"Oh my God." I reach out and touch Jeremy's leg lightly, but he doesn't move. He's staring straight ahead, eyes fixed on a memory I can't begin to imagine.

"When she noticed me, Julia just laughed and said I'd let myself go – and that she preferred her men more fit than fat."

"Bitch," I breathe, then curse myself for being so unprofessional. But at least I was right in my initial assessment.

Jeremy shoots me a half-grin. "I know. Anyway, that's what happened. And that's why I need your – and Dr Lycett's – help."

No wonder the poor man wants to remake himself from the ground up. I'd want to jump off a bridge. "We're here for you, Jeremy," I say, then glance at my watch. Christ, it's almost eight-thirty. Kirsty's going to kill me. Funny that she hasn't texted back to bawl me out – usually she does that when I'm going to be even five minutes late.

"Why don't you put on your normal clothes, I'll get a quick photo of you in your usual outfit for comparative purposes, and we'll call it a night? I think you've made real progress today," I say gravely.

Jeremy tilts his head to the side. "I think so, too. It's really good to have someone like you to talk to."

His eyes meet mine and that funny feeling sweeps over me again. "I'll wait outside," I say, standing quickly and moving toward the door.

A couple minutes later, Jeremy's back in his T-shirt and jeans. As handsome as he looked in the formal wear, this is more natural; more *him*. I snap a photo, then gather up the discarded outfits and shove them in the shopping bags to return later.

"So where are you going tonight?" I ask in a chipper voice as we head down the stairs toward the front door.

"Just off to visit my parents," he says.

So he's not from London, then. I forgot he hadn't actually answered my question. I open my mouth to ask where his parents are from, but he lunges back up the stairs.

"Here, you forgot this," Jeremy puffs once he's returned, handing me the foul salmon shirt. "Please take it with you."

I laugh at his grimace, then put the shirt in a bag and stick out my hand before he can swoop in for the traditional kiss on the cheek. My face heats up as I picture his soft lips – well, they look soft, anyway – against my face, and I clasp his warm hand in mine.

"Bye!" Yanking away my hand, I wave like a maniac as I back out the door. On the dark street, I pick up pace as I move away from his house. I'm practically running by the time I get to Kirsty and Tim's, and I have to bend over to catch my breath after ringing the buzzer.

"Hi, Serenity," Tim whispers, cracking open the door a few inches. "I didn't know you were coming over. Kirsty's sleeping."

"Sleeping? It's not even nine." Kirsty's a night owl if I ever met one.

Tim shrugs. "This pregnancy has really wiped her out. I'll tell her you came by." He looks at me closely, opens his mouth as if he wants to ask me something, then shakes his head. "Night."

"Night," I say, as the door swings closed. I peer up at the darkened bedroom window, hoping my friend is okay. This pregnancy thing might have thrown her for a loop, but Kirsty is the most unflappable person I know. I'm sure she'll be playing Mozart to her belly and teaching the embryo Latin verbs in no time.

I'll come by bright and early tomorrow with Kirsty's favourite *pain au chocolat* and that caramel-toffee thing from Starbucks she loves, and explain to her what happened. If anyone understands work commitments, it's her.

I head for home down the dark and quiet streets. Even Marylebone Road – usually clogged and noisy – seems empty and deserted for a Friday night. I quicken my steps, eager to hop on Google. If Jeremy and this David guy started a company together, I might be able to find something on them. Even if I can't, at least I have a juicy titbit to work with for the column, thank God.

Peter's sleeping on the sofa to the constipated tones of that BBC announcer, so I open up his laptop as quietly as possible and click on the browser. I've been so busy I never thought of Googling Jeremy until now – shocking, really, since in the dead hours between five and six in the evening, when all the women who've had their fat sucked out are busy replacing it by chowing down at the Ritz – I'm a Google fiend, searching everyone I can think of.

I type in Jeremy's name plus David plus property and hit 'Search'. Hundreds of results filter onto the screen and I scroll down until . . . bingo.

Earlham Property Founder Sells Shares for £20 million. Earlham Property founding partner Jeremy Ritchie today sold his shares to former partner David Chase for £20 million, giving up his stake in one of Britain's most successful and rapidly growing property enterprises . . .

Twenty million! I blink. Jeremy has twenty million pounds? I knew he was rich, but rich to me is a million or two, not twenty. I click the link to read the rest of the article.

Earlham Property was founded by Ritchie and Chase, who set up the business in a converted petrol station in King's Cross and laboured around the clock to ensure the company's success. Chase interfaced with clients while Ritchie oversaw the renovation of the company's portfolio. From its humble beginnings, Earlham Property has now grown to over two hundred employees in fifty branches across Greater London.

While Ritchie cites his decision to sell as simply 'time to move on', inside sources claim the breakdown of the founders' friendship is the real reason. Earlham Properties has since been renamed Chase Estates and has continued its exponential growth despite the recent market meltdown.

There's a photo of Jeremy and David standing proudly with their arms around each other's shoulders, the Earlham logo shining out from a building behind them.

I squint at the screen. Jeremy's so young – and about fifty pounds lighter. He looks handsome, fit and happy, and my heart squeezes as I think about the sad man I've just met.

I type in David Chase plus Julia, just on the off chance I can find something.

Chase Estates Owner Weds Girlfriend Julia Adams comes up straight away. Oh God, I think as I look at the date: October fifth, just a day before Jeremy turned up at the clinic.

```
In a lavish ceremony in front of
three hundred family and friends,
millionaire and Chase Estates
owner David Chase wed girlfriend
Julia Adams at their country manor
in the Cotswolds. Celebrity guests
arrived by helicopter while the
bride made her entrance in a
horse-drawn Bugatti.
```

Horse-drawn Bugatti? For real? I can't help snickering at that one. A large colour photo to the side of the article shows David and Julia smiling smugly at the camera in front of a massive house set in groomed gardens. Julia *is* beautiful, with a perfectly proportioned face that looks like it belongs in a painting, and a model-thin body. But there's something about her, even in the photo, that just feels cold.

He might be a millionaire, but David is every inch the typical estate agent: hair gelled to within an inch of its life, smarmy expression, and natty suit. Together, the two of them make me feel nauseous, and even more so when I think of what they did to Jeremy.

Is all this *really* a valid reason for Jeremy to have such drastic cosmetic surgery? Would he feel differently if he had a bit more time to get over the shock of the wedding?

I shake my head to dispel the thoughts – I'm probably being silly. As ambitious as Peter is to build his clinic, he wouldn't agree to perform procedures on someone who wasn't psychologically fit. And Peter *is* a doctor. He knows the right questions to ask to uncover such patients. Jeremy must be fine or Peter wouldn't have agreed to operate, I'm certain of it.

Jeremy's surgery is just what he needs to move his life forward. And with me as his life advisor, he can meet the future head on, new nose and all.

It's a win-win situation for everyone.

CHAPTER TEN

I open my eyes the next morning to the sound of Peter clanking dishes in the kitchen, the BBC at an ungodly volume. I jerk upright, my heart beating fast, before remembering it's Saturday.

Thank goodness, I think, slowly lowering myself back onto the rock-hard mattress. Last night was a late one and my head still feels fuzzy. I stayed up until three working on my column, trying to strike the right balance between drama and sympathy – and making sure not to give away too many details to maintain anonymity. The words filter into my mind and I smile proudly.

```
            DON'T FEEL PATHETIC:
              GO COSMETIC

    What do you do when you catch your
    girlfriend cheating with your best
    friend? For our Build a Man James,
    the answer's easy: redesign
    yourself completely with cosmetic
    surgery.
```

Jeremy – or James – comes out looking a bit like an

abandoned puppy, but when people read this column, they'll want to tear Julia and David limb from limb for what they've done. I know I do. It's such a shame I can't actually reveal who they are.

Hopefully Leza will like it. I emailed it to her late last night, along with the photos for the wardrobe poll so the graphics man could work his magic.

"Oh, good, you're awake." Peter strides into the bedroom. Yanking open the wardrobe, he selects one of the neatly hanging blazers and shrugs it on. "I'm at the hospital until six. Can you take Smitty to his grooming appointment at four?"

I struggle into a sitting position and let out a giant yawn, quickly covering my mouth when I notice Peter staring.

"Sure, no problem." I have no plans of my own, anyway, apart from a visit to check on Kirsty this morning. I swear, that cat has a more action-packed social schedule than I do. Not that it would take much.

"Goodbye, then. I'll see you later."

"Later," I echo, rubbing my eyes.

Peter leans down and pecks me on the cheek – he refuses to kiss on the mouth until both of us have brushed our teeth – then I hear him grab his work bag. The front door creaks open.

"Oh, and Serenity?" he calls. "Please don't forget to ask the stylist to clip Smitty's nails this time. They're much longer than appropriate." I roll my eyes at the thought of an appropriate length for cat claws.

The flat door thuds closed, and silence descends. Sighing, I stare up at the ceiling, my eyes tracing the elaborate plaster decoration in the centre where a light used to hang, back in Victorian times. Another weekend. And while I'm happy the Botox Bitches aren't part of it, I have to admit that sometimes, I feel a little lonely. Peter often has surgeries booked at the boutique hospital up the street, Kirsty's usually busy with work, and that just leaves Smitty and me. And quite honestly, a cat isn't exactly the best company, especially one as snooty as Smitty. The damn thing will barely deign to look in my direction.

If I had a normal job – in an office or something – I'd have tons of friends by now. We'd go out after work for a pint, like all those suited workers I see standing on the street, laughing and drinking every Friday afternoon.

Soon, I tell myself, turning my head to stare out the window at the heavy grey sky. Soon I'll have a whole new crowd of tabloid pals. They'll show me the city, maybe take me to some of those cool East London bars they're always raving about in *Metro* . . .

At least this morning, I'm going to see Kirsty. I slide off the giant pedestal bed, perking up a bit as I imagine us poring over all those wonderful bridal and baby magazines I'm sure she's collected by now – or, at the very least, the brochure from the registrar's office. I turn on the ancient handheld shower and climb into the steam, trying to picture Kirsty cradling an infant. It takes a few attempts, but I can't help smiling as an image of her and Tim, beaming beatifically at their shiny newborn, comes to mind.

Wow, I think as I furiously rub my body with my favourite apricot scrub (thank God The Body Shop has it over here). Kirsty's going to be a wife. A *mother*. A strange feeling comes over me, like she's all grown up now and moving on to a new phase . . . without me. I stick my head under the hot stream of water to wash away the unease.

Standing in front of my jumbled closet, I choose a pair of jeans, my favourite black turtleneck, and a thick checked blazer. Back home, this is the kind of day where I'd snuggle into the fleecy warmth of a tracksuit. But no one wears tracksuits here – unless it's a thousand-pound designer suit and you're a fake-tanned footballer's wife.

Embarrassment rises inside as I remember the time I pulled on my comfy sweats, when Peter and I were about to hit Pain Quotidien for a rare Saturday morning breakfast in the outside world. He took one look at me, asked why I was still in my pyjamas, and told me to hurry up. I know he wasn't trying to be mean – he genuinely thought they were nightwear – but I've never been able to wear that tracksuit again. Dress how you want to be perceived and all that. It's hard to muster up the energy to care on the weekends, but even *I* don't want people to think I'm cruising down the street in my PJs.

Too bad Peter can't take me to grooming sessions like Smitty, I think, twisting my damp hair into a bun. Sighing, I put on a bit of mascara – narrowly avoiding losing an eyeball – jam on my favourite Zara boots, and I'm out the door.

A few minutes later, after popping into a busy patisserie on Baker Street to grab some steaming chocolate croissants, I'm banging on Kirsty's door.

Tim answers. "Hi, Ser. She's upstairs."

I say hello and trot inside. "Kirst!" I yell as I race up the steps. "I've got breakfast."

"In here." Her voice floats from their bedroom.

"Hey," I say in surprise as I round the corner. She's still in bed, reading an old book on – I squint at the spine – military manoeuvres from the Second World War? Her hair is pulled back in a ponytail and her face is scrubbed clean. I can't remember the last time I saw Kirsty without make-up. I always tease that she should have worked for MAC, not a bank.

"Hey, yourself. Come sit down." She waves me over.

I hand her a pastry and squeeze in beside her on the bed. "So! Ready to start planning?"

I wait for her usual assured voice to launch into next steps and outlines for moving forward. Instead, an awkward silence descends, a kind I've never felt between us. Then she shrugs and starts devouring the *pain au chocolat*. Little flaky bits drift onto the pillow like snowflakes, and I resist the urge to sweep them away. Maybe some of Peter's principles are finally rubbing off on me.

"Sure," Kirsty says finally, sounding anything but. Her usually expressive face looks like it's been Botoxed into an unreadable mask.

God, I was certain she'd be raring to go with this whole thing. I stare at my friend for a second, unsure what to do.

"Let's go for a walk." Grabbing her arm, I haul her off the bed. Some fresh air will set her straight and help put things in perspective. She's had a shock, of course. Maybe I was expecting too much of her, too soon. After all, trying to absorb becoming a wife and mother is a lot, even for my efficient friend.

"Aw, come on, Ser," Kirsty whines in a voice I've never heard from her before. "I'm tired."

"Get dressed." I throw a pair of jeans at her, and a few minutes later we're strolling through the Rose Garden at Regent's Park under a grey sky. There's something about the grey in London that's so oppressive, like it's compressing the atmosphere and pushing in on you.

"Talk to me," I say as we jostle past a group of noisy Italian tourists. "What are you thinking?" Strange, I've never had to ask her that before.

Kirsty sinks onto a nearby bench and I plop beside her. "I don't know. Have you ever thought you wanted something, but when you actually got it, you realised . . . you're not sure it's what you wanted in the first place?"

I think back to the events of the past week. "Um, no." I can't even begin to imagine not being happy with my tabloid assignment after craving it for so long. I swivel toward her, unable to believe she means what she's saying.

"I'm sure how you're feeling now has nothing to do with not wanting – er, well, what's just happened," I say, tiptoeing around the recent issues. "You just need time."

"Yeah, time." Kirsty stares straight ahead for a minute, then shrugs. "I'll figure it out. Tell me what's going on with you."

"Well . . ." I pause, wondering if now's the right moment to share my news. *"The Daily Planet* asked me to write a column for their new health and beauty website!" The words burst out of me.

Kirsty raises her eyebrows. "Really? Wow. That's awesome!" She squeezes my arm. "When did this happen?"

"A few days ago," I answer, my heart doing a happy dance that I can finally talk to someone about it.

"Is it the one about the guy who's redesigning himself?" Kirsty stands, pulling me up from the bench.

"That's the one. His name is Jeremy, and he's really nice." A memory of our eyes meeting as I fixed his bow-tie flashes through my mind, and my tummy does a wonky flip.

"So Peter's agreed to all this?" Kirsty asks as we crunch along the gravel path.

"Um, well, that's the thing." I stop to finger a

withered blossom. "He doesn't exactly know I'm writing the column. I'm working undercover."

It feels funny saying that out loud, like I'm some kind of modern-day spy. I guess I am, in a way.

Kirsty stops and turns toward me with an incredulous expression. "Undercover? For real?"

I nod. "Yup, for real."

She stares for a minute, then shakes her head. "How the hell are you managing that?"

"Jeremy thinks I'm a life advisor, working for the clinic. He's signed up for my services. And Peter, well, he has no idea. But there's no reason why either of them needs to know," I add quickly, before Kirsty can say a word. "All the names are changed in the column, so there's no way anyone can find out who – or where – I'm writing about."

"You'd better hope not," Kirsty says as we start walking again. "It's kind of risky, isn't it? What if someone *does* connect your column with the clinic or Jeremy? Peter's going to be furious – not to mention Jeremy."

I huff impatiently. "They *won't*, Kirsty. The chances of anyone reading my column, thinking it might be Jeremy, then being able to find him and tell him are, like, one in a zillion."

"Okay. Just be careful." She gives me a quick hug. "I know how much you wanted this. I hope it turns out to be everything you'd hoped."

Normally I'd dismiss her words as the kind of pleasantries friends automatically exchange, but in light of recent events, they feel more weighted.

"It will, I'm sure." As we tramp down the path, excitement grows inside. I'm more than sure this is everything I want, actually. I'm . . . two hundred and ten percent sure, like they say on *The Apprentice*.

I meet Kirsty's eyes, happy to see some life in them again, and give her a grin so big even Botox couldn't keep it down.

CHAPTER ELEVEN

I wake up Monday morning practically vibrating with anticipation. My column on Jeremy and Julia – or rather, James and *Jemima* (ha! Isn't that a horrible name?) – comes out today, and since the only thing I heard back from Leza was a quick 'thanks', I must have got this one spot on.

Lifting my head, I see it's only six, but there's no way I can lie here a second longer. Sliding out of bed, I tiptoe from the room and over to Peter's laptop, humming the *Rocky* tune again. I peck in the *Beauty Bits* address, then hold my breath as the page loads.

```
ONCE SAD AND PATHETIC, NOW
       GOING COSMETIC!
```

Yikes. I didn't write that Jeremy was sad and pathetic – Leza obviously changed it. Thank goodness for hidden identities; I'd hate to see Jeremy's face if he ever read that. What else has Leza fiddled with? I scan the rest of the article, relaxing only when I get to the end and see that everything is just as I'd written.

To the right of the column, the blank cut-out paper doll now sports a Sean-Penn-like nose – obviously the winner of the last poll – floating oddly in the otherwise featureless face. Today's poll on wardrobe is positioned underneath the cut-out, along with three Jeremy-shaped mannequins, each sporting the outfits I'd brought him but in slightly different shades.

I shake my head as I read the captions: *Messy Mister*, under Jeremy's own T-shirt and jeans; *Suits You, Sir*, under the tuxedo snapshot; or *Fashion Passion*, under the terrible skinny trousers and the salmon shirt that's now violently pink. I cast a vote for *Messy Mister*, eager to see how many people have participated this time. 1,557!

I blink, barely able to believe the number. One thousand, five hundred and fifty-seven people have not only read my column, but have voted, too – albeit, many for *Fashion Passion* (how anyone can find a man attractive in skinny trousers is beyond me – they make everyone look like they're wearing a nappy).

Whooping as quietly as possible, I throw a few punches in the air. Seeing my column onscreen is like that buzzing feeling after one glass of wine – no, better: each of my words gives me a rush unlike anything I've ever known. I can't wait to get started on my next article now, to experience the same thrill again. And if it's this good online, imagine the feeling when my words are in print. I leap up, excitement filling every cell of my body. If I can make every column stronger and secure even more readers, that job will be mine.

To celebrate my future success, I decide to buck routine and make a big breakfast. Peter prefers eating his organic yoghurt only once he's safely installed in the clinic, but he does enjoy a cheeky crumpet now and again. After padding into the kitchen, I click on the kettle to make Peter's tea, and carefully place two crumpets in the toaster. He likes them perfectly golden brown, and if I stand sentinel, I might get it just right. As I wait, I can't help reaching up into the cupboard and grabbing a handful of Jaffas. Chocolate has caffeine, and who doesn't like a little pick-me-up in the morning?

"Serenity?" The bedroom door creaks open, and my head snaps up from the toaster. "Keep it down, please. It's only six-fifteen." Peter sniffs the air. "What are you burning?"

Oh, the crumpets! I jiggle the toaster handle frantically, but it's too late – the tips of the silly things are singed. "Sorry, I was making us breakfast. I didn't realise it was so early." Whoops. In all my excitement, I'd forgotten there were still forty-five minutes to Peter's daily rising time. But surely he can forgo a few extra winks for a yummy breakfast. Well, breakfast.

Peter shakes his head. "I'm not really hungry. I'm going back to bed."

I sigh as he closes the bedroom door, then chuck the crumpets into the bin. A celebratory breakfast was nice in theory, but Peter isn't exactly one for spontaneous gestures – giving or receiving. Still, even my disastrous crumpets and routine-loving boyfriend can't bring me down today.

My exhilaration propels me all the way to the clinic, where it's a quiet Monday morning, as usual. Most women are lying low, detoxing (aka purging) from their weekend binges. I click onto my column for the billionth time – almost three thousand poll votes now! I'm just about to cast another vote for *Messy Mister* when the phone rings.

"Transforma Harley Street, how may I help?" I answer automatically.

There's a silence, then a woman sounding close to tears says: "It's Sara Collins. I'm at the hospital. My consultant says I need an urgent mammogram. I'll have to cancel my Botox appointment this morning."

"Absolutely. No problem." God, imagine having the presence of mind to cancel at such a stressful time. She must be one of those rare nice patients we've been known to have. I'm about to hang up when she stops me.

"Wait! I'm calling to reschedule, silly girl." Mrs Collins's voice is dripping with disdain. "Is there anything available this afternoon? I can pop in after my scan."

I can barely speak for a second, I'm so stunned. She's about to be screened for breast cancer and she's worried about Botox? Really, I couldn't make this stuff up if I tried. I check the schedule, then slot in a new appointment and hang up.

It shouldn't surprise me these people exist – I've been reading about them ever since I came here. The woman with Britain's largest breasts; the one who had her appearance altered to match her toy poodle; the lady who hated her ears so much, she had them removed. But now that such crazies are in front of me, sometimes I can't believe they're genuine. In a way, I guess Jeremy's one of them. But there's something about him that makes him *real*, down to earth.

"Hello? Anybody home?" I glance up to see a woman with skin so tanned it resembles a rotten banana.

"Can I help you?" I try not to let distaste show on my face.

"'Course you can," she twitters. "That's why I'm here, innit?" She smoothes back a lock of bleached hair so fried it's a wonder it doesn't fall out of her head. "Call me when the doc's ready, eh, hon?"

Prancing over to the leather chairs, she crosses her

PVC-covered legs and grabs a magazine, blowing a bubble with her chewing gum as she flips the pages.

"Do you think you might be able to tell me your name?" I attempt to make my request sound genuine, but instead it comes out a little sarcastic. Thankfully, it goes straight over her (oddly large) head.

She chomps away for a few seconds, then turns to look at me. "Aw, hon, you don't need to pretend. You know who I am."

We lock eyes for a second as she waits for me to recognise her, but sadly (well, *thankfully*, for me) I haven't the slightest idea who she is. As inconspicuously as possible, I glance over at the appointment schedule on the screen.

"Princesz Gayle?" I ask, crossing my fingers it's her.

"Hellz, yeah!" She raises her arms and legs in the air as if I've cured malaria instead of identifying the first cast-off from *Big Brother* Season 1098 – or whatever she's 'famous' for. "You know it."

"Princesz? Ready to look beautiful – er, even *more* beautiful?" Peter appears in the reception area and bustles the masticating Princesz into his consulting room.

I shake my head as the room falls silent again. This place is a loony bin today. I certainly don't need to worry about Jeremy's sanity with patients like Princesz around.

My email pings and I look at the screen to see Leza's name. There's no subject line, so I quickly open the message.

> Great response to column. Need another for Wednesday.
>
> Deadline tomorrow by five.

My mouth drops open. Launch party? I never
received any invitation! I quickly type a response
saying a column by Wednesday is no problem –
Jeremy's coming in tomorrow for his first Botox
injections and I can write about that – and yes, I am
definitely attending the party. I hug myself, my heart
fluttering with excitement. My first launch party!

Keying 'Hospital Club' into Google, I stare at the
screen as a brick building comes up – apparently, it
used to be an eighteenth-century hospital. Only in
London would that have morphed into a club. I scroll
down, catching my breath as modern rooms
resembling an art gallery flash on the monitor.

Gnawing my lip, my brain flits through my
wardrobe of black polyester trousers and jeans. No way
am I hitting this trendy venue looking like I've rolled
up from *Hicks R Us*. A trip to Oxford Street is most
definitely in order. Okay, I don't have any money and I
don't get paid for another two weeks. But that's what
credit is for, right? After returning Jeremy's clothes, my
card should still have room. And when I get this job at
the paper, I'll be able to pay it all back, no problem.

Picking up the phone, I punch in Kirsty's number.

"Hey, you. Up for a trip to Selfridges after work
today?" I ask when she answers. "We can meet in the
champagne bar, have a bit of bubbly . . ." My voice
trails off when I remember that she won't be having a
bit of bubbly for quite some time. "Or a coffee," I add
hastily.

"Today's not great," she responds, sounding

distracted. "It's insanely busy here right now, and I have a client coming in this afternoon."

I stare at the receiver, wondering where my best friend has gone. Normally Kirsty would risk life or limb to go shopping. Which she actually did once, on a corporate trip to Moscow when she had to navigate through a protest to get to a mall. That bump on the head was totally worth the Prada discount she scored, or so she says.

I'm not letting her off that easily. "Come on, I really need your help. I'm going to a launch party for the *Beauty Bits* website and I have no idea what to wear." That should get her – she knows what a terrible shopper I am under pressure. When I had to buy a graduation outfit with just an hour until the ceremony, I ended up in Wal-Mart with a belted jersey dress from the kids' section.

Kirsty sighs. "Okay. Meet me in the café on the fourth floor at six-thirty."

I smile victoriously. I knew she'd come around. "See you then."

The rest of the day passes in a 'what the hell am I going to wear' haze, and I barely even register the appearance of the Botox 'n' Breast Cancer patient. Finally, Peter comes into the reception area and I realise I've barely seen him all day. No, scratch that, all weekend. He came home exhausted both nights and, after our usual organic chicken fillet and greens, fell asleep in front of the TV.

It's not like we've ever had a particularly romantic relationship – more like *Love Mediocrity* than *Love Actually* – but these days, we seem more flatmates than boyfriend and girlfriend. Middle-aged flatmates. My parents stay up later than he does. Actually, he behaves more like a parent than they ever did. Hmm.

Even now, Peter's yawning and his eyes droop at half-mast. "Ready to go? After that weekend, I could really use an early night."

I picture the darkened, tomb-like flat, and a feeling of claustrophobia slides over me. "Kirsty and I are going shopping. I'll be back around eight. I can bring us something for supper, if you want to wait." He won't though, I know – he and Smitty always like to 'ingest' on schedule.

"No, that's fine. I'll grab something from the Organic Kitchen on the way home. Say hi to Kirsty."

My mouth drops open – I've totally forgotten to fill him in on Kirsty and Tim's big news. But Peter's already halfway out the door, and it's not something I can share in ten seconds or less.

"I'll see you back home," I call after him. After locking up, I hurry through Marylebone and across St Christopher's Place toward Selfridges. Pushing inside the department store, I breathe in the scent of a thousand different perfumes, gleaming in jewel-like bottles behind glass counters. A few minutes and several escalators later, I spot Kirsty jammed in a corner of the busy fourth-floor café.

"Hey there!" I say, swinging into a chair across from her. A bottle of sparkling water rests on the crowded table top, and a half-eaten sandwich balances on the edge of her plate.

Kirsty glances up from a magazine. "Hey."

I almost do a double take as I examine her wan face and the bags beneath her eyes. Aren't pregnant women supposed to glow? Kirsty looks more like a corpse than a mother-to-be. "You all right?"

"Jesus Christ, I wish people would stop asking me that," she snaps. "I'm fine."

I hold up my hands. "Okay, okay! Relax."

116

"I'm sorry," she sighs. "It's just, between Tim and everyone at the office, I must have answered that question a million times today. I know I look like shit."

"No, of course not," I say, though really, she does. "So have you told everyone at work about the engagement?" If I was her, I'd be shouting it from the rooftops.

"Not yet." Kirsty looks straight at me, and again I'm struck by how pale her face is. "I'm worried they'll think I won't be focused on my job if I'm planning a wedding. Wait until they hear about the baby." Her lips tighten.

"It's not like you're doing anything wrong." I touch my friend's cold hand, anxious to reassure her. "They have to give you time off, right?"

"Of course. Legally, they do. But that doesn't stop them from making comments, or taking away clients because they think you can't deal with it." Kirsty opens her mouth like she's going to say more, but then just shrugs. "So, tell me about this party. And before you ask, I'm sorry. I didn't have a chance to check out your article yet. I will when I get home, though."

Normally I'd let Kirsty have it for not taking the time to read my masterpiece, but she looks like she's about to fall over, so I decide to go easy on her. "That's all right." I clear my throat, shifting in the chair. "Any thoughts on what I should wear to the launch?"

Kirsty sips her water. "You're going to need a killer dress. One that will show everyone you're ready to take on the tabloid world, undercover or not."

My heart starts beating fast. Kirsty's right. In a way, this party is my debut. I need to look and act the part.

"Have you decided what you're going to do with the rest of you?" She stares pointedly at my ponytail, then lowers her gaze to include my ragged fingernails.

"Er, no." I tug the elastic from my hair, letting my lank locks fall to my shoulders. "What do you suggest?"

Kirsty tilts her head. "Well, I've always thought you could get away with quite a few blonde highlights, something to jazz it up a bit." She leans forward and lifts a clump of my hair. "And when was the last time you had a trim?"

I grimace and sit back, away from her clutches. Actually, I can't remember the last time I had a trim; it's so damn expensive here in London, and it's easier to throw my hair back in a bun or a ponytail, anyway. "Okay, okay, point made. I'll book in for a haircut tomorrow."

Kirsty gets to her feet. "Ready to find the perfect party frock, then?"

I nod. "Let's go."

We hop on the escalators and head to the street fashion (i.e. affordable) section. Scanning the forest of clothing rails, I thank my lucky stars Kirsty's here. There's so much choice I don't even know where to begin – and I don't recognise half the brands. It *almost* makes me long for Main Street in Harris, where I could just duck into JCPenney and be done with it.

"What about this one?" Kirsty holds out a sparkly red cocktail dress.

"I don't know," I say, twisting my mouth to one side as I consider it. "A bit much, don't you think?"

Kirsty shrugs. "I like it." She presses the garment against her, the vibrant red giving her cheeks colour. "This would be perfect for the office Christmas party. I might give it a try . . ." She starts to drape the dress over one arm then abruptly thrusts it back onto the rail.

"What are you doing?" I ask. "Thought you wanted to try it on."

"Not much point, is there?" She laughs hollowly. "By Christmas, I'll probably be wearing a shapeless sack and shopping in the maternity section."

I sneak a look at her grim face. "Kirsty, you can talk to me about it, you know."

She gazes down at the rack where the red dress is hanging in all its sequined glory, then meets my eyes. "You know how you said I just need time? That's what I've been telling myself, too. But I'm not sure that's it."

"What do you mean?" I ask slowly.

Kirsty lets out a sigh. "Look, if I really wanted to get married and have a baby right now, wouldn't I be happy? Sure, it's what I planned for the future – far in the future. But I can't get my head around the fact that it's happening now. I just feel . . . trapped."

I stare, unsure what to say. "Does Tim have any idea how you feel?"

Kirsty shakes her head, hair flying out like a halo. "No. He's walking around like I've handed him the winning lottery ticket. I don't even know how to start that conversation." She takes a deep breath. "The thing is, I still love him. That hasn't changed. But none of this is like I imagined. For God's sake, when Tim proposed, I was holding a mug full of pee!"

"Can I help you, ladies?" A bored-looking salesgirl saunters over to us.

"Damn," I say under my breath, as Kirsty flashes a bright smile at the woman.

"Actually, yes. Ser?" She turns away and busies herself with another rack of dresses, and I make a mental note to pick up our conversation where we've left off.

"I need a dress for a launch party," I say to the salesgirl, hoping she'll have more of a clue what that means wardrobe-wise than I do.

"What kind of launch party?" The salesgirl snaps her chewing gum, then examines her glossy, green-painted nails. Yikes. Do I really want to take fashion advice from a girl with green nails?

"For *The Daily Planet's* new health and beauty website," I respond proudly.

Her head jerks up. *"Beauty Bits?"*

"Yes. You know it?" My heart thumps as I await her response. This could be a real, live reader right in front of me!

"It's the one with that *Build a Man* thingy, innit?" The salesgirl arches an eyebrow and gives me a once-over, likely wondering how someone wearing viscose could be invited to such a trendy party. But for once, I don't care. I'm way too excited I've spotted a reader in the wild.

I nod, grinning like a fool. I'm just about to tell her *Build a Man* is my column before remembering my undercover status. Damn. Oh well, I'll get my recognition once I'm a full-fledged tabloid reporter, I'm sure.

"So you need a dress, huh? Let's get you kitted out."

I nod with excitement and let the salesgirl pile my arms high with garment after garment. But as I shimmy into one after another, none feels right. They're all nice, but I want to be noticed; to hit the tabloid world with a bang. Then, just as the store is about to close, I pull a soft chiffon dress by All Saints over my head. It falls to mid-thigh, the Grecian draping creating curves where none exist *and* making my legs look longer – although the skyscraper sandals definitely help. Small sequins sewn along the artfully distressed hems sparkle as I pivot under the lights, and the grey brings out my eyes. I look like I belong in London now; to the funky-media-type crowd; to the tabloid reporter club.

"And?" Kirsty yells from the waiting area down the corridor.

I push aside the fitting-room curtain and step out. "I think we've found it."

Her lips curve in a grin. "What do you mean, *you think*? This is it! It's perfect. And once you have your hair done, a bit of make-up . . . you'll knock 'em dead."

I scoot back into the fitting room and carefully disrobe, then saunter over to the salesgirl at the counter, handing her the sandals and dress. I dig in my bag for my credit card as she totals the sale.

"Three hundred and ten pounds, please," she says.

My mouth drops open. Three hundred and ten pounds? I'd been so caught up in the excitement of trying on dresses that I hadn't even looked at the price. That's almost five hundred dollars! But I need to spend this money – it's an investment in my future. After all, this launch party is my introduction to the media world. And appearance *is* important: I want people to treat me seriously, not like some redneck 'from America', as they say over here. If ever there was anything worthy of debt, then this is it.

I hand her the card. "Here. God, I hope this pays off," I say, turning to Kirsty.

"It will, don't worry." She glances at her watch. "Oh shit, I have to run. I've got a conference call with some clients in San Fran and I want to be on a landline to do it."

I shake my head, marvelling at her non-stop working ability. "Okay. I'll see you later, then." "Don't forget to make that hair appointment," Kirsty calls over her shoulder as she weaves between the racks of clothes. "Split ends are, like, so last year."

CHAPTER TWELVE

The next morning, I fidget (as much as one can fidget on a small circular stool one's butt keeps sliding off), awaiting Jeremy's arrival for his Botox appointment at ten. My questions – in the guise of a 'pre-surgical therapy session' – are all ready, and I'm feeling almost as nervous as if *I* was the one getting Botox (heaven forbid). It would have been much safer to conduct this interview away from Peter and the clinic, but my desperation for a dress last night and the lack of time to get my article to Leza mean it's now or never.

To distract myself, I run through my preparations for the launch party tomorrow. Tonight I've got a hair appointment at Aveda. Then tomorrow, I'm heading to Kirsty's so she can do my make-up and give me the party-ready seal of approval. I wonder if any celebs will be at this do? Or paparazzi?

I shiver with nerves and anticipation, picturing me, *The Daily Planet's* hottest new columnist, sauntering down a red carpet as all the paps snap my photo . . .

"Hello. Sorry, I'm a bit early."

My head jerks up and I see Jeremy standing in front of me, wearing his usual black T-shirt and – thankfully

– a pair of un-skinny jeans. Has he lost a bit of weight?

"Hi!" I smile, thinking it's good to see him.

"Hi, yourself." He tries to mock my accent but it comes out sounding more Australian than American, and we laugh together. "So today's the day. Botox." He props himself up against the desk, his face pinched and pale.

"It's normal to be nervous," I say in what I hope is a soothing tone. God, if he's this jittery now, what will he be like when he's about to have his face ripped apart in a hospital? I glance around to make sure Peter's tucked away somewhere, then lean forward. "Typically, I conduct a pre-treatment session to calm nerves and put you in the ideal psychological state. Sound good?"

"Sure." Jeremy fixes his brilliant green eyes on me. "Fire away."

I grab my notebook then scoot around the desk, motioning him to sit on a leather chair. Plopping into the one beside him, I flip to my list of questions. "Okay. First of all, let's go through the areas you're having done today. To have you focus on the specifics instead of the fear." Gosh, that sounds good, doesn't it? Sometimes I can't believe the stuff I come out with.

Jeremy points to the cute crinkly lines by the sides of his eyes. "Right here, and these wrinkles on my forehead are going today, too."

I bite my lip to stop a sigh of dismay from escaping. I love the way his face moves with almost every emotion. If he gets Botox, that'll be wiped clean.

"Anything else?" I ask.

"Dr Lycett did mention an acid . . . something to give my face more definition. I might go for that, as well." Jeremy looks almost giddy now.

"Hyaluronic acid," I say. "It's a filler; really popular to plump up cheekbones and lips. But if you're getting more work done on your face, you're probably better off waiting. Peter will explain it all, I'm sure." Yeah, right, I add in my head. Peter's a great salesman and a good doctor, but explaining things to patients isn't exactly his strong suit. I've had women present their bill to me without any clue what they've been injected with. And the sad thing is, they don't really care, as long as they appear younger.

"Oh. Okay, then," Jeremy responds, looking deflated.

"What are you hoping to achieve with Botox?" I ask, trying to get all the basic stuff out of the way before I can probe deeper.

"Nothing too dramatic. I just want to be 'fresher'."

I barely refrain from rolling my eyes. The number of times I've heard people say they want to look 'fresher', as if they were a rotting vegetable.

"How do you feel, getting a treatment that's generally used by women, not men?"

Jeremy smiles. "I don't care if it's used more by llamas, as long as it helps me look my best."

"Llamas?" I can't help snickering at that one and Jeremy joins in, our laughter echoing around the empty waiting area.

"Thank you, Serenity." Jeremy's face is serious again. "I was really nervous, but you've helped me relax."

"That's my job." My tummy turns over as my eyes meet his. "How about we try another relaxation technique," I say, to break the moment. "Just close your eyes and count slowly to ten. Now breathe in . . ." I watch as his broad chest expands, wondering where the hell I'm going with this. At least he's not staring at me any more. "Now out . . ." His dark lashes quiver against his cheeks and I wonder what he's thinking.

"Serenity?" Peter pokes his head into the reception area. "Oh, hello, Jeremy." Jeremy's eyes fly open and Peter shoots me a funny look. "What on earth are you two doing?"

Shit. My heart starts beating double-time. "Just helping Jeremy relax," I warble, before Jeremy has a chance to respond. Please God may he not say anything!

"Sure, sure, fine," Peter mutters, barely even registering I've spoken. He gives Jeremy his trust-me-I'm-a-doctor smile. "Ready to go?"

Jeremy nods, then turns toward me. "Wish me luck. And thanks for the pre-session therapy."

"Good luck," I croak, collapsing back against the chair. Thank goodness Peter's already halfway down the corridor.

As I settle onto my stool, it hits me that Jeremy and I are both starting on our journeys – except all his changes are on the outside, while most of mine are taking place internally. Already I feel more successful; more confident about staking my claim in the realm of tabloid journalism. Just like Jeremy, by the end of this *Build a Man* thing, I'm sure I'll be the person I've always wanted to be, with the life I've always dreamed of. Serenity v2: the newer, upgraded version.

I daydream my way through the mind-numbing task of filling in new patient forms on the computer, my head snapping up when I hear Peter's voice. Yup, ten minutes, I think as I glance at the clock. That's Jeremy's Botox done, then.

"Serenity, can you get some ice, please." Peter gently manoeuvres Jeremy into a chair. "Now, Jeremy, you'll be fine. Bruising is a normal part of the procedure, along with extra redness, too. Just have a seat here with some ice for ten minutes."

I rush to the freezer in the supply room, grab an ice pack we keep on hand for moments like this, then head back to the reception area.

"Here you go." I hand the ice to Jeremy, trying not to recoil as I take in the angry red bruises ringing the injection sites on his forehead and beside his eyes.

"Thanks." Jeremy tries to smile, flinching in pain.

"So I'll leave you in Serenity's capable hands," Peter says. "Any problems, please don't hesitate to give me a ring. In the meantime, we'll schedule in your blepharoplasty, rhinoplasty, and chin liposuction – probably for a few weeks from now, depending on availability. And I'll see you next week for the laser-skin resurfacing."

God, if Jeremy looks like this now, I can only imagine the state of him once the top layer of his skin has been singed away.

"Thank you, Doctor," Jeremy responds weakly, pressing the ice pack against his forehead. He glances up at me with an embarrassed expression. "I know, I'm a wuss. I'm sure women just take it in their stride."

I sink down beside him. "Looks like you've had a particularly strong reaction. It does vary, from person to person." I touch his arm as he grimaces again. "So . . . are you sure you want to go through with the rest?" The question is out of my mouth before I can stop it. The last thing I want is to give him any doubts, but he just looks so uncomfortable.

Jeremy nods and a whoosh of relief – mixed with something else – goes through me. "I'm sure. This probably looks worse than it is, and, well, I'm tired of being a loser women only want for money. I've got to go through with it." He turns to face me and I feel a jolt as his green eyes connect with mine. "This is it, Serenity. I'm not going to back down now."

126

I hold his gaze. "I understand." God, do I ever.

Ten minutes later, the swelling on Jeremy's face has reduced and the redness has faded slightly. He pushes out the clinic door, looking relieved to escape. The day drags on and finally, it's time for me to head to the Aveda on Marylebone High Street. As I sit in the stylist's chair listening to the same wailing whale CD we have back at the clinic, I await my own transformation. Sure, it's minor compared to what Jeremy has planned, but it's symbolic of much bigger changes inside. New look, new life! I almost snort as my patter from Jeremy's wardrobe session floats into my head.

"So what are we doing today?" Zach, the stylist, eyes my limp sandy hair with distaste.

"I don't know . . ." My voice trails off. "I'm thinking blonder?"

"Too right. I'm thinking a lot blonder." He squints in the mirror at my reflection. "And one of those asymmetrical cuts. You know, like Ciara Mattos. They're really in right now."

An image of the lead singer from DoMe flashes into my brain, and I swallow hard. No way do I want to look like I've had half my head shaved. "Um, I don't think I'm ready for that."

I grab a magazine and flip through it, looking for something close to what I want. A photo of a model, standing on top of a globe as if she owns it, catches my eye. I stare at her hair, cut in a blunt line just grazing her cheekbones. Power oozes from her and I gaze at the image, entranced. I'd kill to be like that. Confident. Taking over the world.

"How about this?" I shove the picture toward Zach, who raises his over-plucked eyebrows in surprise.

"Well, hell, yeah!" He moves my hair around this

127

way and that, lifting it up and yanking it back. "You have the face to pull it off. It'll be a big change, though."

I think of Jeremy and his determination, and my lips lift in a smile. "That's exactly what I want."

After paging through the magazine for a few hours (yes, *hours*) as Zach works his magic, he finally stops toying with my locks and swivels me toward the mirror. "Ta da!" he says with a flourish, fluffing my hair a final time.

My eyes pop as I stare at a woman with a short blonde bob. Is that *me*? I lift my hands to touch the now-golden hair. "Wow."

"I know," Zach crows. "What a difference. You look brill."

My stylish new cut actually gives me cheekbones, and my eyes seem even bigger. Somehow, Zach's managed to make my hair shinier and full of light, like I've been sitting outside in the sun. It's blonde, but it's not the Leza white-blonde I was dreading. I look trendy and cool.

I look like a real, live tabloid reporter.

CHAPTER THIRTEEN

Big Pricks First Step to Meeting Dream Woman, the
headline on my *Build a Man* column says the next day,
and I can't help giggling even though I've read it a
million times already. I was sure Leza would like that
one. Jeremy probably would, too, if he knew the
column featured him.

> James says the painful pricks of
> the Botox needle are nothing if it
> gets him closer to his ideal
> woman. Yesterday, our Build a Man
> endured multiple shots of Botox to
> the forehead and eye areas in the
> first step of his transformation.
>
> "It hurt like hell, but it'll be
> worth it if I meet the woman of my
> dreams," he said, once the
> treatment was completed.

The woman of his dreams. Is it possible? Does the
perfect partner *really* exist? I let out a puff of air,
thinking of Peter's reaction to my brand new image.
When I got home from the salon last night, he barely
looked up from his brushing session with Smitty. It

was only when I climbed into bed that he noticed my hair, saying it was 'very nice; more clinic appropriate . . . but a touch too blonde', before flipping over and snoring within five seconds.

It's funny, but I never noticed how everything in our life revolves around him. His job, his eating habits, *his* needs. I guess it's because I didn't have anything of my own. Now that I do – even though I can't share it with him – it's becoming more and more obvious how lopsided our relationship is.

Just wait until I get that job, I tell myself. Then I'll quit the clinic and we'll be on equal footing. I'll be a strong career woman, Peter will respect my ambition and drive (if not my place of employment; I can't expect miracles), and things will be fine. Serenity v2 will be that perfectly pulled together person I've been striving for.

I glance at the screen again, grimacing at the cut-out paper doll with Sean Penn's nose, now dressed in the skinny trousers and pink shirt combo. I can't believe *Fashion Passion* won! Who on earth is voting in this thing?

Today's poll focuses on eyes, asking readers to choose from Tom Cruise (not bad); Justin Bieber (seriously?); or Simon Cowell (what? Can anyone really get past the high-waisted jeans and gleaming teeth to *notice* his eyes?). I shake my head, thinking Jeremy's eyes are a million times better than any of these celebs. Tom Cruise comes the closest, so I click on him and blink as the screen refreshes. Almost eight thousand readers have voted. A grin spreads across my face and my heart starts beating fast. *Eight thousand!* That's more people than live in Harris.

The phone rings and I glance at the clock. It's almost six, and I should be racing out the door to Kirsty's for my pre-party hair and make-up.

'Hello, Transforma Harley Street,' I say in a tired voice, hoping whoever's on the other end will take the hint. Instead, a woman unleashes a torrent of angst about her droopy eyelid, a possible side effect of her recent Botox injection.

"I must see the doctor," she demands. "I look like a retard."

A retard? I shake my head as she continues her tirade. Peter always mocks my over-the-top penchant for political correctness, but I'm pretty sure even in Britain it's considered offensive to call someone a retard.

"I can't go to this charity benefit looking like a one-eyed wonder," she screeches. I hold the phone away from my ear, thinking how ironic it would be if the charity was something to do with helping the developmentally delayed or the blind.

"Just let me talk to the doctor," I interrupt, jabbing a finger at the 'hold' button.

"Peter!" I shout. "I need to leave, but there's a woman on the phone who wants to come in and see you. Droopy eyelid or something." I'm desperate to get out of here now.

"Put her through. You can go if you want."

I quickly transfer the call and hear it ringing in his office.

"I'll be home in a few hours," Peter yells before picking it up. "Hello, Doctor Lycett here. What can I do for you?" he says in smooth tones before his door swings closed.

I haven't had the chance to fabricate an excuse for tonight, so I quickly scribble down a note that I'm over at Kirsty's – not exactly a lie, since I *will* be there (for about thirty minutes, anyway). Then I grab my bag, dash home for my dress and shoes, and rush over to her house. By the time I get there, I'm dripping with sweat and more in need of a makeover than ever.

"Sorry, Kirst," I pant when she answers the door. "I got caught up with a crazy woman at the clinic."

She shakes her head, but she's too busy staring at me to launch into her usual speech about the importance of timekeeping. "Wow. You look amazing, Ser. Great haircut!" There's an admiring look in her eyes that I've never seen before. Not that I blame her – it's hard to admire mousy, flat hair.

"Oh, thanks." I reach up and stroke my locks tentatively. In my haste to get here, I'd completely forgotten about my new look.

"When I told you to get a trim, I didn't expect you'd chop it all off." She ushers me up the stairs and into the bedroom.

I shrug and collapse on the bed, trying to catch my breath. "I just felt it was time. Peter's always saying 'dress for the person you want to be' and all that . . . well, this" – I point to my hair – "is who I want to be."

Kirsty nods, looking impressed. "It's awesome." She rubs her hands together, then picks up her bulging cosmetics case. "And once you have your make-up done and you're in that dress, you'll be fabulous. Now, hurry up and change so we can get started."

I pull off my usual clinic outfit of black trousers and blouse. Then I reverentially lift the grey dress from its clinging cellophane wrapper, admiring the sequins and floaty chiffon. I don't think I've ever owned anything quite so beautiful (or expensive, for that matter). I carefully ease myself into the garment, holding my breath as I zip up the side. It catches my soft skin and I yelp, cursing the extra Jaffa I shoved down my throat this morning.

"Okay, I'm ready." I lower myself onto the bed. The dress barely covers the tops of my thighs, and I tug at it nervously.

"Right, well, your hair is fine," Kirsty says after bursting back into the room. "I'm just going to backcomb it a bit for some body." I can feel her moving my locks around, then the *whoosh* of the hairspray. "And a little foundation, some powder and blusher . . ."

"So what are you doing tonight?" I ask, expecting her to say that she and Tim are off to the latest client dinner or the bank's box at the opera, as usual.

"Not much." She sweeps a soft brush over my cheek. "The firm's really cutting back on all the corporate entertainment stuff. And I'm so tired these days. Now, press your lips together for a sec."

As Kirsty works her magic, I think about how strange this is. Usually, she's the one preparing to go out and schmooze at big client dinners, getting all dressed up. Now, it's me.

"Look my way," she commands, picking up a mascara wand.

I meet her hazel eyes, noticing they're still red with even bigger bags than before. Snippets of our conversation at Selfridges yesterday drift through my mind and I bite my lip, recalling her words about feeling trapped.

"Kirsty, tell me how I can help," I say suddenly, dodging the wand nearing my eye.

"You can stay still and let me get on with it." She comes at me with the wand again.

I force myself to relax as she glides mascara over my lashes. "Tell me how I can help with what's happening. You now, the baby and stuff." The gliding stops and I look up, my heart sinking when I notice her eyes glinting with tears. God, I wish I knew what to say. But Kirsty's so strong and confident that I've never been in this situation with her before.

She leans back and heaves a sigh. "Just be there for me. Like you always are." Her voice is sad, and I reach out and touch her arm.

"Oh, before I forget, Tim wants me to invite you and Peter over for dinner tomorrow night. Six okay?" Kirsty grabs a pink lipstick, back to her efficient self. "Sorry for the late notice. Tim's had his head buried in something the past few days and he only just told me about his grand plans now."

"Okay, sure. I think we're free tomorrow." I *know* we're free – we always are. I'll have to drag Peter from the clinic, but anything other than chicken fillet is a welcome change.

I sit in silence as Kirsty paints on a few coats of lip-gloss, then brushes some loose power over my face.

"There, finished. Have a look."

I glance into the compact, gasping at my reflection. Kirsty's lined my eyes with black kohl and piled on the blush. Along with my new haircut, I could fit right into that super-stylish newsroom. I slip on my new sandals and stalk over to the full-length mirror beside the door.

"So? What do you think, Madame Tabloid Star?"

"Thanks, Kirsty. I love it!"

I look tall. I look glamorous. I look nothing like the usual *me*. But that's the whole point. If I wanted to show everyone the usual me, I might as well throw on my cat-hair-covered jogging bottoms and my old Britney Spears T-shirt. This is the confident, eat-you-alive woman I want to be – Serenity v2, with bells on – and I just might be getting there.

What will Jeremy think when he sees me? I'm certainly different to the receptionist he met just a week or so ago. My cheeks heat up as I picture his eyes raking over me, his face full of awe and admiration (as much as the Botox will allow) as he takes in my makeover . . .

"Ready to go, then?" Kirsty's voice cuts into my daydream and my cheeks flush even more.

I turn away to hide my glowing face, grabbing my belted red H&M trench coat.

"Um, no." Kirsty wags her finger at me as I shrug it on. "You're not wearing that over your dress."

I grimace at myself in the mirror. She's right – the casual red jacket really doesn't go with the urban-cool dress, not to mention my make-up and hair. I look like Little Red Riding Hood on her way to a street corner. "I didn't bring anything else."

Kirsty shakes her head. "I'm not letting you ruin my handiwork by wearing that. You don't need a coat, anyway. Just grab a cab."

I nod, not wanting to tell her that I don't have cash for a cab right now. The last time I mentioned not having money, Kirsty launched into a tirade that Peter really should be paying me more, so at least I could live each month without relying on my overdraft. It's hard to ask for a raise from your boyfriend, though – especially when you're living rent free. "Yeah, okay."

Swinging open the door, Kirsty gives me a quick hug. "Good luck!"

Wrapping my arms around my chest to try to keep warm, I watch the door close behind her. God, I wish she could come, too – break the ice with everyone for me, the way it's always been. Now, I'm on my own.

Taking a deep breath, I let my arms drop to my sides and stride along, the sharp staccato of my high heels echoing down the street. The old me might have been a little shy, but this is the new, upgraded me. And

Serenity v2 can face a room full of strangers, no problem.

Clattering down the stairs into the Tube, I ignore the looks of interest from the stodgy, tired men bundled into ill-fitting polyester business suits, and race toward the platform where a wonderfully warm (if smelly) train awaits.

CHAPTER FOURTEEN

Thirty minutes later, I'm standing in front of the brick exterior of the Hospital Club. It's just after seven-thirty, and judging from the shouts of laughter and music I hear from the open windows, the launch party is in full swing. There aren't any paps and there's no red carpet, but this is it – my debut into the tabloid world.

I puff up my hair, smooth down my dress, and adopt a confident stride over to the door, where a man in black is guarding the entrance.

"Serenity Holland for the *Beauty Bits* launch party," I say to the guard, cursing my quavery voice.

"Right." He scans the list in front of him, then puts a tick on the clipboard and points to some stairs. "First floor."

Nodding, I head up the steps toward the noise, almost dizzy now with nerves.

At the top of the staircase, I scan the room in front of me, looking for Leza . . . or anyone I might be able to talk to. The small space is packed with bodies, and the soft glow of pink lights makes everyone look like featureless blobs.

People cluster together in tight little groups with

their backs to me, and I can't even begin to make out where the bar might be. I'm dying for a drink to take the edge off my nerves.

I push my way through the braying crowd, grimacing as I bang my knees against a glass bar. A couple bruises are a small sacrifice for alcohol, and I practically collapse in relief as I order up a Cosmopolitan. Yes, I *know* I'm not Sarah Jessica Parker – I'm practically *Celibate and the City* – but this doesn't seem like a rum-and-Coke kind of venue. Cold fingers grasp my arm and I spin around.

"Aren't you that *Build a Bloke* writer?" A girl around my age and about a foot taller – with long, sleek auburn hair and a pale complexion to die for – is studying me through narrowed eyes.

"Hi. Yes, I am. It's *Build a Man*, actually." It must be okay to ditch my undercover persona if she already knows it's me. I stretch out my hand to shake hers, but I end up knocking her glass. A few drops splash out onto her metallic shift dress. "Oh, sorry!"

The glamazon laughs. "Don't worry. It's Teflon-coated, specially made by Kenzie King. You know, the up-and-coming designer from Saint Martins."

Kenzie who? "Oh yes, of course." I nod, making a mental note to look up Kenzie King and Saint Martins (whatever the hell that is) as soon as I get home.

Glamazon smirks, arching her eyebrows like she can read my mind. "So . . . what do you think?" She throws out her arms and looks around the room with a smug expression.

"Um, yes, it's great. Great party," I stammer. Who the hell is this person?

She nods. "I know. I organised the whole thing. I was worried you wouldn't make it. For some reason, your email invite kept bouncing back."

Glamazon's eyes are wide and innocent, but I'm not sure I believe her. Leza's emails got through fine, along with several thousand spam. Why wouldn't this person want me here?

"So we haven't been introduced," I say, trying to figure out who she is. Judging by the way she's acting, she must be some bigwig reporter.

Her thin lips stretch in a smile and she holds out a skeletal hand. "Mia Sutton."

"What do you do on the paper?" The barman finally passes me my drink, and I take a giant slurp. If I was desperate for one before, now I'm practically gagging.

Mia flips a section of perfectly straight glossy hair over a bony shoulder. "I'm an intern. For now. But I'm a dead cert for the junior reporter position that's opening up."

"Junior reporter position?" I croak, her words swirling around my head. That can't be the same one Leza's promised me, can it? "That's great. Me too."

Mia's spine stiffens. "There's only one position coming up. I should know; I had to do a week's work in HR, and I saw the files." She narrows her eyes again, then shrugs like she couldn't care less.

She can squint at me all she wants in her plasticized dress, I think, still reeling from the fact that I now have competition. It doesn't matter – that job's mine. I'm *not* going to back down.

I turn away to rearrange my features into the perfectly blasé expression Mia's adopted, and my heart drops.

No.

No way.

Latched onto a man dripping with gold chains, and – if possible – even more tanned than when I saw her yesterday, is Princesz Gayle. My eyes widen as she throws back her head in a loud, grating laugh, then downs her pink champagne in one gulp.

'Who do I have to fuck to get another drink around here?' Her elephant-sized head swivels in the direction of the bar and, as if she senses my gaze, focuses in on me.

Shit.

I drop my head and examine my drink, hoping she doesn't come any nearer. If she recognises me from the clinic . . . I don't even want to think what might happen. I shuffle closer to Mia, wishing there was a bit more of her to hide behind.

"Hiya!" Princesz Gayle's nails claw at my arm, and I lower my head even more, praying she'll go away.

"Don't I know you from somewhere?" The scratching intensifies to a persistent poking.

"What the hell's wrong with you?" Mia hisses.

I've no choice but to face the harpy. "Hello. Um, no, I don't think so," I say in as bland a tone as possible, staring at a point just over Princesz's shoulder to avoid meeting her eyes. There's no way I can escape that biscuity smell of fake tan, though, which hangs around her like an ominous cloud. The odour makes me long for my Jaffas and my stomach grumbles. I haven't eaten since I slurped back my Pot Noodles at lunch.

Princesz's eyes bore through me and I hold my breath. With my new look, there's a chance she won't be able to place me. I was nothing more than an insignificant receptionist to her, anyway.

"I'm really good with faces." Tilting her head, she leans in to peer more closely. I jerk away, my drink sloshing over the edges of my martini glass. "Were you at the *Porn or Die* show at the O2 last week?"

I shake my head. "No. I'm sure we've never met."

"Maybe I've seen you around Stringfellows? Because

you look so familiar . . ." She's staring at me so intently, I feel like there's a sign blinking above my head spelling out: BOTOX CLINIC! BOTOX CLINIC! I've got to get away.

"Is that the time?" I make a big show of looking at my watch before realising I'm not actually wearing one. *Idiot.* It's too late to stop my little charade, though, so I plough ahead, ignoring Mia's smirk. "I've got an appointment, so I have to jet. Goodbye!" I throw a manic smile over my shoulder and push through the crowd. My breath's coming fast and I can feel sweat breaking out on my forehead.

"I'll give Leza your best, shall I?" Mia shouts after me.

I turn and see her smiling to herself as she wraps a fistful of hair around her hand. God, she'd fit right in with the Botox Bitches at the clinic.

I clunk down the stairs as fast as my high heels will let me, stumbling into the guard at the bottom.

"Whoa," he says, helping me upright. "You can't take that with you, love." He points to the martini glass in my hand, where a hint of liquid pools at the bottom. I swig it quickly, then push the glass at him and head into the street. It's cold and wet, and without a jacket, every bit of moisture against my bare skin feels like a prick of ice.

I glance up at the bright windows – lights, laughter and music still streaming from them – as drizzle drips down my face, likely taking half my make-up with it. Wrapping my chilly arms around me, I try to stop shivering.

Maybe I shouldn't have run out, but my only thought was escape. Seeing Princesz amidst all those tabloid people was like a collision of my two worlds, as if two separate colour spheres overlapped for a second, creating a scarily ugly shade. And what if Princesz *does* figure out where she knows me from?

A wave of fatigue sweeps over me, and it's all I can do to stay on my feet as the jumbled mix of nervous tension, excitement, and determination drains away. The dress, my hair, my make-up – this party – seem like part of another life, and all I want is to throw on my shapeless tracksuit, curl up with my Jaffas, and watch sitcoms for hours until sleep overtakes me. But I know that as soon as I get home, Peter will have the TV tuned to some educational yet oh-so-boring programme, and I'll sit there, mute, until he falls asleep and I can change it over to *Friends*. I enjoy being with him, of course I do. Sometimes, though, I wish it wasn't such an effort; that I didn't have to continually try to be neat, organised, and everything else I'm not. Not yet, anyway.

I rummage in my bag for my mobile, then punch in Kirsty's number. It's still early, and if I jump on the Tube now, I can be there in thirty minutes.

But the phone just rings and rings, then clicks through to voice mail. No point leaving a message; it'll probably be tomorrow before she calls back. I stare at the mobile in my hand and watch as my fingers – like they're separated from the rest of my body – scroll through the contacts, find Jeremy, and hit 'Call'.

What the hell am I doing?

I'm about to hang up when Jeremy's warm voice comes on the line. I smile, feeling better already.

"Just checking in to see how you're feeling," I say. That sounds plausible, right? He really wasn't in great shape post-Botox. And some people *do* have severe reactions to injections. It's good practice to follow-up.

"I'm fine," he responds. "The swelling's gone down, and my face is almost back to normal. Well, except for the fact that my forehead doesn't move." I can almost imagine him trying to wiggle his eyebrows.

"Good, good." An awkward silence descends and I cough. "Well, um," I say, just as Jeremy starts to talk, and we laugh.

"You go first." I gesture for him to carry on, then realise he can't see me and drop my arm to my side.

"What are you doing tonight?" he asks.

"Nothing right now." Sighing, I look up at the still-rollicking party.

"Well, if you're not busy, do you want to come round to mine?" he asks. "In your official capacity, of course – maybe for some wine therapy?"

For a split of a second, I'm not sure what to say. Jeremy's not asking me out, is he?

Don't be stupid, I tell myself. He did say 'official capacity', after all. It's not a date; it's a life advisory session. And I should jump at the opportunity to get closer to my subject, right?

"That would be awesome." I'm already envisioning a large red in Jeremy's cosy, warm house. "I mean, yes, that sounds delightful."

"Great. I'll see you soon." He hangs up and I scurry toward the Tube as fast as I can.

Half an hour later, Jeremy's door swings open and I practically swoon with relief. The straps on my new sandals feel like razor blades, cutting deeper into my skin with every step. My hands are so cold, my fingernails have turned purple, and I've just spent an uncomfortable twenty minutes on the Tube being ogled by a group of butch lesbians out on their hen night.

Jeremy's eyes widen as he scans my outfit. "Wow! Look at you. Where have you been?"

I flush. In my haste to get here, I hadn't thought up an excuse for my rather un-life-advisory outfit. "I was at a convention for life coaches. Just an evening session."

"You lot are certainly a classy bunch," he says, ushering me inside. "I like your new look." The heat hits my bare skin and I stand still for a second. Bliss.

"Yes, well. You know. Dress for the person you want to be and all that." I glance up at him and smile. The after effects of yesterday's injections are barely visible, and the skin around his eyes and forehead is tighter and smoother. He looks 'fresher', all right, but I miss those tiny crinkles.

"Does not wearing coats fit into that? You're soaking." Jeremy reaches out and touches my arm, and I can't help but take a step closer into his warmth. "And you're absolutely freezing. Why don't I give you something dry to put on? Go take a hot shower, if you like, and get yourself warmed up. You're going to catch your death, as my gran used to say."

The thought of a steamy hot shower – especially in Jeremy's wonder-bathroom – and comfy dry clothes is irresistible. "That sounds fantastic."

"Come on. I'll find you something to wear." He beckons for me to follow him up the stairs. I slip off my grimy, wet sandals and pad after him into the bedroom, squealing as I catch sight of myself in the mirror. My hair is plastered to my head, mascara and kohl have seeped down my eye sockets like Alice Cooper gone wrong, and my All Saints organza dress looks like a sodden bin liner. I quickly wipe under my eyes as best I can, slick back my hair, and pluck the dress from my skin.

"Why didn't you tell me I looked like something the cat dragged in?" I ask as Jeremy rummages through the wardrobe.

"I happen to like what the cat drags in. Anyway, you

always look great." He ducks his head, rifling through a drawer. "Hope this is all right." Jeremy hands me a worn sweater in the same shade as his eyes, and a pair of drawstring jogging bottoms. "Not exactly 'dress for the person you want to be', but it's all I have that might possibly fit you."

"It's perfect." Already, I'm imagining the feel of soft, yielding fabric against my skin. "Right now, that" – I point to the clothes – "is exactly who I want to be. Warm and comfy."

Jeremy shoots me a grin like he completely understands, then hands me a fluffy white towel. "Use whatever you like in the shower, and give me a yell if you need anything else. Do you want me to pop that dress in the dryer?"

"No!" I yelp, cringing at the thought of my precious dress shrinking. "I mean, no thank you, that's fine. Thanks again, Jeremy. I'll be ready to start wine therapy as soon as I'm down." He just shakes his head and keeps grinning, then turns to go.

Fifteen glorious Rainshowered minutes later, I'm standing in the middle of Jeremy's bathroom, wrapped in a soft towel. I scrub some steam from the medicine cabinet, pausing as a thought hits me. Is Julia's watch still there? Slowly, I ease open the cabinet door, running my eyes over the packets and bottles. I push aside a few to reach the corner where the watch was jammed. But . . . it's nowhere to be found. A small pang of happiness hits me. He must be over Julia! My therapy with Jeremy is working, after all. I *knew* this would be mutually beneficial.

I give my hair a quick rub then scrub the remaining bits of mascara from my face, wishing I was one of those walking-make-up-case women. The best I can do is slick on some lip gloss. Then I pull on Jeremy's drawstring trousers (thank God for the drawstring or they'd be around my ankles) and jam the sweater over my head. A spicy scent rises up around me, and for a second I feel like I'm wrapped in Jeremy's arms.

After arranging my wet dress over the shower rail, I leave behind the lovely warmth of the bathroom and go downstairs. The delicious scent of grilled meat hits my nose and my stomach growls.

"Feeling warmer?" Jeremy asks over the sizzle of something on the hob. "I hope you like burgers, because I'm frying up a storm here."

Burgers! I haven't had one since coming to London (no way would anyone label me a gauche McAmerican, I'd vowed), but back home, I'd considered myself a burger aficionado. "I love them." I smile at Jeremy, my mouth watering.

"Ready for some pre-dinner wine therapy?" Jeremy turns from the stove and hands me a brimming glass of red wine. I take a big sip and sit down at the wooden table, thinking how comfortable I feel here and how nice it is to just *be* with him, without my notebook and questions. There's none of the awkward silence that settles over my conversations with Peter as I struggle to find something intellectual to say.

"So tell me." Jeremy puts two plates with giant burgers on the table. "Why a life advisor? You don't seem the usual type. And you're quite young, aren't you?"

I pause as I breathe in the delicious odour of grease and meat, unsure how to take his words. What does being young have to do with anything? It's not that hard to know what you want out of life. I know exactly what I want, and I'm well on my way to achieving it, too.

"It's just so rewarding, helping people get their lives

on track." I take a big bite of the burger, chewing slowly to prevent having to say more. I swallow, then ask: "What about you? What do you enjoy about your chosen career path?" I sip my wine then motion for him to do the same, remembering we're supposed to be in the throes of a session.

Jeremy gulps his drink. "It's very fulfilling working with wood; doing property reconstructions. I like taking something old – that other people have given up on – and creating something new." He wipes his mouth. "Kind of what you and Dr Lycett are doing for me, I guess."

I nod, turning his words over in my head. If I'm honest, building something new by assembling words is the bit about reporting that I really like, too. Add a little glamour and gossip into the mix, and it's the perfect job.

We chat the rest of the way through our burgers, Jeremy telling me enthusiastically about all the renovations he's done – including a barn he owns in some place called the Wye Valley, which he says is like heaven on Earth – and his most recent project, a flat he's working on for a housing shelter scheme. Finally, our plates are empty and we rub our bellies, laughing at how we've both managed to put away the humongous burger. I haven't seen portions like that since leaving home.

"I'd better go," I say, looking at the clock in horror. It's almost eleven, and Peter will no doubt be wondering where I am. "Do you mind if I rush off? I'll just change first and give you back your things." I shudder inwardly at the thought of climbing into my sodden dress and the sandals from hell, and a thought hits me: without a coat to hide my outfit, how am I going to explain my attire to Peter?

147

Jeremy waves a hand as we walk toward the door. "Don't worry about it – you can return everything the next time I see you. That sweater looks better on you than it ever did on me, anyway."

Phew. At least I can tell Peter I borrowed these clothes from Kirsty . . . or something. "Thank you – and thanks for the great burger, too." I pat my very full tummy, certain that whoever invented drawstrings must have been a woman. Shame there isn't a drawstring equivalent for evil shoes, I think, reaching down for them. I'm not sure I can fit my swollen, bloodied feet back into these things.

"It's quite late. Would you like me to get you a cab?" Jeremy's face is serious, and an expression I can't read has come into his green eyes. He reaches for the door handle but puts a hand on mine instead, and for a second everything freezes.

Suddenly I'm desperate to get out of there and into the fresh air.

"No, I'm fine," I say quickly, turning away from him to open the door. "I'll talk to you soon."

Before Jeremy can respond, I've jammed my feet into my shoes and I'm on the street. The baggy-trousers-with-sandals ensemble certainly won't win any fashion awards, and my feet throb with every step, but the pain is a welcome distraction from the confusion churning inside.

It's only when I'm halfway home that I realise Serenity v2's dress is still hanging, like shed skin, from Jeremy's shower rail.

CHAPTER FIFTEEN

Saw you come in last night. No chance
to chat. Call me.

I try to decipher the tone of Leza's email, but the words onscreen tell me nothing. My head pounds and my stomach is still struggling to digest those burgers, but last night's indulgences are the least of my worries. What's really on my mind is *Mia*. With everything that happened yesterday – fleeing Princesz Gayle, seeing Jeremy, then coming home to a half-asleep Peter, who barely even looked at me (thank goodness drawstring trousers aren't his thing) – I hadn't fully absorbed the fact that I've got stiff competition. Well, I've certainly absorbed it now.

Breathing in deeply, I clutch onto the reception desk. Everything will be fine, I tell myself. I'll probably never see Mia again, anyway. I'll just get on with my column and nail that job.

The waiting room's empty and Peter's office door is closed, so I pick up my mobile and call Leza.

"Leza? It's Serenity, from *Build a Man*."

"Serenity. Hang on a sec; just let me grab Mia."

There's a click as she puts me on hold, and my head

starts racing. Why does Mia need to be in on this? Mia has nothing to do with *Build a Man*.

"All right. We're back." Leza's voice sounds far away, and I realise she's put me on speakerphone.

"Hello," Mia says smoothly. I can almost imagine her flipping that flame-coloured hair over her shoulder. "Lovely to meet you last night. Brilliant party, wasn't it? Shame you had to leave early. Guess you couldn't reschedule your appointment for something as unimportant as a launch party."

I grit my teeth. *Remember, put a smile in your voice!* I stretch my lips wide, hoping it will translate into my tone. "No, I couldn't. But anyway," I say, eager to change the topic, "I have some great ideas for my next column."

"Well, that's exactly why I'm calling," Leza says. "We're low on content this weekend and with your column doing so well, I want to make it Sunday's lead story on the site. We'll put it right up under the banner."

"Awesome." Already I'm picturing the *Build a Man* logo at the top of the webpage. Only my fourth column and already the lead story! But why oh why is Mia in on this call?

"Yeah, it's *awesome*," Leza mocks my accent. Mia breaks into a snorting laugh, and I vow never to use that word again. "Anyway, look. For this article, I want you to get more detail on Jeremy's ideal woman and his dream date, blah blah blah. We've an inbox full of emails from readers just gagging to know, silly idiots. We need to throw them a bone."

"Okay." That's going to be an easy one – getting more detail out of Jeremy shouldn't be an issue.

But *why is Mia on the line*?

"And I want Mia to go with you when you meet

Jeremy. I don't care how you explain it – come up with something. The story's getting too big now to have just one of you on it. If anything goes wrong between you and Jeremy, we need a backup."

My pulse pounds in my head. "But Jeremy's *my* source." I will the words to come out strongly and confidently, but instead my voice sounds shaky.

Leza laughs. "Your source? You're an unpaid contributor, Serenity, not fucking Lois Lane. If you do want a position here, you'd better learn teamwork."

I swallow, feeling about as big as a squashed bug. "Fine." Teamwork with Mia is the last thing I want – right down there after cleaning the loo, which Peter insists is part of my reception duties. But if I have to show Leza I can do it, then I don't exactly have a choice. Anyway, Mia will see how good my relationship with Jeremy is, and how much we don't need her around. Memories of my time with him last night flood into my head, and a warm feeling grows in my belly. And no, that's not acid reflux.

"Have the copy to me by Saturday at five," Leza says. "Serenity, you'll be writing the main feature. Mia, I want you to come up with a new poll. I'll leave you girls to get on with it now. If you have any problems, I don't want to hear about it."

There's a silence, then Mia's voice says: "She's gone. I can't wait to work with you." Her tone is so syrupy I almost want to gag – no way am I buying that act. She weaselled her way into this, and I'm certainly not going to behave all buddy-buddy.

"Yeah. Look, this is my feature. I'm working with you because I have to, that's all." I'm keen to set her straight right now, before we even get started.

Her laugh tinkles through the phone. "For God's sake, relax. I have no intention of taking over your precious column. It was Leza's idea I provide backup, that's all."

"Whatever." My voice is tight. "I'll need to talk to Jeremy first to set things up. I'll call you once I have the time and place arranged."

She gives me her number and I hang up as fast as I can, not sure I can keep a lid on the emotions boiling inside me any longer. Anger, fear, and a fierce determination that Mia will *not* push me out are bubbling away to form a very unpleasant cocktail. I take a deep breath.

Calm down, I tell myself. The column's yours; everyone knows that. Jeremy trusts *you*. Leza's impressed with what you've done. Mia's just an intern. There's no way she can compete.

But . . . she does have direct access to Leza *and* she knows everyone in the office, whereas I left the launch party early and didn't even manage to talk to my editor, let alone meet any other staff.

Pressing my hands against my hot cheeks, I try to put everything back in perspective. So I have a little competition for the job I'm after. So what? That's to be expected. With *Build a Man*, I'm head and shoulders above anyone in line, least of all Mia.

The day passes in its usual Botoxy way, and finally Peter and I are locking up the clinic and heading over to Kirsty and Tim's for dinner.

"What's all this about?" Peter asks, looking at his watch as we charge down the street toward their house. "Six o'clock is pretty early to start a dinner party."

Suddenly I realise I haven't told him about Kirsty and Tim. God, we've barely had a chance to even say hello these past few days.

"Peter, guess what?" I huff, trying to keep up with

him. "Kirsty and Tim are engaged!"

"Are they?" He doesn't even look that interested. "Well, they've been a couple for quite a while. Not really surprising. Once you've lived together, it's the next logical step."

Is it? I shoot Peter a look, but he's staring intently at the lights up ahead on Baker Street. I guess it does make sense. An image of us married, with me cooking dinner in the dimly lit flat, goes through my mind and a vague feeling of unease slides over me.

"That's not everything," I say as we wait to cross Marylebone. "Kirsty's pregnant."

"Crikey." Peter turns to face me, eyebrows raised. "Is she going through with it?"

I nod, realising the thought of not going through with it never occurred to me – and Kirsty hasn't mentioned it. With all her hesitation, I can't help wondering if it ever crossed her mind, even briefly.

"Hi, guys," Tim says when he answers the door a few minutes later. He shoos Peter and I into the house. "Thanks for coming."

"What's going on? Where's Kirsty?" I peer over Tim's shoulder as people pass by holding champagne flutes, and a waiter circulates with daintily wrapped hors d'oeuvres. Tim's cheeks are flushed, and he's still wearing his shirt and tie from work.

He hurries us into the lounge, then plucks two glasses of champagne off a tray and hands them over. "This is a surprise engagement party for Kirsty. I made sure Kirsty got tied up with work so everyone could come by before her." Tim glances at his watch. "She should be here any second."

"Cool," I say, clutching my glass nervously. Kirsty didn't want anyone from work to know about her engagement. How will she feel when she returns to see her house full of colleagues? And who ever heard of a surprise engagement party, anyway? Tim's so excited he's practically bouncing from one foot to the other.

"Sorry I didn't let you in on it." He grins at me. "But you and Kirsty are so close, and I know you guys tell each other everything. I couldn't take the chance."

Before I can respond, someone shouts "She's coming!", and the lounge plunges into darkness. The music switches off, and the muffled whispers and giggles of thirty people crouching on the floor float through the room. Peter swears softly when I tramp on his polished leather shoe, and I poke him in the side to be quiet.

A sliver of light streams in as the front door opens, and the sound of footsteps echoes in the hallway.

"Tim? Why is it so dark?" Kirsty's voice calls as she switches on the light.

"Surprise!" the room erupts. Kirsty's eyes widen and she takes a step back.

"Wow." Her gaze flickers around the room then over to Tim. "Just . . . wow. Everyone's here!"

Smiling proudly, Tim pushes through the crowd toward her. "Yeah. You don't know what a feat that was, coordinating everyone's schedule. But now that we're all here . . ." He fumbles in his pocket and draws out a tiny box, then sinks down on one knee and takes Kirsty's hand in his. "I know you've already said yes. But I wanted to do this properly, in front of our friends. So, Kirsty Grainger: will you marry me?"

A deadly silence falls over the room. Then Kirsty nods almost mechanically. "Of course I will." A high-pitched laugh escapes from her, one I've never heard before. "Now come on, get up."

Rising to his feet with a smile so big even collagen couldn't compete, Tim slides a large, glistening diamond onto Kirsty's finger with a flourish. He slings an arm around her and pulls her up against him, turning toward the smiling faces. "And we have another announcement to make."

Oh no. I cringe, praying he's not going to let the cat out of the bag about Kirsty's pregnancy. Judging by Kirsty's expression, she's hoping the same thing.

"Kirsty and I are having a baby!"

Shit.

The room erupts into applause and cheers, but I can't tear my gaze away from Kirsty. A maniacal grin is nailed to her face, but her cheeks are ashen and her eyes have a hunted look in them. Colleagues swarm toward the happy couple, patting them on the back and offering up congratulations. Although Tim radiates happiness, to my practiced best-friend eye, I can tell Kirsty's movements are forced.

Someone switches on the music and *Baby Be Mine* blares through the speakers. God, Tim's even created a party soundtrack. I look around for Peter so we can join the impromptu receiving line. Where on earth has he got to? Oh, there he is, performing a mini-consultation on one of Kirsty's colleagues, turning her head this way and that as he examines the wrinkles around her eyes.

"So." An elegant woman sporting a tailored grey suit appears at my side. "Romantic, eh?" She nods toward Kirsty and Tim, who are still shaking hands and accepting congratulations. "How do you know them?"

"Oh, we go way back. Kirsty and I went to school together."

"American, huh?" The woman raises an eyebrow and I nod. "What are you doing over here?" She scans the room as she speaks, no doubt looking for someone more interesting to talk to.

I almost say 'I'm a reporter' before remembering I'm undercover. "I'm a receptionist," I answer glumly, staring down into my champagne.

The woman nods, sipping her drink. Five seconds later, she's off. God, I can't wait until I really am a full-fledged tabloid reporter. Then everyone will want to chat to me; I'll have to beat people off with a stick.

Feeling slightly self-conscious standing here on my own like a party pariah, I make my way over to Peter's consultation corner. He's got another woman with him now. As she tilts her head, he traces lines by her lips so fine, you'd practically need a magnifying glass to see them.

". . . and a bit of filler should get rid of that, no problem," he's saying. "Pop by any time this week and we can take care of it for you." He hands her a card and the woman – with beautiful long dark hair and features straight out of *Vogue* – stares at it like it's a precious metal.

"Thank you," she says with a hint of a Spanish accent.

It never ceases to amaze me how people with such perfect looks feel the need for cosmetic surgery, but I've long since learned not to try to figure it out. Quite honestly, you'd need someone along the lines of Freud to get to the bottom of it, and I'm sure Freud has better things to occupy his time. Isn't he dead, anyway?

"Ah, here she is," Peter says as he spots me beside him. "This is Serenity. She's the clinic's receptionist and she'll make you comfortable before you come in to see me."

I give him an incredulous look. *Clinic receptionist?*

"Oh, and my girlfriend, of course," Peter adds, catching my eye. He eases an arm around my shoulders.

"Hello." The woman shows off her blindingly white teeth and holds out a manicured hand for me to shake. "So both of you work in the cosmetic surgery industry? How fascinating." She strokes her gleaming hair. "Have you been reading that column about the man who's completely doing himself over through surgery?"

Oh my God. She's been reading *Build a Man*? I'm caught between pride and horror.

"No, I haven't heard of that." Peter sips his champagne. "But I've long predicted male cosmetic surgery would become a trend. In fact, just the other day, a man came into our clinic seeking a comprehensive makeover."

"I think it's fantastic men are taking the initiative now. This man in the column has just had Botox, and he's doing a nose job" – she touches her nose – "and quite a few other procedures, too."

Peter stares. "What a coincidence. My patient just had Botox, and he's doing a rhinoplasty, as well. I wonder if it will become a discernible pattern?"

"Let's go congratulate Kirsty." Heart thumping, I grab Peter's arm, and his drink splashes onto the floor.

"Serenity!" Peter exclaims as I drag him across the room. "I wasn't finished talking." I don't care how annoyed he is – I have to get him away before he twigs that Jeremy and *Build a Man* are actually one and the same. I risk a glance at his face. His forehead is scrunched up in irritation, but thankfully he doesn't appear to have made any connections. I let out my breath and my heart rate slowly returns to normal.

The party goes on, the crowd getting louder and the champagne supply lower. As people start trickling out the door, Kirsty comes over and touches my shoulder.

"I need to see you upstairs for a second," she says, in

a low, urgent voice. Before I have time to open my mouth, she's propelling me forward and up the narrow staircase. She leads me into the bedroom and closes the door, creating a cocoon from the noise below.

"What's up?" I ask, scanning her white face. Her normally confident features are pinched.

She shakes her head. "I can't do this."

"I know, I can imagine. The party must have been a bit of a shock. I'm sorry, Kirst. I didn't know about it until I got here."

"No, no. That's not what I meant." Sinking onto the bed, she buries her face in her hands.

"Kirsty?" I sit down beside her, alarmed at her strange wheezing and the way her shoulders are heaving.

"I can't breathe. I just can't breathe!"

Oh God; Kirsty's having a panic attack. I've seen so many at the clinic – usually when I tell patients we're closed on the weekends, so they'll have to wait until Monday for their Botox – that I can diagnose it in a heartbeat. I scrabble around for a paper bag or something, but I can't find anything. Unsure what else to do, I rub Kirsty's back until she takes a shuddering breath, then straightens up.

"I thought I just needed time to accept everything. But the truth is, I need to get away from it all. Away from Tim. Away from" – she touches her hand to her abdomen – "this. I need space to think."

She looks over at me, liquid pooling in her hazel eyes. "Can I crash with you and Peter tonight? And maybe for the next few days, until I clear my head?"

Wow. I can just imagine Tim's expression when Kirsty tells him she needs space. "Kirsty, are you sure you want to do that?" I ask gently.

She nods, pushing a few curls back from her face.

"Yes. I am."

"Well, of course it's no problem. You can stay as long as you like." It's the least I can do – be there for her, like she asked. And Peter will understand. A friend in need and all that. "I'll just go let Peter know."

I head back down the stairs, thoughts banging in my head. Kirsty's uncertainty has thrown me completely. I knew she was overwhelmed with everything that happened. But I'd chalked that up to shock, and I was positive she'd come around in time. Never in a million years would I have suspected my confident friend, who always knows just what to do, was floundering over her future.

Downstairs is deserted, with empty glasses and wine bottles littering every surface. Peter's sitting on the sofa – ramrod straight with that perfect posture he's been practising lately – watching the BBC News discuss something boring to do with the economic crisis. The humming of the dishwasher comes from the kitchen, where Tim's whistling as he clears up.

"Oh, good. There you are." Peter practically leaps off the sofa when he spots me. "We should get going."

"Um, Peter?" I lower my voice. "Kirsty's going to stay with us for the next few days. She says she needs a bit of space."

Peter stops fiddling with the buttons on his blazer and glances up at me. "Did you already say she could?" he asks in a tight voice.

"Well, yes. She won't mind sleeping on the sofa." In our university days, Kirsty once slept in my bathtub.

Peter's shaking his head as if I've done something naughty. "I wish you'd asked me first, Serenity. You know Smitty doesn't react well to strangers. And the flat isn't set up for an extra person; it won't be comfortable for her – or us, for that matter. Doesn't she have other friends she can ask?" He pushes past me toward the door as if the case is closed. I stare at his rigid back, anger swirling through me.

"Peter!" My low whisper sounds more like a hiss. "She does have other friends, but she asked *me*. I can't say no. Please – it's only for a few nights."

Peter's shoulders heave in a sigh and he swings around, face set in that super-calm expression I recognise from the clinic when he's dealing with a difficult patient. And, increasingly, when he's talking to me. "I'd like to help, but this is a very busy time for me, and we don't need the stress of an extra guest. Now let's head home, shall we?"

My mouth drops open. I can't believe he won't interrupt his precious routine for someone so important in my life, someone who needs my help. I *know* he's busy, and I understand he requires his eight point five hours of 'brain regeneration time', as he calls it, but still.

"No, you go," I say, my voice hard as my heart pounds with anger. "I'll see you back home."

He narrows his eyes like he's trying to understand what thought processes are running through my mind, then shrugs and hands me a five-pound note. "Make sure you call a cab. It's late. And please be quiet when you come in." Leaning down, he pecks my cheek then goes out the door, shutting it firmly behind him.

Irritation swirls through me as I stare at the closed door. Just now, it hits me that Peter probably *doesn't* have any idea what I'm thinking, or how annoyed I am. I don't tell him how his little jibes make me feel, probably because I've always wanted to be as ordered and pulled-together as he is. Serenity v2, and all. And I've never asked him for anything that would interfere with his daily life; there hasn't been any reason to. But I always thought if I needed something – or someone close to me did – it would be a given. Guess not.

An unsettled feeling washes over me as I drag myself back up the stairs. If my boyfriend won't even bend a little to help me . . . what kind of relationship is this, really? I know in a heartbeat I'd do whatever I could to help a friend of his, if he asked. I shake my head and push away the thought. Right now, I need to face Kirsty and tell her that no, I *can't* be there for her when she needs me. My jaw clenches as anger fills me again.

When I open the door to the bedroom, Kirsty's already packing.

"Everything set?" she asks, jamming closed the heaving suitcase. God, it looks like she's moving out, not just leaving for a few days.

"Um . . ." Shoving aside a few empty hangers, I sit on the bed. "Peter didn't tell me, but we're having some painting done in the flat tomorrow. He's worried it might make you feel ill." I trace the stitching on the white duvet cover, feeling terrible. I hate lying to her, but there's no way I can tell the truth. Kirsty's never been a massive Peter fan to begin with, and this would put him even lower on her list than Justin Bieber (and believe me, that's low).

"It's okay, Ser," she says in a tone that tells me I haven't fooled her at all. "Don't worry about it. I'll check into a hotel for tonight then figure out where to crash."

"Isn't there anyone else you can stay with?" The thought of Kirsty all alone in a bland hotel room makes me even more furious at Peter.

"No, not really." She pulls her hair back into a ponytail. "I don't want to ask anyone from work. They know too much as it is – I can't *believe* Tim told them everything without even checking with me first. He knows what it's like there." Sinking down on the bed, she runs a hand over her face.

"I'm so sorry, Kirsty. You know I'd help if I could." I squeeze her arm, my mind racing. There must be something I can do. For a second, I consider bringing her over to the flat, despite Peter's words. He's way too polite to kick up a fuss in front of her. But as much as I'd like to, I can't. It's his flat, *his* space . . . as he's made all too clear since I've moved in. And who am I to argue? He's the one paying the mortgage. It's times like this I long to have somewhere of my own.

"Want me to wait while you talk to Tim, and help you find a place?" I ask, reluctant to go until I'm sure she's okay.

Kirsty shakes her head. "No, that's all right. Who knows how long it'll take? Anyway, the bank has a corporate rate with the hotel across the street, so I'll just grab a taxi and head there."

"Call me later if you want to talk." I scoot off the bed, little fingers of guilt and worry jabbing at my gut. It feels so wrong, leaving her like this.

Kirsty nods and her shoulders lift in a huge sigh. "Okay."

I throw my arms around her, then head back down the stairs. "Bye, Tim," I shout toward the kitchen. Oh jeez, he's still whistling. I can't bear to think about his reaction to Kirsty's coming words.

Outside, the damp air bites at my exposed skin, and I pull my coat around me. I don't want to head back to the flat; quite honestly, I'm still fizzing with fury.

But there's nowhere else to go and the night is dark and cold, so I quicken my pace and stride toward home.

Peter's home, that is.

CHAPTER SIXTEEN

The next day at the clinic stretches on forever, and I can't stop thanking my lucky stars that it's Friday. I'm so tired even a shot of Botox to the brain wouldn't perk me up. Kirsty called around one last night to say she'd settled in at the hotel. I sigh, recalling the strained sound in her voice when I asked how it went with Tim. She didn't even want to talk about it.

I couldn't bear to lie next to Peter, so I fidgeted on the sofa for hours as his snores drifted from the bedroom. The low rumble – and the fact that he was clearly enjoying a good night's sleep – sparked off even more irritation inside. With every passing minute, my indignation grew, until it was a blistering spot ready to pop. For God's sake, it wasn't like I'd asked the man to deliver Kirsty's baby (there's an image I don't want in my head). Underneath it all, though, that uncomfortable feeling I'd experienced back at Kirsty's was brewing.

What kind of relationship is this, when it's so lopsided; when the man I live with doesn't really know – or, in the case of my tabloid ambitions, seem to *care* – what's important to me? What would happen if I got pregnant, like Kirsty? Is Peter a man I'd want to be with?

When Peter got up this morning, he acted as if everything was normal, not even clocking my less than enthusiastic grunts in his direction. We've barely exchanged more than ten words today, but I don't think he's noticed – adding further fuel to my growing questions. He *did* notice the few Jaffa Cake crumbs I left lying around in retaliation, though.

At six o'clock, the last Botox Bitch has scuttled off to her mansion in the country, and I finally have a second to breathe before I need to hightail it out of here to rendezvous with Mia. Jeremy agreed to meet tonight at quarter to seven to discuss 'dating strategies designed to ensnare his ideal woman', and I've arranged to see Mia thirty minutes earlier at a nearby café to talk through our plan – after she reluctantly agreed to pose as my life advisory intern (ha!). I scan my list of questions, then cash up and yell out to Peter that I'm leaving.

I wait for a second, but there's no response. Sighing, I slide off my stool and trudge to his office.

"I'm going now," I say to his bowed head.

"All right." He doesn't even look up from the papers on his desk.

I turn away, dreading the thought of yet another silent, empty weekend ahead with only a supercilious cat for company. Grabbing my bag, I head into the street, breathing in the noise of the city.

It's a nice night – the air feels almost balmy for mid-October – so when I get to the café, I plonk down at one of those shaky metal tables they always have out front. Mia's not here yet, thank goodness, so I get out my notebook and pen to signal that *I'm* the one in charge of what's happening tonight. Sidebars and polls are one thing, but if she thinks she can take over my relationship with Jeremy, she has another thing coming.

My bum gets progressively colder as time passes with no sign of Mia. I glance at my watch. It's almost six-thirty now. She's fifteen minutes late, and she hasn't even had the courtesy to text me. Typical! I try to stir up righteous indignation, but inside I'm just thrilled she hasn't turned up. It's much better if I get Jeremy to myself – for research purposes, of course. He's comfortable with me, and adding someone new to the mix could make things awkward.

At quarter to seven on the dot, I gather up my things and round the corner to Welbeck Street and number nineteen. Again I'm struck by the gleaming white facade of Jeremy's house – even more impressive now that I know he renovated the whole thing himself. Through the open window, voices drift from inside. I stand on tiptoe, trying to peer through the glass. Who's in there?

I'm just about to ring the buzzer when I hear a tinkly laugh that sounds suspiciously like Mia's, with Jeremy's low guffaw booming in return.

Anger shoots through me and I jab at the buzzer so hard my finger feels like it will snap in half.

"Serenity! Come in. We were wondering where you were." Jeremy's eyes are dancing and his face is rosy. He looks more animated than I've ever seen him.

"I was waiting for Mia at the café, like we'd planned." I try to keep my tone light. "Oh, there she is!" I act surprised, but inside I'm fuming. She *knew* we were supposed to meet at the café, and she deliberately kept me waiting so she could ambush Jeremy.

Mia smiles up at me from where she's draped over the sofa in a 'lady of the manor' pose that immediately sets my teeth on edge. With her perfectly casual outfit of jeans and a skin-tight turtleneck – finished off with platformed riding boots I could never wear without resembling a hick farmer – she fits right in here. In my boring ensemble of black trousers and white blouse, I look like I should be serving in the kitchen.

"Sorry, I guess I got the details mixed up. Were you waiting long?" Her eyes are wide but I'm not fooled. Judging by the empty wine glass in her hand, she's obviously been here for a while.

"Here you go, Serenity." Jeremy hands me a glass of red wine and I take a sip, trying to get my emotions back under control. The last thing I want is for Mia to think she's upset me or thrown me off kilter. My eyes narrow as Jeremy squeezes beside Mia on the sofa. She scoots even closer to him then looks over at me, a triumphant gleam in her eyes. An uncomfortable feeling presses against my stomach and I gulp my drink. If ever there was a need for wine therapy, it's definitely now.

I clear my throat and whip out my notepad and recorder, trying not to look at Mia edging closer and closer to Jeremy. "Well, let's get started. Jeremy, can you tell me what you look for in a woman?"

Jeremy shrugs. "Sure, but I just answered that question for Mia. She said you would pool your notes."

Mia smiles smugly over the top of her wine glass. "Since you weren't here, I thought I'd get started. I didn't want to keep Jeremy waiting."

"If you wouldn't mind repeating your response, Jeremy, just so I can get it on the recorder. It's important for your files." I keep my voice even and calm, but I can't wait to get Mia alone after we're done.

Who the hell does she think she is, taking over my interview?

"No problem," Jeremy says easily. "Well, my ideal woman is someone who doesn't take herself too seriously. You know, who can laugh and have a bit of fun. Who's not afraid to get mussed up or dirty." His eyes lock onto mine, and that strange feeling he's seeing straight into me returns. I feel my cheeks start to colour, and I quickly drop my head to scrawl notes on my pad.

"Great, great. What about appearance?"

Jeremy shrugs. "I don't really have a type. Just someone I like the look of, I guess."

"Didn't you say you like the typical *English* woman?" Mia interrupts.

"English or American. Or, er, African, whatever," Jeremy says quickly. "It doesn't really matter where they're from. Just as long as we click."

"How do you define 'click'?" I ask, curious.

"I don't know if it can be defined," Jeremy says. "It's just, you know, when someone's easy to talk to. When I feel really comfortable with them."

He gazes into the distance. "As much as I loved her, I never had that with Julia. I always felt on edge, like I had to live up to her expectations. To be someone I'm not."

I nod as the thought that I always feel on edge around Peter niggles at me.

"So what is your dream date?" I ask, pushing Peter out of my head.

"Well, it would have to be something to do with food," Jeremy responds, lips lifting in a smile. Mia mumbles something under her breath I can't quite catch, and I throw her an evil look. "I've always thought if you can feel comfortable sharing a meal with someone, it says a lot about your connection on a deeper level."

Mia snorts and Jeremy shrugs, an embarrassed expression on his face. "Anyway, all this isn't going to help me with my dating skills," he says, moving away from the probing emotional questions. He looks at me expectantly, as if I can wave my magic wand and transform him into a leading contender in the world's *Next Top Lothario*.

"Um . . . let's do some role-play," I say. "Just pretend I'm someone you're interested in." I can feel my cheeks tingeing red again. Oh Lord. "How would you approach me? What would you say?"

Jeremy's face is pinking up, too. "You want me to do it right now?"

Nodding, I stare at a spot over his shoulder to avoid meeting those green eyes. "We'll assess your skills first, then work with you to improve them." Like I'm someone who can assess dating skills. My dating skills usually consist of paying the bill when the guy sticks me with it at the end.

"Okay," Jeremy says slowly. He walks self-consciously over to where I'm sitting, then loops his thumbs in his pockets and rocks back and forth on the balls of his feet. "Hello. I'm Jeremy. I noticed you from across the room and I wanted to come say hi. Would you care for a drink?" His face is flaming now and sweat is beading on his brow.

"Sure. That would be great!" I warble like a parakeet on speed. God, if only it were that easy. I don't think anyone has ever asked to buy me a drink, although my ex in Harris did get me hooked by offering a Creme Egg. Sadly, that was a one-time deal and the free sweets dried up once we started dating.

"Aw, aren't you two cute," Mia oozes. "Jeremy, that approach might work with a few losers here and there." She raises an eyebrow at me. "But if you really want the right woman, I can show you how it's done." Mia uncurls her long legs and gets to her feet, sashaying over to Jeremy, who looks terrified.

"Hello there," she purrs, putting a hand on his arm and sliding it up and down. A small pang of something I can't identify stirs inside. I want to look away, but my eyes are glued to the tableau before me.

"I'm going to buy you a drink. And you're going to like it. And then we're going to go to my place, and—"

"That's fine!" I yelp before she can go any further. Jeremy's staring at Mia with an expression of horror, slowly backing away. "Um, I think that's more of an advanced method." For complete skanks. "Jeremy needs to start out at a basic level and get confident with that. And I, for one, think his method is fine."

"You would." Mia rolls her eyes. "Look, I've got to get going, *boss*. There's a party in Shoreditch I was supposed to be at half an hour ago. Goodbye, Jeremy. Lovely to meet you." She kisses Jeremy's cheek, then turns and strides for the door. Stumbling to my feet, I rush after her.

"Hang on, I need to talk to you for a second," I hiss through gritted teeth, grabbing her arm before she can reach for the door handle. No way is she getting away with leaving me back at the café while she chatted up Jeremy.

Mia turns to face me. "What?"

"About that stunt you pulled earlier." I step back so I'm not staring at her neck. Thank God I have on my high heels or I'd be looking at her chest.

Mia feigns an innocent expression. "What?"

I roll my eyes. "You know exactly what I'm talking about. We were supposed to meet earlier to discuss our plan. But you went right to Jeremy's without even telling me." I straighten my spine to try to gain some height. *"Build a Man* is my column. You're only an intern – and you're only here to help. Remember that." I stare at her meaningfully, noting with satisfaction that she's momentarily stunned into silence. Ha! I can be serious and scary when I want to be.

But the silence only lasts seconds before Mia breaks out in a snorty laugh. "Don't get your knickers in a twist." Shaking her head, she wags a finger at me like I'm a puppy who peed on the floor. Next thing you know, she'll be rapping me on the head with a rolled-up newspaper. "Aren't you just an unpaid contributor? That puts you at the same level as me – lower, in fact, because at least the paper covers my Tube fare. Don't worry, darling. I don't have any grand designs on your little column. Feel free to slave away and write the whole thing. I'm happy being backup."

I don't know whether to be insulted or relieved. And I'm not sure I believe her, either. "So why did you bother heading right to Jeremy's without telling me?"

Mia shrugs. "I wanted a chance to build some rapport with him, in case things ever go wrong between you two. Honestly, I was glad when you came in. I've never met a more boring bloke. All that business about building the house from scratch . . . whatever."

"He's not boring," I say, much louder than intended. "He's one of the nicest guys I've met here."

A smirk nudges up a corner of Mia's mouth. "Sounds like someone has a little crush. You'd best watch that, you know. It's not good for objectivity."

"I don't have a crush," I say, silently cursing the colour flooding into my cheeks. Why on earth am I blushing?

"Reeeeeally." Mia raises an over-plucked ginger eyebrow. "Anyway, I've got to go," she says, dismissing me like I'm a plaything that's now become boring. "Oh, hello there, Jeremy. I was just leaving. Have a great night."

The door slams behind her and I turn quickly, my heart in my throat. Jeremy? Just how long has he been standing there? Please God, may he not have heard the bit about the crush.

"Um, hi, Jeremy." My face must be almost purple now. "So Mia's gone," I ramble foolishly, flinging an arm toward the door. "How about that drink?" God knows I need it.

Jeremy's lips curve into his slow, crinkly smile. "Sure."

I follow him over to the kitchen and settle into my usual place at the table, keeping my head down so my face can return to a state that wouldn't rival a radish. Maybe he didn't hear anything, I tell myself. He probably didn't. We weren't talking *that* loudly, right?

Jeremy hands me another glass of wine and I take a giant gulp to calm my nerves. Instead of sitting across the table, he settles onto the wide wooden bench beside me, and I swivel to face him.

"Any big plans for the weekend?" he asks.

"The usual. Nothing." I force a laugh to make the words seem less pathetic.

"I was wondering if I could book you for an extra session and take you to Borough Market with me tomorrow. So you can advise me on diet and things like that," he adds quickly.

"Sure, sounds good. What exactly is Borough Market?"

Jeremy's eyebrows lift. "You've never heard of Borough Market? It's brilliant – I do my weekly shopping there every Saturday. Great for foodies. You need to do some exploring of London. What else have you seen? Have you been to Hampstead Heath?"

I shake my head.

"Primrose Hill?"

"Wait, I know that one. That's where Gwyneth Paltrow lives, right?"

He grins. "Right. But did you know there's also a fantastic view over the city? And have you ever been to Greenwich?"

"No. I have a lot of London to see, I guess." His enthusiasm is infectious, and I can't wait to get out and discover more. When I first moved here, I had grand plans to see every part of my new home. But with work and Peter, somehow those fell by the wayside.

"Tell you what. Why don't I pick a London location to introduce you to each weekend? I love showing off the city."

"That would be awesome – er, great!" I say, eager to leave the confines of Marylebone and experience new bits of London with Jeremy. Peter usually works on the weekends and he's always saying he hates 'tourist stuff', anyway. And, of course, it's all in the name of duty. The more time I spend with Jeremy, the better my column will be.

"It's a deal then. First up tomorrow: the market. They have the best coffee there – Monmouth, my favourite."

"What, you're not a tea drinker? I thought all Brits loved tea," I joke.

Jeremy waves a hand in the air. "Sod tea. If I need caffeine, I'm going for coffee."

Silence falls as our laughter fades away, and the only thing I can concentrate on is the warmth of his leg pressed against mine. As much as I know I should, I can't move away. I can barely breathe, let alone send any commands to my body, which seems to have gone all gooey and marshmallow-like. Ever so slowly, Jeremy leans closer and closer.

So close I can smell his musky, spicy scent. So close I can feel the bristle on his skin. So close I–

The ringing of my phone jerks us apart. I give my head a little shake and spring to my feet. What the hell was that? It was like I was in a trance, as if my body wasn't my own. Well, whatever it was, it was just . . . one of those things. I glance at Jeremy, who appears just as confused as I feel.

"Hello?" My voice is shaky, and I take a deep breath to steady myself.

"It's me," Kirsty says. "You okay?"

"Fine, fine. One sec." I put a hand over the phone and turn to Jeremy. "I'll just be a minute," I say, grateful for the chance to scoot into the hallway and let my heart rate return to normal.

"So how was the day?" I ask softly, knowing Kirsty would have faced Tim at work.

"Terrible," she says. I can hear her sigh through the phone. "Tim didn't come in today or answer his phone. I got called into the director's office to talk about my 'future plans'."

"So what *are* you going to do?" I ask, hoping she's got it all figured out.

"I don't know," Kirsty says. "I still love Tim, but this is too fast. I just want to get away."

Unsure how to respond, I nod silently. It's such a strange role reversal: usually it's me in a mess, uncertain what to do.

"Maybe some time apart will do you both good," I say finally, raising my voice over the clanking of pots and pans coming from the kitchen. "And whatever you decide, you know I'm here for you."

"I know. Thank God! Listen, what are you up to

tomorrow? I have to work in the morning, but do you want to meet for coffee around lunchtime?"

"I'm going with Jeremy, a client," – I throw in, in case he's listening – "to Borough Market. Just let me check and see how long we'll be there."

I stick my head into the kitchen, where Jeremy's levering a huge chunk of pasta into a pot of boiling water. Yum, I'm starving. "Jeremy? How long do you think we might be tomorrow? A friend of mine wants to meet up in the afternoon."

He turns to face me, clad in a plaid apron that should look silly, but just . . . doesn't. "Why doesn't she join us down there for coffee?"

I tilt my head, considering his words. Kirsty knows all about Jeremy and my undercover mission, but I'm not sure I want the two of them to meet. Still, I know she can keep her mouth shut when she needs to, and it will be nice for Kirsty to see that what I'm doing isn't such a bad thing – I'm actually helping Jeremy, too.

I nod then lift my hand from the phone. "Do you want to meet at the market at noon, in front of Monmouth Coffee?" I say to Kirsty.

She agrees and I hang up, then plonk down at the table.

"Ready to eat?" Jeremy calls from the stove. A delicious garlic smell is drifting through the air.

"Ready." I smile up at him as he hands me a plate then sits down across from me. An image of *Lady and The Tramp* filters into my head, where they slurp the same strand of pasta, drawing nearer and nearer until . . . Get a grip, I tell myself. This isn't a Disney film, it's reality. And the reality is, I'm hardly a 'lady' and Jeremy, well, Jeremy's *definitely* not a tramp.

CHAPTER SEVENTEEN

"Crap, crap, crap," I mutter, dodging the throngs of people exiting Borough Tube station. I'm supposed to meet Jeremy at ten this morning, and it's already five past. A bad night's sleep fighting with my pillow as Jeremy's lips floated through my mind meant I'd awoken way too late. Since I'm seeing him in my professional capacity, there's no way I could rock up without at least finding a pair of jeans free from random air ventilation pockets (i.e. holes) and putting on a touch of make-up. I must admit, advisory session or not, it *is* good to be doing something on a Saturday.

Pushing through the turnstile, I catch sight of Jeremy looking fantastic in a dark corduroy blazer and a pair of baggy jeans.

"Hi!" I shout, raising a hand as I approach.

Jeremy smiles warmly. "Hello. Ready to pick up some good, healthy food for the new me? What's that saying: you are what you eat?"

I nod, feeling curiously hollow. So he really *did* ask me here in my official role. Of course he did, I tell myself as we head away from the packed station and down a busy street. Why else would he?

"Okay?" Jeremy throws a look over his shoulder, then takes my hand and pulls me along after him so we don't lose each other in the crowd. I stare down at his strong fingers gripping mine, mesmerised by the tan colour of his skin against my pale hand.

A few minutes later – my palm sweaty and my face hot – we reach an area stuffed with people, food stalls, and smoking barbecues. The air is pungent with the smell of cheese, fresh bread and meat, and I realise we're still holding hands. I drop his quickly and rub my nose, fabricating an itch.

"Here we are! Borough Market. Why don't we grab a sausage, get something sweet, and have a picnic?" Jeremy asks.

"That sounds fantastic," I respond, before remembering I'm supposed to be guiding him toward healthy eats. "But that's not exactly food for life, Jeremy." God, I sound like Peter. He's always talking about sausage like it needs to be burned at the stake.

"Ah, we can get the 'food for life' later." Jeremy shrugs.

Well, if the man wants a sausage, who am I to complain? It's been ages since I've had one. I trail after him toward the smoking barbecue where plump sausages are grilling. Jeremy hands me a bun dripping with onions and sauce, then worms his way over to an organic chocolate brownie vendor, grabs two, and leads us to an empty space in the nearby courtyard of a church. We sink down onto the stones and I tilt my face upwards, feeling the warmth of the autumn sun and taking in the robin's-egg blue sky. What a gorgeous day. When I turn back to Jeremy, I catch him staring and he quickly drops his eyes.

"So." He gestures toward the buzzing market stalls. "What do you think?"

"It's fantastic," I say, meaning it. "I can't believe I've never been here."

Jeremy bites into his bun, nodding as he chews. "Me neither," he says once he's swallowed. "Just wait until you see Hampstead Heath – it's like a piece of wilderness in the city. You can even swim there. Maybe we'll head over next weekend."

"That would be great," I say, suddenly feeling shy. It's so nice of him to show me around London.

We chew companionably for a few minutes, then explore more stalls under a giant metal awning, me pushing random veggies at Jeremy in a bid to appear like I know what I'm doing. Then, before I know it, it's almost noon and time to meet Kirsty. I can't believe how quickly time has flown – and how much fun I'm having. Jeremy leads me over to Monmouth Coffee, where a line snakes down the pavement and the heady scent of coffee beans taints the air.

"There she is!" I wave an arm at Kirsty, who's waiting just out front. Nerves leap inside me for a second, but I tell myself it will all be okay. Kirsty knows the deal, and she's good at keeping secrets when she needs to.

"Hey." She gives me a quick hug, then pulls back and runs her eyes over Jeremy. I take the time to study her face, my heart sinking as I note the dark circles under her eyes and the pale complexion.

"Kirsty, this is Jeremy," I say. "Jeremy, Kirsty."

Jeremy holds out a hand politely. "Nice to meet you."

We join the back of the line, Kirsty and Jeremy chatting easily about how long we've known each other and our hometown back in Maine.

"So Serenity's really helped you, huh?" Kirsty asks when they've exhausted our two-street town.

Jeremy nods. "Oh, definitely – everything from wardrobe, to dating, to getting psyched up for treatments." He shudders. "I really hate hospitals and needles. My younger sister had leukaemia, and she was in and out of the hospital a lot. She lost the battle, in the end."

"Oh, I'm sorry." Kirsty touches his arm.

"I'm sorry, too," I echo. Poor Jeremy; I can't believe he didn't tell me that. God, he must *really* want to change to endure all the hospital visits in his future.

"It was ages ago now, but I still miss her. All those years in the hospital . . . I don't like to go to one, even today. It's why I've waited so long to have cosmetic surgery, even though I've wanted to for a while now."

Kirsty and I nod, and a sombre silence falls as we shuffle forward in the line.

Jeremy's mobile rings and he turns away to answer it.

Kirsty leans closer to me. "Ser, you can't *really* believe Jeremy needs all this surgery stuff. He's actually quite good-looking. Sure, he could lose a little weight, but he has a nice face."

The memory of just how nice his face is up close floods into my head, and I can feel my cheeks getting hot. I shrug nonchalantly to cover it up. "If it makes him feel better, what's the problem?"

Kirsty stares. "What's the problem? The problem is that he's basically risking his life for nothing."

I snort at her melodrama. "He's not risking his life." *I hope.* I make a mental note to talk to Peter about that one later. "And it's his decision."

She shakes her head. "Maybe. But I can't help thinking it's a little unethical for doctors to perform surgeries on patients who clearly don't need it."

"They're just giving people what they want," I

respond. "People should have the freedom to do as they wish to their bodies if it makes them feel better." As the words come out of my mouth, I realise it's the same line I've heard Peter repeat whenever anyone challenges what he does for a living.

"Have you had a shot of Botox to the brain?" Kirsty stares at me incredulously. "You never–" She stops mid-sentence as Jeremy puts the phone in his pocket and swivels toward us, face drained of colour.

"What?" I ask. "Is everything okay?"

He nods. "That was Doctor Lycett."

Peter? What's Peter doing calling Jeremy?

"There's been a cancellation tomorrow afternoon for one of his surgeries. Doctor Lycett asked if I wanted the spot for my eye-bag fix, nose job, and chin liposuction."

My heart starts thumping. Tomorrow! This could be great for the column, really kick off the action. And great for Jeremy too, of course. He'll get started on his transformation even sooner than expected.

"And?" I ask, when I can't bear the silence any longer.

Jeremy drops his head, running a hand through his hair.

A pang of fear shoots through me. Surely he said yes!

"I don't know," he answers finally. "When the operations were a few weeks away, it seemed safer. Like I had a cushion of time to think more about it, to change my mind if I wanted."

I stare, unable to make a sound. Change his mind? *What?*

"I told Doctor Lycett I'd ring back in a few minutes to let him know." Jeremy meets my gaze. "What do you think? Should I just go for it?"

I look into his green eyes, thoughts racing through

my head. This is the first time I've ever thought Jeremy might have doubts about the surgeries ahead – he seemed dead set on everything.

Beside me, I can feel Kirsty's disapproving stare as she awaits my answer. But what does she know? She hasn't listened to Jeremy's tales of woe; heard his Julia horror story. If ever anyone needed this surgery emotionally – to pick himself up and feel more confident – it's Jeremy.

"You should do it," I say. "Just think of your dream woman."

Jeremy swallows and keeps his eyes fixed on mine. "I am."

My stomach shifts at his words, and I tell myself not to be ridiculous. He doesn't mean *me*, of course. "It's a great opportunity for you to get started with your real transformation, sooner than you thought. You should definitely go for it."

An emotion I can't quite pinpoint slides over Jeremy's face – something like hurt and disappointment – and he turns away from me, taking out his phone. Kirsty and I stand mutely as we listen to him make arrangements to be at the hospital tomorrow. When he swings toward us again, his face is an unreadable mask.

"So?" I ask.

"So, this is it." Jeremy shoves the phone back in his pocket. "I'm on my way."

I bite my lip as I notice the stiff set of his shoulders. This is the beginning of his journey; of everything he wanted. Why doesn't he sound happier?

"Do you mind if I head home? If I'm going to do this tomorrow, I have a few things I should take care of." Jeremy's words come out tense and tight, nothing like his usual warm, relaxed tone.

"But what about the coffee?" I ask, unwilling to let him go like this.

He shakes his head. "I'm not in the mood for it any more."

Kirsty and I say goodbye, watching Jeremy's broad back weave its way through the crowds away from us.

"I hope you know what you're doing," Kirsty says, shaking her head.

"Of course." Thankfully, my voice sounds way more confident than I feel.

By the time I've navigated all the weekend Tube delays to get home, I've managed to suppress any earlier doubts about Jeremy's surgery. I'm sure his hesitation was down to cold feet. Peter's always saying patients get antsy pre-operation. Well, he did tell me once about a woman who cried for hours before her gastric-band surgery because she didn't want to give up venison.

I've got two hours to write the ideal woman/ dream date piece for Leza, and I need to let her know about the change of plans for the operation. I scrabble in my purse for my mobile then punch in her number.

"Yes?" she barks when she comes on the line.

"Jeremy's surgery has been moved to tomorrow afternoon," I say quickly, knowing Leza won't want to waste time with pleasantries. "It's the blepharoplasty, rhinoplasty, and chin liposuction." God, that sounds like a lot, doesn't it? Another thread of uncertainty weaves its way back in.

"Brilliant," comes her quick response. "Shadow Jeremy while he's in the hospital. Get into the operating room. I want details. Remember, the more blood, the better."

I swallow hard, my stomach turning over at the thought of Jeremy's blood. I've never been good with bodily fluids, let alone those from people I know. But if that's what it takes to impress Leza and get the job, I'm there with bells on. Or whites. Or whatever you have to wear in the operating room. "Sounds good."

"Get the dream date copy to me by five today, and the surgery copy on Monday. And tell Mia to do a fact box with surgery stats."

"Okay." I can't wait to pass that along; to show Mia *I'm* the one spearheading this and that she really is just secondary.

"Keep me posted on any issues."

"Okay," I say again. "I–"

I realise the phone has gone dead and I slump onto the sofa, wondering how best to go about getting into the operating room to watch. I can tell Jeremy it's part of the life advisory package – seeing him through surgery, etcetera – but what the hell am I going to say to Peter to explain my sudden interest in surgical procedures?

He knows I'm hopeless when it comes to the technical aspects. He'll never let me forget the time I asked what a 'subcutaneous contusion' was after snooping around in Madame Lucien's post-op files (disappointingly, it's just a bruise).

Well, Peter's always after me to take more of an interest in the biology of things, so he should jump at the chance for me to get first-hand experience . . . or first-face experience. I shudder again at the thought of Jeremy lying there, still, as Peter cuts into him, but I draw in a deep breath and sit up straight. I need to do this.

Right, time to get started on the dream date column. I get out my notepad, tapping a ragged nail against my teeth as I think about how to begin.

THE WAY TO A MAN'S HEART:
THROUGH HIS (SOON TO BE GONE) STOMACH

> Before his first major operation
> tomorrow, our Build a Man James
> took some time out of his
> preparations to speak about his
> ideal woman – and his dream date.

I glance down at my notes from last night.

'My ideal woman is someone who's easy to talk to; someone I feel really comfortable with,' I write, remembering Jeremy's laughter and how much fun we had earlier today. Whoever he ends up with is a lucky woman.

The door opens and I hear the click of Smitty's newly trimmed claws on the floor as Peter comes in.

"I'm home!" he calls.

Damn. I snap the notepad closed.

"Insanity at the hospital today." Peter flops onto the sofa beside me and clicks on the television, cranking up the volume.

I wince at the blaring of the TV. "Peter, can you–"

"Shh!" He holds up a hand as a reporter details how one of those fanatics with a metal detector found a stash of Anglo-Saxon gold in a field. Thank God Peter hasn't taken up that yet, although lately he's been making noises about buying a device. Still, where's he going to use it? Regent's Park? The most you'd find there would be a junkie's needle.

Sighing, I scoot closer to him. If I don't ask Peter now about getting into the operating room, I may never get a chance – particularly if Tony Robinson comes onscreen. Thankfully the story's over quickly and Peter leans back, stretching out his long legs.

"So I hear Jeremy's going in for surgery tomorrow," I say, to get the conversation headed in the right direction.

Peter turns to face me, eyebrows raised in surprise. "Yes, he is. He's scheduled for two in the afternoon. How did you hear that?"

Aw, *shit!* With everything running through my mind, I completely forgot I wasn't supposed to know Jeremy outside the clinic. I've been playing the life advisor role so often, I almost feel like I actually *am* one.

"Um, um . . ." My mind works frantically to come up with something plausible. "He left a message on the clinic's answering machine about it." Peter should be happy I've actually checked the messages (not that I did, of course) – he's always reminding me to do it on Saturdays and Sundays in case, heaven forbid, we miss scheduling an all-important Botox shot to the earlobe or something.

"That's strange," Peter muses. "I gave Jeremy the hospital number to ring, just in case. Maybe I should call him to make sure everything is okay." He gets out his mobile.

"No, no!" I practically leap onto Peter's lap. "That's not necessary, I'm sure. Jeremy only wanted to know if . . . if the hospital had a twenty-four-hour room service facility. You know what these people are like." I feel disloyal to Jeremy, lumping him in with the rest of the rude rich, but if Peter calls Jeremy, the jig's up.

I hold my breath as Peter jams the phone back in his pocket. "Okay. You rang him and told him yes, right?"

My mouth drops open. What? The hospital has twenty-four-hour room service? I was just making that up. "Of course." I squish even closer to Peter, the smell of his lemony cologne – so different from Jeremy's spicy scent – filling my nostrils. "Um, Peter? I'd really like to learn more about actual surgical procedures, from a clinical perspective. And, you know, to see you in action and witness your expertise. Could I come to the hospital tomorrow and observe you with Jeremy, maybe?"

After the recent episode with Kirsty, I'm not keen on pandering to Peter's ego. But if I don't get in that operating room, Leza will kill me. I hold my breath, thinking my words are slightly over the top. But a beatific grin is spreading on Peter's face. He's bought it!

"I think that could be arranged. Jeremy's probably a good one to watch, since you've interacted with him from the beginning. You'll need to stay in the corner, out of the way. And you'll have to get Jeremy's consent, too, before the surgery. Otherwise, there's no way I can let you in there."

"No problem." I need to see Jeremy before the surgery, anyway, to ask him a few interview questions.

"But I have to warn you, the procedures aren't pretty. There's a lot of blood, so prepare yourself. I can't have you fainting or causing any disruption in the room."

"I can handle blood. Don't worry." I cross my fingers, hoping that's true. I've never been in the presence of a lot of blood to find out, thank God. But I'll just focus on my work and I'm sure I'll be fine.

"Come to the hospital around noon, then you can pop into Jeremy's room to get the consent form signed. I'll leave you a copy at the front desk. Patients usually don't have a problem being observed, in my experience. But if he does express any discomfort, please don't badger."

Badger? Me? "No, of course not. Thanks, Peter."

Peter reaches out and pulls me toward him. "I don't have to be at the hospital until ten tomorrow. Late start for once."

He tidies my hair back from my face, and just as I think he's about to kiss me, he tilts my head up, touching the small furrow between my eyes. "Hmm. You might want to consider some Botox in the next few months."

Gee, thanks. I bite back my snarky response and smile tightly. He *has* just done me a huge favour by letting me in the OR tomorrow.

"Do you feel like . . .?" Motioning toward the bedroom, Peter raises his eyebrows.

I follow his gaze, trying to remember the last time we actually made love. It's been a couple weeks, but with everything that's happened, I've barely even noticed. And right now, getting busy with Peter is the last thing on my mind.

"Sorry. I'm a bit tired." Not to mention I've got to finish my article for Leza.

Peter shrugs. "Okay, no problem. I must admit I'm knackered, too."

Suddenly I remember my earlier conversation with Kirsty. "Peter, this operation tomorrow . . . it's not dangerous, is it?"

Peter shrugs. "It's as dangerous as any other operation. Whenever patients go under general anaesthesia, there is always a risk of complications."

My heart jumps. "Complications? Like what?" I hold my breath as I await his response.

Peter turns up the TV. "Oh, don't tell me you're turning into one of my hyper-anxious patients. I don't have the energy right now to deal with this, Serenity. Jeremy will be fine."

I shake my head at his abrupt dismissal, then grab the notepad and head to the bedroom to refocus on my story. Peter's a good doctor and a fantastic surgeon. I'm sure everything will go to plan.

CHAPTER EIGHTEEN

Yawning, I force myself from the cocoon of blankets and into the cold air of the bedroom. God, I had the worst sleep *ever* last night. I jerked awake at three, after a horrible nightmare where Jeremy's crimson blood was splattered across the operating room and my pristine white clothes. Then, every time I closed my eyes, all I could envision was the pattern his blood spots made against the stark white.

The flat is silent; Peter must have left for work already. What time is it? I rub my eyes and squint at the digital clock. Only ten-thirty. Phew. Still plenty of time to get ready and head to the hospital.

Thank God for coffee – and hot water, I think, turning up the temperature on our shower and directing the puny flow of water over my head. Why the Brits are so advanced in other aspects but can't seem to fashion a proper shower is beyond me. An image of the Rainshower in Jeremy's house flashes through my mind. I'd give anything to have one of those.

I pull on a pair of black trousers and a matching blazer to resemble an official life advisor, whatever they're supposed to look like. Catching sight of myself in the mirror, I grimace. I'm more Darth Vader than the female equivalent of Dr Phil.

What would Mia wear? Probably something fashioned from a cutting-edge material NASA just discovered. I can't wait to ditch this whole undercover thing and really break out a few Serenity v2 'I'm-a-tabloid-reporter' ensembles. And if I'm honest, all the subterfuge is starting to get to me. I've had some close calls lately and if this keeps up, I'll be in the cardiac unit soon instead of the newsroom. Another few weeks and I'll be home free.

I take off the blazer and throw on a fitted white shirt and a bright red cardigan to give the outfit some colour. Slipping on my red kitten heels, I yank a brush through my tousled hair then slick on lip gloss.

There. Professional, pulled together and still stylish, thanks to the splash of red. I grab my notebook and recorder, throw on my trench coat, and I'm out the door.

The streets of Marylebone are Sunday-morning quiet, and fifteen minutes later I'm inside the private hospital's elaborate entrance, standing in front of a receptionist so perfectly beautiful she looks like she's been airbrushed. Chandeliers hang from the mosaic ceiling, and the whole foyer is done up in Italian marble. If I didn't know better, I'd think I was in a Venetian palace, not a London hospital.

"I'm Serenity Holland," I announce. The receptionist lifts a perfectly sculpted eyebrow, eyeing my ensemble with something like distaste. My face flushes. It seemed stylish back at the flat, but now it feels like I've hijacked Primark's discount rails. "For Jeremy Ritchie?"

"One moment, please," the receptionist responds, voice dripping with derision as she taps away on a Mac computer. "Jeremy Ritchie is in suite three-zero-five, on the third floor. Johnson will escort you up."

Johnson? I turn as a man clad in what looks like a bespoke three-piece suit comes forward, ushering me toward the lift. Jeez! In the Harris Regional Hospital, the most fashionable suit is worn by Ernie the Janitor – and that's an army-green one-piece jumpsuit. And if you think jumpsuits are trendy, one look at Ernie bulging out of his will change your mind faster than you can say 'beer belly'.

"Oh, Dr Lycett left this for you." The receptionist hands me a stapled sheaf of papers. Glancing at the document, I see it's the patient consent form I need Jeremy to sign if I want to observe his operation.

Taking deep breaths, I follow Johnson across the marble floor toward the lift. Now that I'm actually here, it all seems so real. Jeremy will be going under the knife today – the first irreversible step on his way to becoming the man he always wanted to be. For just a second, I feel a sense of loss that he's leaving behind who he is now. But this is his dream, and he needs to go for it. No one understands that more than I do.

The lift pings as it reaches the third floor, and Johnson ushers me down a corridor and into suite 305.

"Hey there! Ready for today?" I sweep into the room and smile at Jeremy. He's sitting on the bed, and his shoulders have that stiff set to them again.

Jeremy lets out a shaky breath and glances up at me. His cheeks are pale and his eyes look greener than ever. "Hi. Yeah, I guess so. Thanks for dropping by. I didn't want to impose on your advisory duties too much on the weekend, but I was kind of hoping you'd come round."

I sink onto the bed beside him, my face flaming as I remember the last time we sat side by side and he leaned toward me . . . Clearing my throat, I force my lips in an even wider smile. Jeremy's so tense I can almost see it pouring from him.

"Of course. Helping you through these difficult moments is part of my job description. And I'll be there during the operation, too, just for your peace of mind," I say. "Don't worry. Peter's done these surgeries a thousand times – probably more. He's very experienced." I take my recorder from the bag and click it on. Jeremy's so used to it now he doesn't even comment.

"I know." He tries to smile but it doesn't quite reach his eyes. "It will all be worth it. I want to show Julia I *can* be a man worth being with, even if she's not the sort of person I want any more."

"Why were you with Julia, anyway? She doesn't sound that nice." It's something I've been wondering about. They're so different it's hard to imagine the two of them laughing together, living together, doing *other* things together . . . Ugh. I push away the thought.

Jeremy shrugs. "She was the kind of woman I thought I wanted back then. I was happy to make her happy. Now I realise that a one-way relationship isn't what I want at all. I want someone who wants to make *me* happy, too."

"I understand." I nod, trying to stop myself from asking why, if he really wants someone who loves him for who he is, is he having cosmetic surgery?

"So, how are you feeling?" Predictable question, I know, but it has to be posed.

"Terrified, actually." Jeremy slides off the bed and lumbers to the window. "You know about my sister and everything . . ."

I walk over and touch his arm. "I'm so sorry, Jeremy." I can't begin to imagine what that must feel like, losing a loved one.

"It's why I hate hospitals – even this one, with all its luxury. It still can't hide what it really is." He sighs, then collapses onto a chair. "It's part of the reason I was considering cancelling the surgery – cold feet, as you say. I couldn't bear to come back to a hospital again. It just reminds me of her."

"I understand. But you're only in here today and tomorrow. You'll be back home and looking hot in no time. Not that you're not hot now. Um, you know what I mean." God damn it, my face is heating up again.

Jeremy smiles. "I know what you mean. Look, thanks for pushing me to do this. I know there's nothing to worry about. It's kind of like going to the dentist, right?"

"Exactly." I smile back, ignoring the jabs in my belly – and Peter's answer that there's always a risk of complications. But this is what Jeremy wants. And he said it himself: his cold feet are mainly down to the earlier experiences with his sister.

A nurse wearing the classiest whites I've ever seen pops her head into the room. With blonde hair pulled into a chignon and chic straight-leg white denim paired with an embroidered tunic, she looks right off the runway. I tug down my own red cardigan and pat my hair back into place.

"Shall we get you into your hospital attire, Mr Ritchie?" The nurse smiles, revealing the glossiest and whitest teeth known to humankind. God, where do they recruit these people from? The Perfect Nurse Planet?

Jeremy nods. "I guess so." He takes the neatly folded stack of hospital clothes from the nurse and glances over at me. "You'll hang around until I'm out of the recovery room, right? I probably won't be in much of a mood to talk, but it'll be good to have someone here."

"Of course. I'll be here all along, and I'll come visit tomorrow, too. Did you know they have a chef in residence? I wouldn't dream of missing out on that. Do you think they do homemade Jaffa Cakes?"

Jeremy laughs. "Not in a high-class joint like this one." He plonks the bundle of clothes down on the bed. "Guess I'd better get changed." The tense expression has reappeared.

I pick up the item on top and shake it out. It's a hospital gown – in black – with a small tag bearing the name 'Versace'. Versace designed the hospital gowns?

"Well, at least you'll be operated on in style." I say, handing it over to him. "I'll wait in the hall."

I go out to the corridor and lean against the pearl-gray wall, feeling like I've stumbled into an alternate universe – the same way I feel when women fork over three thousand pounds in cash without batting an eyelid. A world where hospitals have chandeliers, nurses are models, and Versace designs black hospital gowns. I mean, I read the tabloids. I knew places like these existed. It's just different when you're in them.

Jeremy pokes his head out. "You can come back in now."

"You look great," I say, catching sight of him in his full hospital regalia. No limp pastel ensembles here – Jeremy's wearing the black gown underneath a deep-red Chinese-style tunic. He actually does look pretty damn good.

"I'm like a bloody ninja," he says, making a face. "I can't believe this get-up. Honestly, I'd prefer good old flash-your-bottom gowns to these poncy things."

I'd prefer flash-your-bottom ones too, if there was any chance of seeing his cute butt, I think, sitting back down on the bed.

"How's it going in here?" Peter strides into the room and for some reason, I jump off the bed and over to a Philippe-Starcke-style chair in the corner.

"I'm fine, I guess." Jeremy's voice sounds shaky.

Peter pulls up a chair beside the bed and settles into it, in full authoritative doctor mode. "So what we're doing today is removing the bags under your eyes" – he reaches out and grabs the loose skin under Jeremy's eyes – "and then some chin liposuction, and then the nose job." He tweaks Jeremy's small jowls (very small, I'd say) and I turn away, mortified to watch my boyfriend poke and prod his patient like a side of beef. "All in all, you should be in and out in an hour or so."

"Great." Jeremy sounds a bit embarrassed, too.

"The orderlies will come get you in a few minutes, once we have everything prepped in the OR. And you're sure you're okay with Serenity being present during surgery?"

Jeremy throws me a warm look. "It's the one thing keeping me sane right now. I must say, your clinic does provide a very comprehensive service."

Peter nods, smiling proudly. "Customer satisfaction is our top priority."

"We'll leave you now," I say quickly, before Jeremy can elaborate on how comprehensive the service really is. I leap off the chair and grab Peter's arm, propelling him toward the door. "Good luck, Jeremy." As soon as the words leave my mouth, I realise how ridiculous they sound. Do people wish each other luck for surgery? I smile at Jeremy over my shoulder, noting with chagrin that his face is glistening with sweat and a muscle under his eye is twitching.

"You've got the signed patient consent form, right?" Peter asks as we head toward the lift. "There's no way I'm letting you in the OR without it."

Oh, God. I put the form on a table in Jeremy's room . . . and it's still there. "Just a sec."

"Hurry up," Peter huffs. "I have to start operating in ten minutes or I miss the slot."

I race down the corridor and back into Jeremy's room. He's at the window again, arms crossed over his chest as if protecting himself from a coming blow. "Sorry, I just need you to sign this form for me to be in the operating room."

"Sure." As Jeremy scrawls his signature across the document, I can't help noticing his hand is trembling.

"I'll check in with you after the operation. And I'll even bring you some Jaffa Cakes from my private stash. Now *that's* sacrifice." I smile, worried now at how pale and shaky he is. Maybe he really doesn't want to go through with this. But you wouldn't have something as major as surgery if you didn't want to, would you? He'll be happy when everything's done and dusted.

Jeremy looks so anxious that I put my arms around him in a friendly hug. The thick cotton of his tunic is soft against my skin and his spicy scent envelopes me. He wraps his arms around me and pulls me closer, and I feel a rush of warmth from his body pressed up against mine. Then, without warning, he releases me and takes a step back, his chest rising and falling.

"Right." His voice sounds husky and he clears his throat. "I'll see you after the surgery."

I grab the form and dash down the corridor to where Peter is waiting, tapping his foot.

"Jesus Christ, Serenity. We're going to be late. You all right?"

"Fine, fine. I got the form." I wave it in his face to distract him from looking at me too closely. I can barely catch my breath.

195

But that's probably from all the running around, right?

The lift dings and we start our ascent toward the operating room.

CHAPTER NINETEEN

A few minutes later, my hands and arms have been scrubbed to within an inch of their lives, and I'm wearing a rather trendy tunic and trouser outfit (by Chanel, this time) in Egyptian cotton.

"The patient's ready, Doctor." A nurse pops her head between the operating room doors.

"Great. Thank you." Peter's all business now, tying a mask over his mouth. I do the same, trying not to gag as I breathe in its starchy smell. What, they could get designer gowns, but they couldn't fashion something better than this?

"Ready?" Peter turns toward me, eyes serious. "Just stay in the corner. Don't ask any questions or try to talk." His words are muffled through the mask.

"Okay," I say, suddenly terrified. I can't even bear to watch *Extreme Makeover*. How on earth am I going to witness someone I know being torn to bits in front of me?

I have to, I tell myself, wiping my sweaty palms on my tunic. I'm a reporter now, and I need the detail. If it bleeds, it leads. Blood is a good thing. People love it!

"Let's go." Peter elbows his way through the

swinging metal doors. I take a deep breath then follow him into the operating room.

The first thing I notice is how bright the lights are, and how white it is. Everything gleams, as if it's been polished a million times (it probably has), and there's not a scratch, scuff or fingerprint anywhere. If ever there was a place I'd want to have my face removed and put back on again, then this would be it. Suddenly I'm not quite so nervous. The OR is like something out of a space ship, Peter's a brilliant surgeon, and I'm not even sure they *allow* things to go wrong here.

I let out my breath and look toward the centre of the room. Jeremy's stretched out on a table, covered up to the shoulders in a sheet – no doubt designed by Dolce&Gabbana. Except for the tube running into his arm and the man standing behind Jeremy's head monitoring a bevy of beeping machines, Jeremy could be sleeping. Okay. This isn't so scary.

"Ready?" Peter looks at the nurses. They nod, their twin chignon-heads bobbing up and down in unison.

"Scalpel, please," Peter says, just like in the movies. The nurse hands him a scary-looking metallic instrument, and my face screws up in anticipation of Peter cutting into poor Jeremy's skin. I know he won't feel a thing, but still . . .

Peter makes an incision under Jeremy's left eye and a nurse dabs away the blood. Then Peter pulls back the skin flap to reveal blood and something yellowy – fat, I presume – and a wave of nausea rolls over me.

Gross. I gulp in air, forcing myself to watch as Peter removes extra skin and fat, then stitches up the incision.

He starts in on the right eye, and this time I'm able to observe without the threat of vomit. Still, there's *no way* I would voluntarily do this for a living. I'd never be able to detach myself from the fact that it's a living person I'm pulling apart.

Peter's just sewing up the bit underneath the right eye when there's a bleep from a machine behind Jeremy's head. The man monitoring them springs to his feet.

"Shit!" He fiddles with the device's buttons and knobs.

My heart jumps into my throat. I'm no expert, but I can't imagine 'shit' means something good.

"Patient's aspiration levels have dropped to a critical level," the man says in a controlled voice. Suddenly the relaxed feeling in the OR disappears.

"Decrease anaesthetic," Peter snaps.

"I have," the man shoots back. "But he's not responding. All the levels were fine until now. Must be an allergic reaction to the anaesthetic."

Everything stops as a silence like nothing I've ever known fills my ears. My heart thumps and I start to count to ten, just like Mom always instructed me to do when faced with something scary. When you get to that final number, she'd said, everything will be better. Granted, I was seven when she told me that, but it's always worked for me.

One.

The man's eyes are glued to the monitor and my breath comes in shallow gasps.

Two.

Everything will be fine. It will.

"Well? Is he responding?" Peter barks.

Three.

The man behind the monitor shakes his head.

Four.

Come on, Jeremy, I plead with his silent form on the bed. *Come on!* This is your dream. You *need* to be okay.

Five.

Halfway there. He's got to come around.

Six.

"He's back. Normal aspiration."

I let out my breath and lean against the wall, my heart galloping faster than a race horse. Thank God, I think, as my pulse slows. I knew Jeremy would pull through before I got to ten. I knew it! Whatever the crisis was, it's over.

"Thank you," Peter says, although his tone suggests anything but. "How long without aspiration?"

"About two to three minutes." The man shakes his head.

"Fuck," Peter hisses in a tight voice. My eyebrows fly up. I've never heard him swear in a professional context. "Serenity, wait out there." He points toward the door.

"But–"

"Now!" Peter's expression leaves no room for argument and I don't want to distract him from whatever's happening with Jeremy, so I slink through the doors, trying to figure out what's going on. Something to do with the anaesthetic – did they give him too much? Or too little? That's not such a big deal, is it? Jeremy will be all right, and this incident will add a bit of drama to my column. We'll have a laugh about it tomorrow, when he's resting comfortably eating whatever yummy meal the hospital chef has prepared.

I cross my fingers, praying I'm right. The alternative doesn't bear thinking about.

A few long – very long – minutes later, Peter bursts through the operating room doors. He jerks when he sees me, as if he forgot I'm here.

"So? Is Jeremy okay?" I need to hear Peter say everything's fine.

He peels off his mask and gloves, washing his hands in silence until I can bear it no longer.

"Peter!"

Sighing, he turns toward me, his face anxious and tense. "No. No, Jeremy's not okay."

My heart drops and my pulse starts pounding. "What's wrong? What happened?"

"You know how some people are really sensitive to pollen or seafood? They respond in a way that's different to normal people." Peter dries his hands.

I nod, desperate for him to hurry up and get to the point.

"Well, Jeremy's hypersensitive to anaesthetic."

"What does that mean?" I ask.

"It means that the amount we gave him – based on his weight, age, etcetera – was too much. And when someone has too much anaesthetic, the brain can't get the amount of oxygen it needs to function normally."

I watch Peter's mouth move but I can't quite piece it all together. "So what does that mean, exactly?"

"It's like drowning. If the brain goes without oxygen for too long, certain centres like speech and mobility can be affected."

"How long was Jeremy without oxygen?" I'm almost afraid to ask.

"We reckon around three minutes. Long enough to suffer some damage." Peter's face is serious.

I sag against a wall. Jeremy, brain damaged? My stomach flips, and for a second, I'm certain I'm going to throw up. "What damage has he suffered?" I croak, bracing myself to hear Peter's words.

"We won't know until he regains consciousness," Peter says. "He'll be moved into Critical Care for observation."

"Can I see him?"

"Family only," Peter responds brusquely. "Although it's not common, hypersensitivity to anaesthetic does happen. They know how to deal with it there."

I nod numbly. I don't care how frequently it happens. All I care is that it happened to Jeremy.

"Why don't you go home now. I've got another surgery in thirty minutes, anyway." Peter starts stripping off his scrubs, as if he's already forgotten about poor Jeremy lying prostrate in Critical Care.

He notices my expression and sighs. "Complications can happen, Serenity, I told you. It's part of medicine. Now go on." Peter gives me a little push toward the door, as if I'm Smitty. "I'll see you later tonight. I'll fill you in on Jeremy then." He turns to the sink again, dismissing me.

I stare at his back, unable to believe he can be so cold. Sure, Peter doesn't know Jeremy like I do, but he's so damn clinical about the whole thing, as if Jeremy's just one damaged cog on the surgical production line. Which, in a way, he is.

In a daze, I change from my scrubs, then go out into the gleaming corridor and over to a little kiosk in the corner, serving – I squint at the food inside the case – caviar and sushi, along with a full menu of imported sake. Suddenly I'm disgusted by this place and its over-the-top wealth and luxury. It's just tempting fate to step in and make something go wrong.

I collapse onto a distressed leather chair. Funny, until I asked, I've never heard Peter mention to any patient that something could go wrong during surgery. It's always been about the outcome: how wonderful they'll look; how they'll appear ten years younger. If this anaesthetic thing happens as often as Peter says it does, shouldn't he be telling patients about it?

But as much as I want to pin the blame on Peter for

what's happened to Jeremy, there's one thought blaring in my head. It presses down on me, filtering through every pore and making me shiver with guilt. *I* was the one who convinced Jeremy to go through with the surgery. Part of the reason he's lying in Critical Care is because of me.

There's no way I'm going home. *No way.* I'll get into Critical Care somehow to see Jeremy, to sit beside him so he's not alone, even if he doesn't know I'm there.

Wiping away the tears that have gathered in my eyes, I stand up, full of determination. Heading to the interactive information stand beside the lift, I scroll through the hospital departments until I locate Critical Care on the eighth floor.

As the lift rises, I rehearse my story. I'll pretend I'm Jeremy's sister, and hopefully that should do the trick. If it doesn't, well, I'll sneak back into the OR, grab my scrubs, and impersonate a doctor if I need to. I can't let Jeremy lie there alone.

I walk out into a blinding white corridor with the same grand chandelier as in reception. Potted orchids grace every surface, and the whole thing feels more like an upscale boutique hotel than the Critical Care department of a hospital.

"Hello." Yet another blonde nurse behind a bamboo desk smiles at me with just the right mix of sympathy and empathy. "Can I help?"

"I'm Jeremy Ritchie's sister. From America," I add quickly, remembering my accent might be a tip-off I'm lying. "I believe he was brought to Critical Care after an operation about twenty minutes ago?" I try to look trustworthy but my face flushes.

The nurse's expression doesn't alter, but her eyes narrow slightly. "Just let me check our records." She taps away at a Mac then glances up. "Can I see some

ID, please? Sometimes we get paparazzi trying to sneak in." Her mouth twists like she's tasted something foul.

"Yes, those vultures, I know. They stop at nothing," I say, my cheeks getting even redder. I make a show of searching in my handbag for identification. "I'm sure I have something in here. Just a second . . ." My eyes widen in horror as the notebook I'd shoved in my bag clunks onto the floor.

The nurse stands, peering over the desk. "Did you drop something?" She spots my notebook. "What's that?"

"Oh, it's just, it's just my journal. Journaling's all the rage in the States." I smile shakily, willing her to believe me. At least my accent is helpful this time.

"I need to see some identification," she repeats, sitting back down.

"Um, I don't have any with me. Sorry. I never thought of bringing ID to the hospital." That much is true, anyway. "Please let me see my brother. I'm really worried about him."

Something in my expression must ring true, because the nurse waves me past the desk. "Mr Ritchie is in suite ten. Please use the disinfectant gel outside each room before entering."

I nod then race down the corridor, past numbers one, two, three . . . I pause for a second outside suite ten, wondering what Jeremy will look like. In my mind, he's all wound up in bandages like a mummy or a car-crash victim, but realistically I know Peter only did the bags under Jeremy's eyes before disaster struck. The real damage is inside his head.

Taking a deep breath to steady myself, I rub a squirt of gel from the silver wall dispenser into my hands, then push open the door.

Inside the spacious room, the light is dim and

although they've made an effort to keep up the cool –
with modern art on the walls and a glass sculpture in
one corner – nothing can disguise the row of machines
and the high hospital bed. This is a room for a very ill
person.

"Jeremy?" I whisper as I walk on tiptoes toward the
bed. The room is silent except for the beep of monitors,
and it feels like I've crawled into a cocoon, where the
outside world doesn't exist. Nothing exists but Jeremy,
lying here in front of me.

Wow. If I thought he was pale before the operation,
this gives the word a whole new meaning. Even the
hospital sheet has a healthy glow compared to him.
Angry bruises make his eyes resemble a raccoon's, and
the stitches underneath . . . I wince at the neat black
thread piercing angry-looking skin. But apart from that
– and the tube running into his arm, along with the
various machines he's hooked up to – he could be
resting.

Except he's not.

I slump onto a retro-patterned chair beside the bed,
unable to take my eyes off him. Maybe he'll be fine
when he wakes up. No one really knows what happens
in the brain, right? It's still a mystery. And people can
go without oxygen for a long time – what about that
David Blaine dude? He went up to, like, seven minutes
or something holding his breath.

I watch Jeremy's chest rise and fall, then lean over to
take his hand. God, it's freezing. I rub his fingers
between my hands to try to warm them up, then place
his hand back under the sheet and cover it with my
own. I sit like that for hours, observing Jeremy's still,
bruised face, and praying he'll be okay when he
awakens.

The shrill ring of my mobile jerks me from my

trance. I answer it quickly, ducking out into the corridor.

"Hello?" I whisper.

"How's the column coming?" Leza's sharp nasal tone blares out at me and I hold the phone away from my ear. Oh God, the column. With everything that's happened, writing it has been the last thing on my mind.

"I'm sorry, Leza. There were complications with the surgery, and Jeremy's still not awake." I cross my fingers for the millionth time that when he does come to, everything will be all right.

"Complications?" she interrupts. "Like what?" Instead of sounding angry, her voice is kind of . . . happy.

"Well, Jeremy had a reaction to the anaesthetic. The doctors think he may have suffered brain damage as a result." I lean back against the cool wall, struggling to breathe against the heavy weight on my chest.

"Brain damage?" Now Leza sounds downright gleeful. A flash of anger goes through me. How can someone be giddy about brain damage? "What kind of brain damage?"

"They don't know yet. The doctors are waiting for Jeremy to wake up to assess him."

"This is good shit, Serenity. Seriously good shit."

Good shit? Jeremy lying in bed, damaged, is good shit? I try to form words to respond, but my mind can't even begin to conjure up anything coherent.

"Hang tight there, Serenity," Leza continues. "Discover the extent of the damage. Jeremy should wake up in the next few hours, right? Write the column, and add in the damaged bits once you find out. Even if it's just a bloody eyelid twitch, I want to know. We couldn't have asked for a better story, really.

This is drama at its best, and our readers deserve to know *everything*."

I shake my head, unable to process what she's saying. Leza wants me to offer up Jeremy on a plate because our readers deserve it?

"Serenity? Serenity! You're not getting wussy on me, are you? You wanted to be a tabloid reporter. This is what tabloid reporters do. Forget the Monday deadline – get me the copy by eleven tonight, and that job is yours. I want to make a big splash with this tomorrow morning."

Thoughts swim round my head like caffeinated goldfish. If I can do this, the job will be mine. Everything I've wanted – a full-fledged reporter on London's top tabloid. But–

"Or should I get Mia onto it?" Leza's voice is low and threatening.

My head snaps up. Mia? "No. No, I'll do it." The words fly out of my mouth.

"Good." The line goes dead.

CHAPTER TWENTY

I stare at the phone in my hand, feeling like I've done a deal with the devil: Jeremy, in exchange for my coveted job. Kind of like that Faustus guy who offered his soul in return for knowledge. I shiver, remembering what happened to him in the end. Let's just say it wasn't good.

Easing open the door to Jeremy's room, I slink over to the corner. The room is deathly silent, and the chair squeaks loudly as I shift on its hard surface.

Right. I can do this, I say to myself as I flip open my notebook. I'm a reporter; I need to act like one. *Dream it, live it.* I'm pretty sure Mom might not approve of me using her mantra in this instance, but hey, a mantra is a mantra.

Tapping my pen on the pad, I try not to stare at Jeremy's pale face or his unmoving body – or think about those terrible moments on the operating table, when the doctors struggled to get oxygen back to his brain. But the more I try to push away the memories, the more they demand centre stage.

I slam the notebook closed and walk over to the window, drawing in deep breaths. It's not like I'm using Jeremy's real name. It's perfectly anonymous – and Jeremy *will* be fine. All I need to do is concentrate on separating the broken man in front of me from James, the fictional guy in my column. I sit and open my notebook again.

Okay. First things first: the headline. Maybe I can focus on what went right. *The Eyes Have It*? I shake my head – that's not what Leza wants. She's craving every gory detail of the surgery gone wrong, and then some. I stare at the lines on the paper, willing the right combination of words to come to mind.

What about . . . *Brain Drain*? I scrawl down the opening sentence as fast as I can, almost on auto-pilot.

```
James didn't want to choose
between brains and beauty, but
when his surgery for a 'fresher'
look went wrong, the choice may
have been made for him.

Today was supposed to be the day
our Build a Man really kicked off
his quest for transformation.
Checking into a luxurious private
hospital, James was nervous, but
happily anticipating his new
chiselled jaw, Romanesque nose,
and bag-free eyes.
```

A moan fills the room, and I glance up to see Jeremy's head move slightly to one side. I rush to the bed. "Jeremy? Jeremy!"

He keeps groaning, as if he's trying to fight his way through to consciousness. A doctor and nurse burst into the room. I step back as they check Jeremy's monitors.

"He's coming around," a doctor says. "Jeremy. Mr

Ritchie. Can you hear me?"

Jeremy opens his eyes, and I swallow back a gasp. His right eye is perfectly fine – or as fine as you can imagine with all the bruising. But the left one sags, struggling to open halfway. My heart plummets and all the air squeezes from my chest.

The doctor leans over Jeremy, waving a light in his face. "Abnormal pupil dilation." He lifts Jeremy's limp right hand. "Jeremy, squeeze my hand if you can."

I focus on Jeremy's fingers, willing them to move. Relief floods through me when I see his fingers twitch, closing the doctor's hand in his.

"Good, Jeremy, good." The doctor takes Jeremy's left hand. "Now, can you try squeezing again?"

Watching closely, I wait for Jeremy's fingers to move. But they don't, and I notice the doctor give the nurse a meaningful look, then scribble something on his clipboard.

"What?" I ask, unable to stay silent any longer. "What's wrong?"

"Please let us finish, Miss," the doctor says as Jeremy starts moaning again. Jeremy's eyes look more alert now, but his left lid still droops.

"Can you say your name?" the doctor asks him.

What a stupid question. Of course Jeremy can say his damn name.

I stare in horror as Jeremy's lips move and he struggles to form the sounds. The right side of his mouth looks normal, but when he tries to speak, the left side doesn't move. He manages a word, but it sounds nothing like 'Jeremy'.

Oh my God.

The doctor pats Jeremy's arm. "Excellent. Thank you." He glances at me. "Let's talk outside."

I lean over the bed, watching Jeremy's eyes as they

focus on my face. He struggles to speak, and I touch his shoulder. "It's all right, Jeremy. You're going to be fine." Tears gather in the corners of my eyes and I dash them away. "I'll be right back."

I follow the doctor from the room and into the private consultation pod outside the door. With a padded, circular banquette and calming lounge-style music, it seems more restaurant than hospital. I can't imagine anyone giving me bad news in a place like this, but judging from the doctor's serious face, it's definitely not going to be good.

"Have a seat." The doctor points to the bench and I sit down, every muscle in my body quivering with tension. He swivels to face me awkwardly. "So. Your brother is suffering from brain damage."

I nod, still trying to absorb the words.

"The lack of oxygen to his brain appears to have affected the muscles on the left side of his body," the doctor continues. "The severity of it still needs to be determined by a CT scan, which he's booked in for tomorrow. In the meantime, we'll do a full neurological exam to see what other responses and brain centres might have been affected."

"He will get better though, right?" I study the doctor's face, desperate to spot a glimmer of hope. I can't imagine Jeremy like this forever, unable to speak or move the left side of his body. He loves working with his hands, building things. What will happen if he can't?

"It's hard to say at this stage," the doctor answers. "Jeremy will need to undergo rehabilitation, certainly. How fast and how much he recovers can't be predicted, but the good news is that he's regained consciousness. He should be more alert tomorrow."

I nod mutely.

"It's a lot to take in, I know. If you want to stay the night here, the nurse can book you into one of our complimentary relative rooms. They come with a free massage and unlimited broadband access." The doctor sounds like he's reading off a cue card.

I stare, unable to believe he thinks I want a massage and free broadband when my friend is lying brain damaged next door.

"No?" the doctor says when I don't respond. "Well, you can call our twenty-four-hour patient hotline any time for a status update. Jeremy's key-in code is" – he consults his chart – "six-six-seven-five. I'll be back later to check on him." He pats my arm and leaves.

Slouching back against the soft leather, I try to take in what the doctor's just told me. No matter how desperately I want to pretend it's not true, Jeremy's *not* fine – he's brain damaged. I repeat the words in my head, trying to get to grips with them. *Brain damaged. Brain damaged. Brain damaged.* It's a game Kirsty and I used to play when we were kids: take the worst word you know (back then, it was 'bitch'), and say it over and over until it loses its badness; until the jumble of letters becomes meaningless. But as many times as I chant 'brain damaged', it still sends a sharp pang through me.

But, of course, it's not just that. *I* encouraged Jeremy to have the surgery when he questioned going forward. What's he thinking, lying there now? Will he ever be able to forgive me?

Rubbing my tired eyes, I leave the pod and head back into the room, steeling myself to face him. But when I walk over to the bed, Jeremy's lids are closed, and his chest is moving up and down in a regular rhythm. I reach out and smooth a lock of hair from his forehead. God, I hope he'll be all right, with time. Lots of people have recovered from brain damage and gone on to lead successful, productive lives. People like . . . okay, so I can't think of anyone right now, but they're out there.

I sit on the chair by Jeremy's bed for hours, watching his chest rise and fall as the room darkens. My eyes pop with surprise when I finally glance at my watch. It's already ten o'clock. One more hour to deliver the goods on Jeremy and his botched operation. One hour until that job – the job I've dreamed of since forever – is mine.

Can I do it? Can I write about the man in front of me – the man I now know is not okay – as if he's some other person; someone I'm offering up to the tabloid gods and the 'deserving' public, like he's a piece of meat on a platter?

My phone bleeps and I click on the 'New Message' icon.

```
I need the copy now. And get a
photo - a close-up of his eyes.
We'll crop it later.
```

A photo? I shake my head, anger building inside as I picture myself focusing in on Jeremy's limp form, snapping away as he lies there, ill. I shudder at the thought of it; of how I would feel, sinking to that level. Invading his privacy and taking advantage of him at his most vulnerable.

No. No way. No matter what name I give him, I can't separate Jeremy from the anonymous Build a Man any longer. Going undercover seemed so harmless before, when it was just Botox and beauty adjustments. But now that Jeremy is brain damaged . . . I *can't*. My head throbs as I think about what I'm giving up – everything I've ever wanted, since those boring, dreary days back in Harris.

I look over to where Jeremy's lying so still and I know, beyond a shadow of a doubt, I'm not going to write that article.

Creeping from the room, I call Leza before I lose my nerve. This is it: the end of my tabloid career.

"Serenity. Where's the copy?" she barks when she comes on the line.

"I can't do the column," I say in a low voice.

"What?" A sharp banging noise hurts my ears. "The reception's terrible here. I thought I heard you say you can't do the column." Her voice is almost menacing.

"I did say that." I pause and wait for her response, but there's just silence. "He's really ill, Leza. Maybe I can write about the risks of cosmetic surgery, the percentage of things that go wrong . . ."

"You know as well as I do that's not what our readers want. You got them to know this James bloke personally. They don't fancy a clinical explanation of bloody *cosmetic surgery risks*. They want to know exactly what happened."

"I know, but it's just . . ." My eyes fill with tears. "He can barely say his name." Too late, I realise I probably shouldn't have told her anything. I wanted Leza to know the severity of the situation, but I've probably piqued her interest further.

"Even more of a reason to write about it," Leza says crisply. "Look, I think I know what's going on here."

"You do?" My brow wrinkles with confusion.

"You two have a personal relationship going, yeah? If you're a good undercover reporter, you probably do. That's how reporters get inside the skin of their subjects, Serenity. By making friends, building a relationship. Do you think I got that exposé on Scottie

Leon just by asking him a few questions?"

"But isn't he gay?" I wonder out loud. The last I'd heard, the famous comedian had been caught in a loo on Hampstead Heath with a 'lady man', according to *Snap!*.

"Not with me, he wasn't," Leza says smugly. "Look, I know it's difficult being objective in situations like this, when you've got to sever ties and do your job. But you'll get used to it."

I turn her words over in my head. Get used to screwing people over – people like Jeremy, who's lying there defenceless? "I can't, Leza."

She makes a disgusted noise. "I thought you had what it takes to be in the business, but clearly you don't. Well, I'm not going to waste my time with you. Hand your notes and sound files over to Mia. I'll have her meet you outside the hospital. Thank God we got her in on the act earlier."

Yeah, right. I'm not going to let Jeremy be torn to bits by the two of them. Any information I have is staying with me.

"No. Sorry, but no." My voice is firm, but inside I'm terrified. You don't tell Leza no.

She laughs incredulously. "You think you can stop us by holding back the pitiful info you have? We can find out anything, Serenity. Anything. And we will, don't you worry. We'll have that column front and centre tomorrow, *without* your help." She pauses. "Oh, and good luck finding another tabloid job. Once I tell everyone what an absolute waste of space you turned out to be, they won't let you anywhere near their offices." The line goes dead.

I stare at a painting in front of me, the blobby red bit in the centre changing shape as tears fill my eyes. My dream is over – everything I've worked for in the past few weeks, all the excitement of thinking I've finally made it . . . finished.

But if I'm honest, the reality of it wasn't *really* my dream. Sure, I enjoyed having tons of people reading my column and being invited to a swanky launch party. But my dream didn't include the lying bit – and certainly not the part where I'd have to betray friendships. I wanted the gloss, not the accompanying dirty deeds.

Trudging back into the room, I reach out and take Jeremy's right hand. Something inside me gives way when his fingers slowly close around mine. Tears fill my eyes, but they have nothing to do with losing *Build a Man* – it's not my driving force any longer. I just want the man in front of me to be well again.

I picture Jeremy splashed all over the *Beauty Bits* homepage, and a sick feeling washes over me. I've no doubt Leza's right. With or without my help, a *Daily Planet* reporter will worm their way in here. And I can't let that happen. Somehow, I need to protect Jeremy. I grasp his hand harder as the tears drip down my cheeks, falling onto the crisp white sheets below.

Jeremy's eyelids flutter.

"Jeremy?" I whisper. But he just turns his head a fraction of an inch, and the room stays silent.

A couple hours later, Jeremy still hasn't awakened. Thankfully, no *Daily Planet* reporter has shown up – yet, anyway. I'm sitting beside him, staring down and willing him to get well, while fending off the attentions of the hospital's grooming staff. One stylist who came to do Jeremy's hair had the nerve to tell me I need to get my eyebrows threaded. Exactly what I want to hear in the Critical Care unit.

Finally a doctor enters the room, checks Jeremy's machines, and scribbles something on his chart. "You have to go now," he says to me. "The wards are closed to visitors during the night."

There's no way I'm leaving Jeremy unprotected – I wouldn't be surprised if Mia and Leza were shimmying up the wall James-Bond-style right this second. Jeremy is *Beauty Bits'* lead story, and they're not going to let him go without a fight.

"I'm staying," I say to the doctor, in what I hope is a firm voice.

He shakes his head, dismissing me like a school kid. "You're not. Visiting hours are over. In fact, they ended long ago. Now, do I need to ask security to remove you from the premises?"

Oh, God. "No, no, that's fine." I squeeze Jeremy's hand a final time, then ease myself past the doctor and out into the corridor. I'll think of something. I have to. I may have left Jeremy's side, but I'm not going home until I'm sure Leza won't get her claws into him. Maybe I can tip off the hospital that Jeremy's being targeted by the paparazzi?

I push into the private pod outside the room, a plan forming in my mind. Talking to hospital personnel face-to-face is too risky. They'll probably ask uncomfortable questions I don't want to answer. But there's a twenty-four-hour patient hotline – I can call from a pay phone (no chance of tracing my number), and warn the hospital their solid reputation when it comes to patient privacy is about to be compromised. A lot of celebs come here for surgery, so they should take the threat seriously. But what if they don't? Or, even more likely, what if they ask for more details before taking action? After all, they wouldn't want to disturb a patient by implementing protective measures without evidence. It's almost guaranteed I'll need to spill the specifics on *Beauty Bits* to be taken seriously.

If I do, though, the hospital is bound to tell Jeremy about the column when he wakes up, to justify the additional security. And when he reads the posts . . . well, it will be pretty obvious I'm the one behind it. There are things in there only I could have known.

My heart clutches as I picture his reaction to the fact that I'm not what he thought I was; that I tricked him into telling me personal details, and that those personal details were splattered across the internet for everyone to see – even if I *did* protect his identity. And what if Jeremy tells the hospital I was behind the column?

A jab of fear hits me as I hurry through the corridors, down the lift, and out to the payphone I'd spotted right outside the hospital entrance. I'll come to the hospital early tomorrow morning, before anyone has a chance to fill him in, and explain everything. Hopefully, somehow, he'll see how sorry I am and how much I do care. So much that I couldn't carry on writing about him.

No more deals with the devil. I'm done.

I pull open the smeared glass door of the telephone booth. Heart thumping, I dial the patient hotline, then stay on the line as they transfer me to their emergency communications department for 'further investigation'. Just as I suspected, they demand to know more before agreeing to provide extra security, so I give them the *Beauty Bits* website address and explain that 'James' is really Jeremy. Tapping my fingers against the metal of the phone, I wait while they check out the site. Finally, they agreed to station a guard outside Jeremy's room as soon as possible, and I hang up.

As I push out of the booth, I still can't believe what's happened. Jeremy's brain damaged. I've quit the column. And tomorrow, I'll have to face the man I've betrayed and tell him what I've done. Moving like a robot, I somehow manage the short walk back to the flat.

It's almost twelve-thirty when I crawl into bed beside Peter, wondering how on earth I'm ever going to sleep. Every muscle in my body aches with exhaustion and my head throbs, but whenever I even *think* of closing my eyes, all I can hear are the awful noises that came from Jeremy's mouth when he tried to say his name. I turn over on my side and the bed jiggles in response.

"Serenity?"

"Sorry," I whisper, trying to lie still.

Peter flips on the light. "Where the hell have you been?"

Uh-oh. I probably should have called, but it was the last thing on my mind. "I was at the hospital."

Sitting up, Peter rubs a hand over his face. "Until now? Doing what, exactly?"

What does he think I've been doing, getting my nails done (although I'm sure they have a manicurist there)?

"Checking on Jeremy. Did you know he can't even speak properly? Or move his left side?"

Peter shakes his head. "No. I didn't. But I'll look at his chart tomorrow." He flops down on the pillow and closes his eyes. "Let's go to sleep. I've another early start in the morning." He turns off the light.

I lie there for a second with my eyes wide open, exhaustion giving way to anger. I've just told Peter that Jeremy's brain damaged from an operation *he* performed, and he wants to sleep? I flick the light back on and sit up.

"Don't you care at all about Jeremy? He's your patient."

Peter makes an impatient noise. "Actually, Serenity, he's not. He's out of my care now – he's the responsibility of the neurologist."

"What, so you're washing your hands of him completely?" My words are loud and angry in the hushed silence of the room.

"No, I'm not washing my hands of him completely. Jesus, you really don't know how these things work, do you? I'm not an expert in neurology. Why would I even begin to try to treat him? I'll see how Jeremy's doing from time to time, but that's it. I've other surgeries and new patients to focus on."

Peter's practical tone infuriates me. "So job done, even though you messed up?" It's a bit over the top, I know, but I want to prod my boyfriend into some kind of emotion.

Looks like I've succeeded. When he swings toward me, his face is angrier than I've ever seen it. I jerk away, worried I've gone too far.

"I didn't 'mess up'." Peter jabs his fingers in the air as he says the words. "And I really resent the implication that I did."

I stare at him, feeling strangely detached from the man in front of me. I've always admired the calm, unruffled way he goes through life. But now – when it comes to people I care about – it doesn't seem so admirable.

There's nothing I can possibly say, so I lower my head onto the pillow and turn away.

CHAPTER TWENTY-ONE

Light filtering through the window wakes me from my shallow sleep the next morning. I stretch out my arms, grateful the torturous night is finally over. Peering at Peter, I can see his chest rise and fall with soft snores, and an image of Jeremy's chest moving up and down in the confines of his hospital room flashes through my mind.

I slide out of the covers as quietly as possible, then pull on the heap of clothes I discarded by the bed last night. It's still early, but I've got to talk to Jeremy.

Running a brush through my hair, I jam on my trainers and head out into the street. The closer I get to the hospital, the more desperate I am to see him. Guilt and regret mixed with something like hope – hope that we can begin again, hope that he *will* get better – churn inside, and I urge my legs to move faster and faster until I'm practically running.

Finally, I cross the hospital's marble foyer and head straight to Jeremy's suite on the eighth floor. Funny, there's no guard. Maybe he's inside? I heave open the heavy wooden door, anxious to see if Jeremy's awake and if he's doing better today.

"Jeremy?" My smile freezes as I take in the empty space with the bed neatly made. I search for any trace of him, but there's nothing – it looks like a hotel room, awaiting the next guest. I glance at my watch: eight o'clock. Could he be getting the CT scan the doctor told me about?

Heart beating fast, I head back into the corridor and race over to the desk.

"Excuse me," I say to the nurse, a dead ringer for Cindy Crawford. "I'm looking for Jeremy Ritchie. Can you tell me where he is?" Maybe he's been moved or downgraded to a regular ward.

"One moment, please." She smiles coolly at me and taps on the keyboard – I can hear her fingernails clicking from where I'm standing. Come on, I say inside my head. *Come on!* With every passing second, I want to see Jeremy more and more.

"Mr Ritchie requested a transfer earlier this morning," she says.

"Requested a transfer?" I repeat lamely, unable to get my mind around exactly what that might mean. "Transferred where? Is he all right?"

"He is no longer in care of this hospital," the nurse responds, sounding almost robotic.

"Okay. If you could give me the address of where he's been transferred, that would be great." I dig out my pen and notepad. Jeremy is stable enough to be moved, thank goodness. But why would he request a transfer? Unless . . . I gulp as the answer seeps into my mind. Unless the communications department has already talked to him about my column.

Cindy shakes her head, her long ponytail swooshing back and forth. "I'm sorry. Communications has left strict instructions not to disclose this information."

Oh God. They have. They've talked to him.

"I'm his sister." I force a smile as sweat prickles on my forehead. "And I never heard anything about a transfer. Please, can you just double-check?"

She gives me a big fake smile and pretend-clacks a few keys (I know she's not typing, because I don't hear her fingernails clicking). "His file says absolutely no information is to be released to anyone except his immediate-care doctors."

My heart picks up pace. Maybe Peter can find out where he is. "Is Dr Lycett on that list?" I hold my breath.

Cindy rolls her eyes but taps the keyboard. "No. Just Mr Ritchie's neurologist." She raises her eyebrows. "Anything else I can help you with today?"

Unable to force a word past the lump in my throat, I shake my head, backing away from the desk and into the lift. Jeremy's gone. He's gone, and he knows I've lied to him; that I've betrayed his trust. As the lift judders downwards, my heart drops along with it, and I grip onto a steel railing, lightheaded with dismay.

At least . . . at least if I can't locate Jeremy, Mia and Leza might not be able to, either. But I can't muster up any triumphant feelings. Every inch – every last fibre of my being – is focused on Jeremy. I've *got* to find him to tell him how sorry I am, and that I'm through with the tabloid.

Okay. I take a deep breath and try to focus. I have his contact information and I know where he lives. A ray of hope flashes through me as I dig out my phone and call his number, waiting for his easy, relaxed tones on the voicemail. I'll leave a message explaining things. He'll have to pick up voicemail sometime.

But instead of ringing, the number just disconnects. I try again – same thing. And again. Why won't my calls go through? Has he blocked my number?

Unable to think what else to do, I rush down commuter-clogged Marylebone toward Jeremy's. Maybe someone's there – he could have hired his own nurse. He's rich enough to, right? And if he has been moved to another facility, maybe someone's come round to gather up his things.

When I reach his house, the familiar geraniums bob over the black iron railings, and my heart lifts. I pound on the door, willing it to open, but it remains resolutely closed. Leaning back against the white facade of the house, I try to think of what to do next.

If I can't reach Jeremy by voicemail, then I'll do it the old-fashioned way: by letter. I get out my notebook, cringing as I spot the opening paragraph I scrawled down last night. I can't believe I wrote that – it feels like another person did. Well, I guess in a way I *was* someone else: Serenity v2. Funny, now that my tabloid dream is over, I realise how far from being Serenity v2 I actually am – and how I'm sure now I don't ever want to be. Flipping to a fresh page, I hunker down on the steps, tapping the pen against my teeth as I think about what to write.

Hi Jeremy! No, that sounds wrong – too upbeat and casual. I scratch it out then turn to a new page. God, if only the mistakes of my past were as easy to fix.

```
Dear Jeremy,

I hope you're feeling better. I
went to see you today, but you'd
been transferred and they wouldn't
tell me where. I know you've heard
about Beauty Bits.
```

I pause for a second, unsure what to say next. How can I ask him to forgive me for such a massive lie? My cheeks colour with shame as I recall everything I spewed, from wine therapy to how to dress for the person you want to be. *God.*

```
Jeremy, I'm so sorry I wasn't
honest with you. But I've stopped
writing that column now - I just
couldn't carry on after your
operation. Please get in touch and
let me know where you are. I'll
explain everything.
```

Tapping my pen again, I ponder how to close the letter. Yours? No, that's way too formal. Best wishes, from your fraudulent life advisor? I shake my head.

```
Love,
Serenity
```

There. My eyes tear up as I rip out the page, and I realise not everything between us was pretend. There was something there; we *do* have a connection – something like friendship – that goes beyond reporter-subject, and I think Jeremy felt it, too. Hopefully it's made enough of an impact for him to give me a chance whenever he does get this letter. And in the meantime, I still have his number to try. I call it again, and again it clicks off before going through.

My mobile rings and I almost drop it with surprise. Maybe it's him!

"Hello?" I say, almost gasping with nerves.

"Where the hell are you? It's almost eight-thirty." Peter's angry tones buzz through the handset and my heart plunges. Oh. It was ridiculous to think it would be Jeremy, anyway. The poor man could barely even speak yesterday.

"Sorry, um, I just went out for fresh air," I say lamely, tucking Jeremy's letter halfway through the slot in the door, so that if anyone does come by to get his things, they'll be sure to see it. "I'll meet you at work."

I hang up, then trudge the five-minute walk to the clinic. After Peter's response last night, I'm in no hurry to see him. And after what I witnessed in the operating room, I'm definitely not in a rush to watch others treat cosmetic surgery like it's the same as going to the hair salon. I cringe at the memory of Jeremy comparing his operation to visiting the dentist.

Turning into the mews, I can see Peter at the clinic door, impatiently fiddling with the keys. His eyes widen as he takes in my dishevelled state.

"What are you wearing?" he asks as I approach. "Jesus Christ, Serenity." Unlocking the door, he ushers me inside. From the straight set of his shoulders as he marches past me to his office, I can tell he's anything but impressed.

Well, so what? I'm not exactly impressed with him, either. And for the first time since our relationship started, I don't care. I head to the bathroom and stare into the mirror, taking in my pale cheeks, the dark circles under my eyes, and my tousled, greasy hair. This is me – the real me, and I'm not going to try to pretty myself up, today of all days. I go back out behind the desk and perch on my stool.

With a growing sense of dread, I turn on the computer and type in the *Beauty Bits* website. Since Jeremy has disappeared and I only gave Leza the barest of information about his condition, I hope they won't be able to dredge up anything too horrible. The familiar road sign appears.

Fingers shaking, I scroll down.

BUILD A MAN REVEALED!

Disastrous Operation Leaves Property Millionaire Jeremy Ritchie in Coma

Oh my God.

No.

No way.

I stare at the headline, praying it's a figment of my imagination. That's *not* Jeremy's real name on the screen. It's not. I jam my eyes closed to wipe the slate clean. But when I force my lids open again, there it is.

I press a fist against my mouth to stop the rising fury and panic from spewing out. If the thought of Jeremy's story splashed all over the web under a false identity was bad, this is just . . . beyond words.

> *The Daily Planet* can now reveal our Build a Man is none other than property multi-millionaire Jeremy Ritchie. Dumped by his ex-girlfriend in favour of his better-looking business partner, it's easy to understand why Jeremy (or 'James' as we've been calling him) fancied a fresh new look. Sadly, his surgery yesterday didn't turn out as planned.

I tear my eyes away from the car-crash text and look over at the sidebar. The blue cut-out paper doll is now all warped, as if someone's run their hand across it and pushed it out of whack. Underneath it is the same photo of Jeremy and his business partner I'd seen on Google, and under that, the photo of Julia and David when they got married.

I force myself to read the rest of the text.

```
Instead, he emerged a groaning,
moaning one-eyed wonder after a
bad reaction to anaesthetic during
surgery nearly left him dead on
the table. Although Jeremy
survived, the brain damage he
suffered - resulting in left-side
paralysis - means he's more Lurch
than luscious.

Jeremy's a new man all right - a
man better suited to a care home
than the vigours of dating. After
all, what woman wants a life with
a man who needs his nappy changed?
```

Oh, *Jesus!* I drop my head into my hands, pushing my palms against my eyes as if I can erase the words. I thought I was protecting Jeremy by warning the hospital. But by cutting off Leza's source of future stories, I'd given her the green light to reveal his identity. Why would she care about keeping it a secret if her subject had disappeared, anyway?

Off to the side of the column is a poll:

```
         RETURN TO SENDER?

What would you do if a man you
were dating suffered brain damage?
Would you:

A. Make like Florence Nightingale
and happily nurse him back to
health.
B. Check him into a rehabilitation
centre and hope for the best.
C. Kick him to the kerb and find a
man who can take care of you, too.
```

I glance at the results, split between B and C, and my eyes nearly pop out of my head. Over seven thousand people have voted already, on a Monday morning. Leza was right: people *do* love this kind of thing. An image of vultures circling over Jeremy, pecking away at him, flashes into my mind, and I shudder. As much as I don't want to lump myself in with Leza and Mia, I know I played a part in serving him up. A big part. If it wasn't for me, Jeremy wouldn't be on that hospital bed. My gut clenches and guilt floods through me again. I hope he gets my letter soon. Even if he doesn't contact me, at least he'll know I wasn't involved in this post.

I scroll down, marvelling at all the content they've managed to squeeze out of the incident. There are fact boxes, links to other stories of cosmetic surgeries gone wrong . . . and nine hundred and seventy-nine comments. I skim through them, mainly of the 'get well soon' variety. But some berate Jeremy for having cosmetic surgery in the first place, and one even calls him 'a weak male specimen who deserves what he got'. Those people have obviously never heard of a little thing called sympathy.

Come back tomorrow to discover if our Build a Man can put himself back together again, it says at the very bottom. *Is he destined to drool forever? Or can he fight back and find love despite the damage? We talk to the experts to find out.* Jeez, they're going to milk this for all it's worth, even if they don't have direct access to Jeremy.

There's a noise behind me and I look up from the screen, quickly clicking the window closed.

"Cancel everything for the rest of the day," Peter says tersely, shrugging on his suit jacket. Lines are etched into his face and his brows are knit together.

"What's happened?" I'm almost afraid to ask.

"The hospital board has called me in. Apparently,

some sort of column is being written on Jeremy Ritchie without his consent. The reporter gained inside access to the hospital, and the whole board is on a witch hunt. Look, I've got to run." He throws the keys at me and they clatter onto the desk. "Lock up when you've rung the clients. I'll see you back home."

I nod, my already buzzing head trying to comprehend his words as I watch him go. It's like a second punch to the gut, just when I was struggling to catch my breath from the previous blow. What have I done? I was so busy trying to protect Jeremy that I never even thought the hospital might question Peter.

It's just routine, I tell myself. Of course the hospital would want to talk to Peter – he was Jeremy's doctor, after all, and they'd need to examine every angle. Thank goodness Peter knows nothing about what I've been up to. There's no way they can implicate him in anything . . . I hope. But what if Jeremy's told the hospital I was involved, or reported the clinic somehow? I hope to God my letter has made its way to him and he knows I wasn't involved in his big reveal.

I dial the clients then shut down the computer, my skin prickling with tension. Writing about the clinic seemed like such a benign thing, back when I was certain everything would stay confidential – and that even if there *was* a breach, Jeremy would look like a million bucks, the perfect advertisement for Peter's skills. Never in my wildest nightmares could I have imagined things turning out like this.

Before heading back to the flat, I swing by Jeremy's, anxious to see if the note I tucked through the slot in the door is still there. As I approach the now familiar building, my heart picks up pace. I squint at the door, looking for a scrap of white paper.

Bingo! My heart lifts as I realise the letter is nowhere

to be seen. Someone's been by, thank goodness. Now, I can only pray that my words have had some effect – or, at least, have stopped Jeremy from turning me in.

Back at the flat, I try in vain to find something to fill the time, even resorting to a book on customer service Peter bought me for 'professional development'. A couple hours of fruitless page-flipping later, I stick our fillet in the oven for supper and hunt down Smitty for his brushing session, trying not to think about what's taking Peter so long. For the millionth time, I glance at the grandfather clock. It's almost six – Peter's been gone now for hours. Smitty yelps and I realise I've just brushed his face by mistake.

I let him go and pad over to the kitchen, absently taking down the packet of Jaffa Cakes and shoving one after another in my mouth. Even the tangy orange doesn't calm the small knot of tension grinding in my gut.

The flat door swings open and I hastily swallow a mangled hunk of cookie. "You're home! Is everything okay?" My heart is beating so fast that my pulse whooshes in my ears.

Peter places his briefcase neatly by the door in its usual spot, hangs up his coat, then eases himself down on the sofa. "God. What a day."

I settle into a chair across from him. "What happened?" My voice is clogged with fear and worry, but he doesn't seem to notice.

"Well, of course the board wanted to make sure I knew nothing about those columns. Patient confidentiality is critical to the reputation of cosmetic surgery facilities. No celeb will set foot in a place if they think their procedures might end up in a sordid rag like *The Daily Planet*. If anyone at the hospital was involved, it could cause serious damage."

I swallow hard. I hadn't realised the consequences could be so severe – or rather, I'd been so gung-ho to get things going that I hadn't stopped to think about it. Has Jeremy said anything? It feels like someone's sitting on my chest, and I struggle to take in air.

"The hospital cleared me, thank God. If they'd cancelled my operating contract there . . . disaster." Peter focuses in on me, his tone deadly serious. "Look, Serenity. I know you're into the tabloid scene."

"Um, sort of." The banging of my heart is so loud now, it's almost drowning out his voice.

"Have you ever heard of this *Beauty Bits*? I haven't taken too close a look at it yet, but it sounds like whoever wrote it was able to get access to our clinic – or at least had quite a personal relationship with Jeremy. Jeremy's unable to articulate much right now, and the hospital's loathe to press him. They called *The Daily Planet*, but . . ." Peter shakes his head.

"But?" I squeak, caught between relief and horror. Jeremy hasn't turned me in – yet – but I wouldn't put it past Leza to hang me out to dry.

"The legal department just said the paper protects their journalists." Peter shrugs. "Journalists, as if. More like vermin."

I automatically open my mouth to protest, but snap it closed again when I realise Peter's right. What I did wasn't journalism – at least, not the kind I can take pride in.

"Do you think it could be another client?" Peter's brow furrows as he tries to puzzle it out.

"Maybe," I finally manage to say, my mouth dry and my throat scratchy with Jaffa crumbs. Perhaps I *should* tell him; come clean. But what good would that do? He's already been cleared of any involvement, and explaining to him what I've done would thrust him squarely into the 'involved' side of things. No, keeping everything locked up inside as tightly as I can is the only way to go.

"The important thing is, it's over," I say, trying to keep my trembling voice steady. "If I were you, I'd just forget about it." Please please *please* may he just forget about it!

Peter clicks on the TV and stretches out his long legs with a sigh. "I guess so. Anyway, you're right. Jeremy's no longer a patient, so we can put this whole thing behind us and move on. Get back to normal."

"Yeah." I try to smile, but my face feels frozen. Get back to normal? Right now, I can barely breathe.

CHAPTER TWENTY-TWO

"Come on, Serenity." Peter taps his foot as he hovers by the door the next morning. "We're going to be late."

"Okay, okay." Quickly tying a Primark scarf around my neck to cover a toothpaste stain on my blouse, I walk into the corridor. Peter closes the door behind us and practically runs to the lift.

It's Tuesday morning, and my brain is fuzzy from lack of sleep. I lay awake all night, relief that I hadn't harmed Peter's professional reputation mixed with heavy guilt about Jeremy – and a glimmer of hope that somehow he might, he just *might*, respond to my letter.

"Hurry." Peter nudges me into the waiting lift. Suited and booted, he looks polished and groomed, putting his words about returning to normal into effect. Despite my work clothes and heavier than usual make-up, I still look exactly how I feel: like death warmed over.

Inside the clinic, I scoot behind the desk and turn on the computer. Sighing, I open the browser and type in the *Beauty Bits* website, my heart in my throat as I wait for the page to load. Have Mia and Leza managed to find Jeremy? What will they write about today?

I click my fingernails on the desk. Finally, the *Build a Man* icon appears at the top of the screen.

> Getting physical with a beautiful
> woman was our Build a Man's dream
> when he signed up for cosmetic
> surgery. But instead of moving his
> hips, Jeremy's now trying to move
> his lips. After an operation two
> days ago left him brain damaged,
> Jeremy must now begin the long
> journey back to the man he once
> was.
>
> "Jeremy's got it tough," said
> celebrity therapist Keith Kole.
> "He'll need my three-T method to
> recover: time, tenderness, and
> tenacity."

I can't help rolling my eyes at that one. They must be struggling if they had to dig up a quote from a celebrity therapist. Obviously they haven't been able to track down Jeremy, thank God.

At the bottom of the article, small print catches my eye:

> *The Daily Planet* would like to
> thank everyone who has contacted
> us to wish Jeremy well. To respect
> his privacy, *Build a Man* column
> will only run when we receive
> health updates from our Man.
> Coming tomorrow: *Tummy Trends*.
> Read about the latest trend in
> cosmetic surgery – the designer
> belly button – and the pioneering
> surgeon who developed it. Staff
> Reporter Mia Sutton has the inside
> scoop.

I stare at the words. Staff reporter?

Mia's got the job.

I wait for some – any – emotion to hit me, but I feel so removed from it now, as if all my dreams and ambition for that world existed in a former life.

And designer belly buttons? I'm nauseated just thinking about it. Thank goodness they're moving on. I wondered just how long they could keep *Build a Man* going, without any access to Jeremy.

> Please note: *Build a Man* column cannot accept deliveries of flowers, sundry clothing items (including lingerie), perishable goods, or any item apart from standard post. To express your best wishes, please email: **getwelljeremy@beautybits.co.uk**. Any additional items received will be donated to the Knightsbridge Fund for Botox Beauty.

The Knightsbridge Fund for Botox Beauty? My eyebrows fly up. The nerve, donating things sent to Jeremy to a fund supporting cosmetic surgery. I shouldn't be surprised, I guess, but I am.

"Excuse me." My head snaps up. In front of me are two women: an older one with expensive-looking honey-blonde hair and a sharply tailored blazer, and a fresh-faced teenager with wide blue eyes.

"Yes. Hello." I force my lips into a smile. "Can I help?"

"We've got an appointment at nine with Doctor Lycett. Mrs Edith Evans and my daughter, Felicia." She's already turned away from me. "Come, Flic." Felicia trots after her like a puppy.

Jesus Christ. Felicia – whose face is the last place

anyone would *think* to look for a wrinkle – must only be about thirteen. "Excuse me!" I call.

Mrs Evans lowers herself onto a leather chair and points Felicia into the one beside her. "Yes?" she says, once settled.

"Your daughter hasn't been here before, has she?" God, I hope not. "She needs to complete a consultation form."

Mrs Evans waves a hand. "No, no. Doctor Lycett knows us. It will be fine."

I grit my teeth. "Well, if Felicia could just give me a few details for our system . . ."

Mrs Evans sighs. "Flic, go shut that woman up. She's hurting my head."

What a bitch! She *knows* I can hear her. Felicia scurries over to the desk, smiling shyly at me.

"Does Botox hurt?" she whispers, wrapping a chunk of hair around her fingers.

I smile back, debating what to say. I could go with my usual answer – that it's like a pinprick. But according to people who have had it done, it *does* hurt. And the last thing Felicia should be thinking about during her teen years is Botox. When I was her age, my main cosmetic worry was how to put on mascara without poking myself in the eye.

"Yes. It does," I answer solemnly. Felicia's eyes cloud over.

"Crap." She shoots a look at her mother, who's absorbed in a copy of *Tatler*. "I don't really want to do it, you know. But Mother said if I get wrinkles, I'll look ugly."

"Ugly! No way. You're gorgeous." Now I really *do* want to kill Mrs Edith Evans. Imagine telling your adolescent daughter that. Suddenly, I feel so lucky to have the parents I do. They're always saying I'm a beautiful treasure. It's been a couple weeks since we've talked – I really should call them.

"Look," I say, "if you don't want to do it, just tell her. You're too young, anyway."

"I can't." Felicia glances fearfully toward her mother, now flipping through the magazine with such aggression I can hear the snap of the pages from here. "She gets angry and says I'm being stupid."

"Well, I'll tell her, then." I'm not going to let this woman inject her daughter with unwanted substances. That's child abuse.

"Would you?" Felicia's face brightens with hope.

"Sure." I hop off my stool and stride over to Mrs Evans, anger pushing its way up to the surface.

"Yes?" Mrs Evans says when she's noticed me standing in front of her, blocking what little light we do have.

I glance at Felicia, who's hovering beside the desk. "Your daughter has just informed me she does not want to have Botox injections."

"So?" Mrs Evans responds calmly. "I'm her mother. I tell her what she does and what she doesn't want."

"It's this clinic's policy that anyone who has injections must be over the age of eighteen," I say, staring straight into the woman's beady little eyes. It's not – Peter's never had that policy – but hopefully she'll buy it.

Mrs Evans flings the magazine onto the chair beside her. "This is ridiculous. I've been here hundreds of times and I've never heard any such regulation." She stands, tugging down her blazer. "Come on, Flic. Let's go see Doctor Lo. He even does pets. Surely he'll do you, too. "

Felicia gives me a grateful look as her mother drags her toward the door, and I nod back. I may not have saved her from Botox, but at least she won't be getting it on my watch. Before the pair reaches the exit, though, Peter pokes his head into the waiting area.

"Mrs Evans? Are you all set?"

Mrs Evans spins to face Peter, and I can practically see steam coming from her ears. "No, I'm not. This" – she gestures toward me – "*girl* has told me your clinic can't do Botox on anyone under eighteen. Absurd." She marches over to Peter, still dragging poor Felicia. "I tell you, you'd better rethink your policy if you want to stay in business. I have a friend whose baby just got Botox." And with that, she turns up her nose and yanks open the door so hard it bounces off the wall.

"What policy is she referring to?" Peter's voice is dangerously calm as he turns toward me.

"If we don't have one already, then we should. Anyone under eighteen is way too young for Botox."

Peter sighs. "Botox isn't harmful. All we need is parental approval if the child is under the age of consent."

My heart twists. It's what I thought he'd say, but still. "That sends a terrible message to the child."

Peter makes an exasperated noise. "It's a decision they and their parents can make. It's not up to me – I'm just giving them what they want." He stares at me. "Since when do you care? You didn't seem too bothered before."

He's right; I didn't. All this was something funny; something to write pitches about. And when I defended Jeremy's right to have surgery, I even used Peter's 'just giving the people what they want' line. But now, after everything that's happened, I can't stand by pretending to be okay with it all. I'm not.

I take a deep breath. "Peter, I–"

"It's fine, Serenity," he cuts me off. "Just don't do it

again. Your job is simple: take the client's name, give them the form, and get them coffee. I make the policies when they're needed."

My mouth drops open at his condescending tone, and for an instant, I want to tell him where he can shove his policies – right up alongside the giant pole in his butt. Then a wave of guilt hits me at how I've risked the clinic and his dream for mine, and I nod mutely. He's right: it's his business. I'm just a receptionist. Nothing more.

The sooner I accept that, the sooner I can put recent events behind me.

Several mind-numbing hours later, Peter emerges from his office in a cloud of Hugo Boss. "I'm off."

"Where are you going?" I try to look interested, but I shut down sixty minutes earlier after an onslaught from Mrs Hong when I handed her Tiger Balm instead of the pre-injection anaesthetic cream.

"I told you, I have my Society of Cosmetic Surgeons dinner tonight. Remember? The one that was rescheduled? Now, please give Smitty his meds on time. And if you can . . ."

Peter's voice drones on and I tune him out, nodding as my brain flips back to this same moment a few weeks ago – the night I met Jeremy at Providores to get him on-board. Back then, I was so full of hope and excitement. Now, I feel mostly dead inside. And the one bit of me that *is* still open for emotional business is weighed down with fear and anxiety.

Jeremy hasn't notified anyone of my involvement yet, but he hasn't got in touch, either. Does that mean he's still too ill? *Is* he planning to inform the hospital? Will he ever talk to me again?

"Did you get all that, Serenity?" Peter's staring at me, and I jerk toward him.

"Um, yeah. No problem. Smitty, empty dishwasher, fillet . . ." My voice echoes around the empty reception.

Peter drops a kiss on my cheek and clunks the keys on the desk. "Please tidy the files before you go. They're in quite a state. I'll see you later."

I nod again as he leaves. Then, desperate not to be alone with my thoughts tonight, I pick up the phone to call Kirsty. If there's one thing I need right now, it's someone who knows *me*.

Luckily, Kirsty's just as eager for company as I am. An hour later, I've navigated the futuristic Docklands Light Rail and managed to get my exhausted, brain-dead self over to the Hilton at Canary Wharf, Kirsty's home for the past few days. Outside, night has fallen, and the lights of restaurants shimmer in the water and canals. It's a part of London I don't know, and my stomach clenches again as I think of Jeremy showing me the city. I bet he could take me to some great places around here. It's only been a few days since our outing to Borough Market, but I miss him.

"Hey!" Kirsty waves at me from a chair in the reception area. "Is everything okay?" she asks when I reach her side. "I texted you, but you never responded. And God, Ser, you look worse than me. If that's possible."

I take in her wan face and crazy curls flying all over the place. "Gee, thanks. I'm sorry I never got back to you. It's been mental." Quickly I fill her in on the nightmare with Jeremy's operation and how my efforts to protect him backfired, leading to his big *Build a Man* reveal and Peter being investigated by the hospital for suspected breach of client confidentiality.

"Shhhhhiit," Kirsty says in a low voice, drawing out

the word. "If I need a drink after just listening to that, I can only imagine how you must feel. So is Jeremy going to be okay?"

"The doctors don't know." I shake my head. "He might recover completely or . . . he might not." My voice cracks on the last few words, and Kirsty leans over and touches my arm.

I glance up into her sympathetic eyes. "The worst bit of it is, if I hadn't pushed Jeremy into having that surgery, none of this would have happened."

"Look, you know I didn't agree with Jeremy having the operation," Kirsty says, "and sure, you might have given him a little added shove. But he wanted that surgery – I could see how excited he was about the whole thing. No one could have predicted the outcome."

I nod, drinking in her words.

"And you did the right thing, not writing about him after what happened, and trying to protect him by warning the hospital. You couldn't have known Leza would reveal his identity. Jesus, what an absolute witch." Kirsty's eyes flash in indignation.

"I just hope Jeremy gets in touch, so I can make sure he's doing okay and explain everything," I say, sighing deeply.

Kirsty shoots me a worried look. "Listen, Ser, I wouldn't expect too much from him. First of all, who knows how long it will take him to recover? And secondly . . ." She bites her lip.

"I know, I know, I totally betrayed his trust," I rush out before she can say anything. "But I really did think it was in his best interest." Now that I've said it, I realise how silly those words sound. His best interest, right. More like *my* best interest. I drop my head into my hands. How could I have been so selfish? Kirsty's right – it's naïve to expect Jeremy to respond to my letter after everything that's happened. The weight inside me gets heavier.

"I take it you haven't told Peter you wrote the column," Kirsty says gently.

I lift my head. "No. I just thought, it's over now so there's not much point. Jeremy hasn't said anything yet, and I'm praying he won't. And if I did tell Peter, it would put him in a terrible position at the hospital – you know, that someone working for him was involved. Can I imagine the damage to his reputation and the business?"

"It wouldn't be good, and he definitely wouldn't be happy. He's practically married to that clinic." She makes a face.

"Yeah." Peter *is* practically married to the clinic – my relationship with him has always come second. Underneath all my practical reasons for staying silent, I suspect if I tell him what I've done, even if I say how sorry I am . . . that will be it.

Is that what I want? To be with someone who has more passion for his business than our relationship – and who might choose it over me, if push comes to shove? And can I really stand sleeping beside someone each night who doesn't care how his practice affects people? I picture Peter's response to Jeremy's disastrous outcome and think of Felicia, just thirteen, and how Peter was only too willing to jab her full of Botox.

I can't even begin to examine all this right now.

"So how are things with you?" I ask Kirsty, aware I've been fixated on me since I arrived and dying to think about something else.

"Horrible. Tim keeps trying to talk to me at work; I keep hiding in the bathroom to avoid him. Between that and morning sickness, it feels like I spend most my time in there these days."

"God." I don't know what else to say. It sounds so grim.

"Yeah." Her eyes well with tears. "I do love him. It's just a lot to handle right now." Kirsty shakes her head. "Look at the two of us! Ten years ago, would you ever have thought we'd be in such a state? I was sure I knew what I wanted back then. But once I had it, I couldn't run away fast enough."

"I know exactly what you mean." I lean over and put my arms around her. I wish there was a pill we could swallow to fast-forward past all this confusion. The days when we knew beyond a doubt what our futures held seem so long ago. I'm afraid nothing will ever be that clear again.

CHAPTER TWENTY-THREE

The next few weeks pass in a blur as I go from clinic to home to clinic again, with a weekend outing here and there to visit Kirsty in Canary Wharf. Neither of us has made a move in any direction. It feels like we're floating aimlessly through life, unable to break free from our inert state.

The only thing I *do* care about is hearing from Jeremy. I should just be happy he hasn't reported me – and I am, of course – but I'm longing for him to get in touch. With each passing day, though, I'm more and more convinced Kirsty's right: it's too much to expect. I've lost him.

Things between Peter and me have reached a similar inertia. I do what he asks at the clinic and home, moving like an automaton most the time. Peter's so absorbed in his own world that he doesn't notice my lack of response, and since he's been doing paperwork at the clinic most nights, I'm usually alone at the flat.

Peter's working late as usual when my phone buzzes. I scrabble between the sofa cushions to find it, thinking it's probably him asking me to pop the fillet in the oven.

"I'll put them in now," I answer.

"Ser, it's me." Kirsty's voice is tense.

"Are you okay?" I sit up, my heart beating fast.

"I'm bleeding. I'm worried something might be wrong with the baby. Can you meet me at the hospital? I'm about to call a taxi. I tried to get Tim, but he's not answering." She sounds close to tears.

"Of course. But maybe you should call an ambulance?" Horrific images of women lying in pools of blood flash through my head, courtesy of *ER*. "Lie down, put your legs in the air, and call 911. Or whatever it is here."

"It's not serious enough for an ambulance," Kirsty says tightly. "But it's still pretty bad."

I'm already on my feet, shrugging on my coat. "Okay. I'll grab a taxi. What hospital are you going to?" I've no idea which one is closest to her.

"Limehouse Hospital. Hurry, please." She hangs up, and I snatch my keys and two tenners from Smitty's emergency fund, then dash down the corridor and into the lift, willing it to go faster. Outside, it's raining, and little wet beads patter onto my face as I rush toward Marylebone High Street, where there's sure to be a taxi. I flag one down and climb in, instructing the cabbie to go as quickly as possible to the hospital.

Finally – after what feels like forever – the driver pulls up in front of the brightly lit Accident and Emergency Room (why Accident and Emergency? Isn't an accident, by default, an emergency?). I hand him some money then run through the doors, spotting Kirsty on a row of dingy chairs. Her face is paler than I've ever seen, and even her normally springy hair looks flat and lifeless.

"Are you okay?" God, what a stupid question. Even by the way she's sitting – both arms crossed over her womb as if protecting herself from invisible forces – it's obvious she's anything but fine.

Kirsty just shakes her head.

"How much blood was there?" I ask softly.

"There wasn't much, but enough," she says, brow furrowed with worry. "It seems to have stopped now." Kirsty grasps my hand and I almost gasp at the coldness of her fingers. "What if I've lost the baby, Ser? What if it's gone?"

I cradle her hand between mine to get it warm again. "There's no point thinking about that now. Let's wait until the doctors take a look at you before we jump to any conclusions. Have you checked in?"

Kirsty nods. "About ten minutes ago. They asked me to wait for a second."

The nurse behind the glass check-in desk beckons us over, and I can't help making comparisons with the private hospital where Peter works – the contrast is as stark as the difference between an army barracks and a luxury hotel. The chairs here are battered and mended with duct tape, the linoleum tiles worn, and even the plants look like they've been resurrected from the eighteen-hundreds.

"Right," the nurse says busily. "Let's get you in to see a doctor. First things first, they'll do an ultrasound to make sure everything is all right with the baby, and a blood test to make sure Mum is fine. I'm sure it will be okay, love. You say you're about twelve weeks? Bleeding during the first trimester is very common. Just give me a few details, and we'll sort you out."

Kirsty's face relaxes slightly under the nurse's warm, reassuring tone, and she lowers herself gingerly onto a metal chair, scrawling her details on a form the nurse has handed her.

"Now, if you're finished with that paperwork, I'll

get someone to transport you to the ultrasound unit." The nurse points to a rusty wheelchair in the corner. I help Kirsty into the stained seat.

"Can my friend come?" Kirsty asks.

The nurse nods. "Of course. She can take you up. Fourth floor."

I wheel Kirsty down the corridor and over to the lift in silence.

"Want me to try Tim again?" I ask, as the lift creaks and clanks its way upwards.

Kirsty nods slowly. "Yes, please."

Digging out my phone, I find Tim's number in my contacts and hit 'Call', but it goes right to voicemail. "Hi Tim," I say quickly, conscious of Kirsty listening to me. "Kirsty and I are at Limehouse Hospital, in the ultrasound unit. Please call." I don't know what else to say, so I hang up.

"I have no idea where he could be. He's been at work every day – not that we talk. Guess he took my request for space to heart. But he's always there." Kirsty twists her neck to look up at me. "I might have blown it, Ser. Everything. Tim, the baby . . . what if I lose them both? God." She presses her fingers to her forehead.

"I'm sure everything will be fine." I touch her back, hoping my words will come true.

Two hours later, there's good news. The ultrasound shows the baby's heartbeat is steady and strong, and a bit of life has flooded back into Kirsty's face. We're sitting in the ultrasound department waiting to see a doctor to discuss the possible cause of the bleeding, and I've already made three trips to the cafeteria to pick up food for Kirsty.

I've ducked down the corridor to ring Tim several times and I've left more messages, but there's still no sign of him. Even though Kirsty hasn't said anything, her hopeful glances toward the door each time it opens give her away.

"I could have five more of these." Kirsty licks her fingers as she polishes off yet another pastry.

I stare at her with horror. "That's the last of them at the cafeteria. I could head over to McDonald's and grab you a burger, if you want."

"Relax, I'm just kidding." She grins over at me and I smile back, happy to see some colour in her cheeks.

"Kirsty Grainger?" the nurse at the counter calls.

"Come with me?" Kirsty asks, looking nervous again.

I nod and take her arm as we approach the counter.

"Room one," the nurse says, pointing down the corridor.

Inside the small space, the two of us settle into chairs across from a Formica desk. A doctor sweeps in and plonks a file down in front of him.

"Hello, ladies. I'm Dr Chandler. Which one of you is Mrs Grainger?"

Kirsty raises her hand, like we're back at school. Dr Chandler just has that authoritarian air about him. "That's me, Doctor." Her cheeks colour a bit. "And actually, it's Miss."

"Well, Miss Grainger. You have placenta previa." He pauses, takes in the blank look on our faces, and says: "That means your placenta is lower than normal, and, in your case, almost completely covering the uterus."

"How does that affect the baby?" Kirsty asks.

"It doesn't. As your pregnancy progresses, the placenta should move into the right position. We'll keep an eye on it through ultrasounds, make sure everything is all right. And if you have any more bleeding, come to the A&E straight away."

"So the baby's going to be okay?" Kirsty still looks worried.

Dr Chandler nods. "Yes. If you take it easy – no heavy lifting or straining – the baby will be fine."

Kirsty slumps and lets out a deep breath. I can almost see the pent-up tension draining from her.

"I've scheduled you for a follow-up ultrasound in another two months. So if that's everything–"

The door bursts open. "Kirsty? Are you okay? What's going on?"

Kirsty and I turn in surprise as Tim rushes into the cramped room, crouching down beside her. His face is beaded with sweat and his hair sticks up like horns.

"I'm so sorry," he pants. "I just got your messages now. I was at the gym." He's wearing the ratty old Spandex biking shorts Kirsty always mocks, and a flimsy, faded T-shirt.

But Kirsty doesn't seem to notice his clothes. With an expression of absolute relief mixed with joy, she reaches out and draws him to her, burying her face in his neck. Tim folds her in his arms, and the two of them rock back and forth. Kirsty's shoulders heave in silent sobs and I glance away, embarrassed to be witnessing such an intimate scene.

Dr Chandler clears his throat and they look up, as if realising for the first time where they are. Tim straightens, still grasping Kirsty's hand.

"Would you like to have a seat?" Dr Chandler points to a small stool squeezed into the corner.

"Here, have mine," I say, standing. "I'll wait outside." Now that Tim is here, it feels like I'm intruding.

Kirsty shoots me a smile, and I head out into the

corridor, closing the door behind me. Leaning against the wall, I picture the two of them, arms entwined, each gripping the other like they're the only thing that makes sense.

Something shifts in my chest, and a longing pulls at the very core of me. I want that: the closeness, the overwhelming strength of emotion, the knowledge that no matter what life throws their way, they can handle it – together.

How do you know someone's 'the one'? Jeremy asked me, back at Providores. I remember running Peter through my mental checklist: handsome, ambitious, successful . . . he had everything I thought I wanted.

But for the first time, I realise I've left off something critical from my list.

I've left off love.

CHAPTER TWENTY-FOUR

Scanning my wardrobe a few days later, I try for the millionth time to muster up the energy to throw on a clinic-appropriate outfit. The morning is gloomy, with rain falling in big, steady drops, and my mind is buzzing from the relentless questions that have been tormenting me since I saw Kirsty and Tim together. Do I love Peter? Does he love me? Is he really the man I want?

I picture the two of them clinging onto each other in the hospital that night, and the same strong yearning sweeps over me. They're back on solid ground – stronger than ever, Kirsty says – and after everything she's been through, it's good to see Kirsty's finally found her way to what's really important. If only I could do the same.

Reaching into the packed wardrobe, I select a pair of trusty black trousers and a soft cashmere top that always makes me feel like I'm wearing a fuzzy blanket. I've been craving comfort all week – or, at least, a respite from the storm raging inside me.

It's always been obvious Peter and I are different: he's so rational, while 'irrational' could have been my middle name. But we both had ambition, wanted stability and, well, I thought I could somehow make myself be a cool, calm person like him – the now-defunct Serenity v2, perhaps. I've come to realise it's just not possible, though, and I don't even *want* to be like that. So where does that leave us?

"Ready?" Peter pushes into the bedroom, neatly turned out as usual in a dark suit with a perfectly matching paisley tie.

"Almost." I step into my flats. I'm *not* going to wear high heels, no matter what he says. I've had enough of cramps in my arches.

He doesn't seem to notice, placing his hand on the small of my back and propelling me out the door.

A few minutes later, we're in the claustrophobic world of the clinic. Without my tabloid dreams to distract me, it feels like the walls are closing in more and more, until one day they'll finally crush me, and all the fillers in the world won't be able to plump me up again.

I'm so absorbed in my personal nightmare that I barely notice the clinic door opening.

"Hiya!" A chirpy voice cuts across the silence of the waiting room.

My head snaps up. And my mouth drops open.

There in front of me – so tanned she's now the colour of peanut butter – is Princesz Gayle.

"Oh, hello." I turn my head away, hoping she won't look too closely. Thank God I'm completely different from when she last saw me at the launch party – my hair is a mess, I'm not wearing make-up, and I'm sporting a saggy sweater. "Do you have an appointment?" I mumble, staring at the computer screen to avoid meeting her eyes.

"Yeah, at nine, innit?" She props herself up against

the desk. "I'm sure I've seen you somewhere recently."

Oh, shit. "Well, you were here a few weeks ago." I try my best to smile, still gazing at the screen.

"That's right, just before that *Beauty Bits* launch party." She squints, then clicks her fingers together. "Snap! I *knew* I'd seen you somewhere. You were at that party, weren't you?"

"Princesz?" Peter walks into the reception area, and my heart drops. "You ready?"

Her bracelets jingle as she holds up a hand. "Just a sec, Doc. So what did you think? It were a great knees up, hey? Why were you there, anyway? Market research?" She snorts.

"What are you two talking about?" Peter asks in his conversational, yes-I'm-interested-in-my-patients tone.

"Oh, nothing." I make a big show of looking at the clock. "You'd better get started, Doctor. Madame Lucien's at half past, and you know she likes to be prompt."

"Pffffff! Madame Lucien can wait." Princesz puts a hand on her hip. "So, did you have a good time?" She turns to Peter. "We're on about that launch party last month, innit? Your girl here was there, looking fierce."

Peter laughs. "No, I think you're mistaken. Serenity wasn't at any launch party."

Princesz nods, stamping her stiletto on the floor for extra emphasis. "Oh yes, she was. *Beauty Bits*, just last month. I never forget a face, me. That were her."

Peter freezes. "*Beauty Bits*?"

"Yeah, the one with that bloke who wanted to pull birds, but he was too ugly? He was going to get *everything* done, you know." Princesz leers at us.

My head swivels back and forth between the two of them as if they're actors on a stage and I'm in the audience, unable to interrupt. I'm not sure I *could* interrupt, even if I wanted to. My mind has gone blank.

Peter turns toward me, eyes colder than I've ever seen. "Serenity?" he asks in a dangerously calm voice. "Were you at the *Beauty Bits* launch party last month?"

I focus on his face, my mind racing. I'm so tired of hiding things; of playing games; of uncertainty. But I know how important the clinic is to Peter. If he finds out what I've done – how I jeopardised his baby, even if I didn't quite realise it at the time – will he ever be able to forgive me?

Am I ready to find out?

"Yes," I say. "Yes, I was at the launch party."

Peter's face twists with anger before the mask slides back into place. "We'll talk later," he says through gritted teeth as he takes Princesz's arm and escorts her into the consulting room.

In the ten minutes that follow, I don't know what to do with myself. I can't sit still, so I pace up and down the waiting area, the Norwegian pine floor creaking under my flats. How will Peter react? Will he listen to my explanation, or will he chuck me out faster than I can say 'collagen'? Do I mean as much to him as this place, or am I just a fixture in his life that he's got used to having around, like Smitty? And what do *I* want?

Finally Princesz reappears, pays her bill and departs, leaving Peter and I facing each other.

"So?" he asks finally.

I swallow. His face is so cold he almost looks like a stranger, not the man I've spent seven months of my life with. "Peter, I wrote that column on Jeremy," I say quickly, suddenly desperate to get everything out there. "It was all under different names. No one was ever supposed to know it was about Jeremy – or this clinic. I really thought it might do us some good in the end."

Peter stares at me, a slight redness in his cheeks the only sign of anger. "Jesus, Serenity." He turns away and traces my previous route up and down the floorboards. "You could have written about anything. But you had to choose something that would threaten the clinic, didn't you? What if Jeremy informed the hospital's board of directors? And did you even stop to think what might happen if someone *did* connect the dots? Someone like Princesz?"

I gulp. "What did you tell her?"

Peter waves a hand in the air. "I made up a story about how we like to keep in touch with what the media are saying. She's thick as a plank, so it wasn't exactly difficult to fool her. But it could have been someone else. It only takes one person to ruin a clinic's reputation on patient confidentiality."

"I know that now," I say. "I'm so sorry, Peter."

He keeps pacing as if he hasn't heard my words. "Christ! I even brought you into the hospital. That stunt with the OR – that wasn't because you wanted to know more about the surgeries, was it?"

"No." I shake my head as shame seeps in.

"Here I was telling the hospital board there was no way anyone in my employ could be involved, when all this time my own *girlfriend* was doing it behind my back." He stops pacing and turns to face me, and I jerk back from the venom in his eyes. "I can't even stand to look at you right now."

"Peter, I'm so sorry. I–"

"Just go," he spits out. "We're through. Get your things from the flat tomorrow when I'm at work. I don't want to see you again."

"Let me explain," I sputter. "I didn't realise . . ." My voice trails away as he spins on his heels, and a few seconds later, I hear the slam of his office door.

I stand as still as a statue for a moment. I did something terrible – I know that now – by not telling Peter what I was writing. I *knew* he'd be furious, but I had to be honest, to see if our relationship was based on more than chicken fillet and convenience; to find out if it had the strength to survive something tough. Well, now I know. And even though I'm slightly stunned at how quickly we've folded, I'm not surprised.

"Goodbye, Peter," I say softly. Turning, I force myself to walk at a normal speed to the door. I heave it open then stand in the mews, gulping in air.

With just one word, I've chucked away a job, a boyfriend, and a home – my so-called perfect London life, gone in a heartbeat. But the really funny thing?

I don't think I'll miss it at all.

CHAPTER TWENTY-FIVE

"Morning."

Kirsty's voice drifts into my consciousness and I crack open an eye, squinting against the brilliant sun slanting into her guest room. Sitting up slowly, the events of yesterday replay in my head and I wince, recalling the hardened expression on Peter's face when I told him the truth.

I keep waiting for a tsunami of emotions to hit, for a sense of loss to sink in . . . but it just doesn't. Those months with Peter seem like a life lived by someone else, not *me*. And I can't mourn something I don't feel connected to.

"What are you doing home?" I rub my eyes, trying to focus.

"Called in sick." Kirsty grins mischievously at me.

"Really?" The old Kirsty would have gone to the office even if she had dengue fever.

Kirsty shrugs. "Yeah. I figured, what's the point of being labelled a 'delicate pregnant woman' if you can't capitalise on it every once in a while? Anyway, I want to hang out with you today."

My eyes fill with tears. "Thanks, Kirst."

I lean back and look at her properly. A faint swell bulges from under her heavy cable-knit sweater, and her eyes are sparkling. I give her a quick hug, pleased to see my friend looking so happy and healthy.

"Shower, get dressed, and we'll head over to Peter's. We can grab all your stuff and dump it back here. Then" – Kirsty glances outside, where the sun is almost blinding in the November sky – "I dunno, we'll get some fresh air. Celebrate your freedom." She pumps a fist in the air. "Sound good?"

"Yeah. Sounds good." I slide out of bed and into the shower as Kirsty thumps downstairs.

An hour later, after scrubbing myself senseless and downing some very strong coffee, Kirsty and I are standing in Peter's flat. It's strange being back – already, I feel like I'm invading his personal space. Not that it's much different to how I felt when I was living here, really. It never seemed like my home, too.

My small, battered suitcase rests almost exactly in the middle of the parquet floor. It's the same one I stuffed full of my favourite clothes when I left Maine for London, eight months ago now. I stare at the garish *Feed the Hungry* sticker Mom stuck on it, feeling a tiny thread of connection to the person I was before all this began.

"That's everything?" Kirsty asks in disbelief, eying the tiny suitcase with its jumble of clothing. In my own little rebellion, I've left behind my hideous clinic wardrobe for Peter to dispose of.

"That's it." God, I can't believe after several months in London, this is all I have to show for my life here – exactly what I came with. I'm surprisingly okay with that, though.

"Hang on, what's this?" Kirsty picks up something from the sideboard. "It's got your name on it, Ser." She hands me a slim white envelope and I tear it open, fingers trembling. What could it say? Has Peter changed his mind? Maybe he wants me to stay? No matter what's inside, though, I know we're not right for each other. We never were, despite my efforts.

"Oh my God." My hollow laugh bounces off the polished floor as I examine the envelope's contents.

"What?" Kirsty leans closer.

"It's a cheque," I say, still unable to believe my eyes. "A cheque for five thousand pounds" – I scan the accompanying note, written in Peter's tight, neat script – "to ensure non-disclosure of any event that occurred during my time of employment." I meet Kirsty's eyes. "In other words, he's paying me to keep my mouth shut about the clinic and my connection to Jeremy."

I shake my head. Does Peter really think he needs to give me money to keep quiet? Then, guilt hits full force. Can I blame him? Although I never mean to hurt his business, I did risk his career and livelihood, and all behind his back. No wonder he doesn't trust me now.

"Well, maybe you should take it," Kirsty says, shrugging. "God knows, he certainly didn't pay you enough for working at that awful place."

I stuff the cheque back in the envelope and prop it up on the sideboard. "No way. I can't start over living on Peter's money. And taking it feels like admitting I *do* need a pay-off to keep my mouth closed."

Kirsty pats my arm. "I understand. Tim and I can loan you whatever you need until you get back on your feet." Shuddering, she scans the flat. "Now, can we go? Honestly, I don't know how you managed to live here. It's like a funeral parlour."

I can't help smiling as I glance around. Now that Kirsty's pointed it out, I notice it *does* have the still, solemn air of funeral homes.

"Peter loved antiques," I say, then realise I've spoken about him in the past tense. "Come on. Let's get out of here." I feel like I'm struggling to breathe.

"Bye, Smitty," I call out to wherever he's scuttled off to. I'm certainly not going to miss him and his catty ways.

"And goodbye, Peter," I say under my breath. I look around the room a final time, then close the door.

"I never understood what you saw in him," Kirsty says as we leave the building and walk to her house, where we dump my suitcase before heading into Regent's Park. The sky is a deep blue, but the late-November air is freezing and our breath makes clouds. "I never pictured you with a guy like that."

We stroll in silence for a few minutes as I ponder why I *did* stick with Peter, despite all the signs that we weren't a good match. "I guess I thought that's the kind of man I should be with. You know, to be in a grown-up relationship."

Kirsty turns to face me. "Rigid and boring?"

"Peter's not rigid and boring!" I say automatically, then laugh. "Well, okay, he was. He liked everything just so, and he never wanted to do anything but work and watch TV."

Kirsty raises an eyebrow. "Exactly. I see you with a man who's down-to-earth. Who can laugh and joke around, and not take himself too seriously. You know, someone like Jeremy."

My head swivels toward her at the mention of his name. "Like Jeremy?" What is she talking about?

"I saw how you two acted around each other. He definitely had a thing for you. And I can't help thinking you might have felt the same way?"

"Don't be ridiculous!" I say, quickening my pace. Images of Jeremy's green eyes and his soft lips drawing ever closer in the kitchen that day fill my mind, and I can feel heat spreading through my cheeks.

Kirsty shrugs. "Just sayin'. But think about this: do you want to hear from him so badly just because you feel guilty, or is it something more?"

The crunch of the gravel fills my ears as we continue down the path, and I turn Kirsty's words over in my head. I *do* feel guilty, obviously. I'm desperate for the chance to explain everything.

But I miss Jeremy, too. I miss the easy way we could talk about anything, how I didn't feel I had to act a certain way or watch that I didn't say anything stupid. A surge of emotion sweeps over me. I sag onto a nearby bench and look up into Kirsty's sympathetic face.

"It doesn't matter how I feel now, does it? After what I've done, it's clear Jeremy doesn't want to talk to me. Not that I blame him." I press my hands against my temples, trying to block out memories of Jeremy lying on the bed, so pale, his eyelid sagging and mouth twisting.

Kirsty sits down beside me. "Maybe it's time to stop beating yourself up over it. I'm not saying forget about him, but I think you've tortured yourself enough."

I stare out at the boating lake, watching a few brave souls manoeuvre across the water. It's almost noon, but the shadows are long and the sun is low in the frosty sky. The trees are dotted with a few brown leaves clinging to naked branches.

Kirsty's right: I'll never be able to forget Jeremy. I've made huge errors of judgment, hurting those closest to me, and that's not something I can shake off easily. But despite the guilt pressing down on me, I need to accept that as sorry as I am for the mistakes of the past, I may never be able to get absolution – let alone anything

262

more. My heart throbs painfully as I picture Jeremy and I laughing together, the warmth of his hand on mine.

"So what are you going to do now?" Kirsty asks. "You know you can stay with us as long as you need to," she adds.

"Thanks." I touch her arm, grateful for such a wonderful friend. "That's the million dollar question. I just don't know. All I ever thought about was tabloids. Now that it's crashed and burned, I have no idea. I mean, I only have an English Lit degree. It's not like I've got experience actually *doing* anything."

"Of course you do. You've got experience writing for one of Britain's biggest tabloids," Kirsty says. "That's something."

"There's no way Leza would give me a reference," I respond glumly.

Kirsty rolls her eyes. "You're going to let that bitch stop you? If you explain what happened, it would probably work in your favour."

"Maybe," I say. "All I know is I've got to figure out what I want to do, and get myself on track – for real this time." However that's going to happen.

"Come on." Kirsty stands, dragging me up with her. "Let's go back home, have some hot chocolate, and watch *Sex and the City* reruns."

I nod and take a deep breath, the cold air burning my lungs.

"Let's go."

CHAPTER TWENTY-SIX

November morphs into December, and the days fall into a sort of routine, time marching on toward God knows what end. Kirsty and Tim leave for work before I get up, so the house is empty and silent when I finally do roll out of bed. I'm desperate to move forward – to put time and space between me and the mistakes of the past – but I haven't the slightest idea what to do with my future.

Nights of battling to shut off my brain, waking up in a cold sweat after operating-room nightmares, and the constant questions hammering inside my head are beginning to take their toll. I look like a woman in need of Botox, fillers, and facelifts all rolled into one.

Every day, I sit like a zombie in front of the computer, scanning job site after job site as listings parade in front of me. Assistant manager, advertising executive, copy editor . . . I've read so many advertisements, I can practically quote them in my sleep. Sadly, none of this job immersion therapy is making my future any clearer. Maybe I should try wine therapy, I snort. I probably would, but given the sad state of my finances, I'd only be able to afford a thimble-full. I'm down to the last twenty of my final paycheque Peter mailed through – without a note, or any mention of that five thousand pound pay-off. It's like I'm a stranger he's simply dismissed from his life.

I'm just about to raid Kirsty and Tim's alcohol cabinet when the buzzer sounds.

Who the heck is that? It's twelve on a weekday, and everyone I know is gainfully employed.

Peering through the peep hole, I catch sight of the mailman.

"Hi," I say, opening the door. I run a hand through my hair, hoping it isn't sticking up too much – in its overgrown state these days, it seems to have acquired a mind of its own. Serenity v1 has returned full force.

"Package for Serenity Holland," the mailman says in a bored voice, not even bothering to look at me.

I scrawl my signature on his electronic keypad and take the bulging envelope, smiling as I recognise Mom's familiar scrawl in her favourite glitter pen.

I should have guessed; I gave her this address when I first came to London and, since I never told her about Peter, it's where she still sends all my mail.

Gripping onto the package, a strange feeling comes over me. I stare at the return address, and for the first time since settling in London, I actually feel homesick. I'm in no hurry to move back to Maine, but part of me longs for space; for the smell of damp earth and ripe fruit in the greenhouse; and yes, even the ever-present mooing of cows. I was in such a hurry to leave, I never stopped to consider I might miss some of it.

Ripping open the envelope, I slide out a sheaf of papers, along with a handwritten note.

Dear Serenity,

I was cleaning out an old storage
closet and came across these. I
hope you know your father and I
will always be behind you, no
matter what path you choose.
Remember, follow your bliss and
the universe will open doors where
there were only walls.

Love and miss you,
Mom

I roll my eyes at Mom's habit of inserting hippie quotes wherever she can. Instead of sloughing it off without a second thought like usual, though, I stare at the words in front of me. Follow your bliss and the universe will open doors where there were only walls. I'm trying! I want to scream. Goddamn it, I'm trying. But I don't even know what my 'bliss' is. Maybe my future lies in Jaffa Cakes? Which reminds me, I haven't had any for ages . . .

Lifting the incense-scented note, I stare at the stack of yellowed sheets beneath it. The lined paper is dog-eared, and the smell of mildew rises in waves. Squinting, I can barely make out the pencilled letters.

Oh, God. It's the monthly newspaper I used to put together for the commune alumni, back before I'd ever heard of tabloids. I shake my head, smiling at my eleven-year-old self, as memories of my enthusiasm run through me.

It had been one of those wet, windy afternoons in spring and I'd been bored out of my mind, listening to Mom and her ex-commune buddies drone on and on about the good old days. Without a TV to plonk me down in front of, Mom had pushed a paper and pencil into my hands and suggested I take notes, to keep a record of their memories.

Although it'd sounded suspiciously like an assignment Mrs Tranter had given us the year before, there'd been nothing better to do. I'd grabbed the pencil and started listening, even throwing in some questions of my own. Before I knew it, I'd been interviewing Mom's friends – and they'd been eager to talk to me. I'd loved the heady sense of power and the feeling that *I* was a conduit to share their experiences.

I kept up my commune magazine for almost a year before the evil Clarissa mocked me for not knowing about Oprah, sending me straight into the heady sphere of pop culture, celebrity mags, and tabloids.

I lean back on the sofa now, leafing through the pages. How had I forgotten the simple joy of just *talking* to people? Of learning new things, then putting it all together and sharing? Sure, there'd been an element of that with *Beauty Bits*, but it had got all distorted and tied up in the quest to make everything as dramatic as possible.

If it bleeds, it leads, I think, my mouth twisting in disgust. My desire to be part of what I thought was a glamorous world overshadowed any joy I used to feel in writing.

Now, I know I don't need to be part of that world. Even more, I don't *want* to be. But it's not tabloids or broke: there must be thousands of community newspapers and magazines all across London where I could work.

A small current of excitement stirs within me at the thought of reporting again, this time without all the guilt and exploitation. Just being able to write the facts!

Maybe I do know my bliss, after all. I just hope the universe is listening.

CHAPTER TWENTY-SEVEN

Two weeks later, I'm sitting in front of Simon Thetford, executive editor of *The British Journal of Continuing Medical Education* (try saying that in one breath), as he scans my résumé and portfolio. The office is all done up in various shades of beige, a few wilted potted plants and tattered Christmas decorations providing the only splashes of colour. It's exactly what I didn't want, back when my tabloid dreams were alive and kicking. Now, I find the lack of glitz strangely comforting.

It's been a desperate couple of weeks. I've applied for job after job – everything from editorial assistant to writing obituaries – just waiting for the universe to knock down those walls for me. But whoever's in charge obviously had a build-up of wax, because until now, my appeals have fallen on deaf ears. When Simon Thetford called a few days ago, I practically drooled my gratitude all over the phone.

Now, I cross my fingers and send up a fervent plea for success. The damn universe better have had an ear wash, because this job is perfect for me.

"New Dick for the Right Chick?" Simon asks as he

examines my portfolio, peering over the top of his glasses with a tiny smile.

My cheeks go hot. "Well, yes. That was the editorial style of the paper . . ." Not that I need to explain – everyone and their dog knows *The Daily Planet*. "But whatever you may think of the content, my posts received thousands and thousands of comments, and my column quickly became one of the most popular on the site." It's all true, but I just can't be proud.

Simon raises his eyebrows. "Well, it's obvious you can write, and those numbers are impressive."

I nod, holding my breath.

"But I'm not sure this is the right position for you. Our articles are based on fact, you understand."

"I know. That's exactly what I'm looking for. I can be a serious writer." I stare hard at Simon, willing him to see how much I want this. "Please, give me a chance. I've had experience working in a medical clinic" – if you call Botox medical – "and I have vast expertise in cosmetic surgery procedures." That much is true, I think grimly.

Simon studies me for a few seconds. "Let me grab our managing editor, Ryan Nicholls. I know he'll want to meet you and have a quick word before we make any final decisions."

I nod, my heart thudding in my chest. As Simon ducks out of the room, I wipe away the sweat that's gathered on my upper lip.

"Here he is." Simon returns with a small, wiry man almost vibrating with nervous energy. "Serenity, this is Ryan, our managing editor. If you come on-board, you'll report directly to him."

"Nice to meet you," I say, standing and holding out my hand.

"American?" Ryan asks.

"Yes, I'm from–"

"Great, great. Look, I'm really sorry I can't chat. Bit of a crisis right now – we've had an advertiser pull out last minute and we need to fill extra space."

"Have you got something you can use?" Simon's calm voice is a direct contrast to Ryan's anxious one.

"Dermisin's holding a press conference on their new filler today, so we can do a story on that," Ryan responds. "I just need someone over there ASAP."

"Dermisin?" The word pops out of my mouth. I know that company; I used to see their logo on products back at the clinic.

Ryan glances over at me. "Are you familiar with the cosmetic surgery industry?"

I nod. "Yes, it's my speciality." Unfortunately. "I'd be happy to cover the conference for you, as a kind of trial run. Or a test of my skills. Or whatever you want to call it," I babble, desperate to show how motivated and eager I am.

The two men exchange a look, then Simon turns to me with a broad smile. "Well, Serenity, you've convinced me. Welcome to the team. We'll take you on as a junior medical reporter, probationary for three months as usual, then a permanent position after that – all things being well, of course."

"Thank you!" Happiness gushes through me as I shake his hand.

Simon smiles. "Welcome to the team."

Before I can respond, Ryan takes my arm and ushers me from the office. "Thanks so much for mucking in with the Dermisin press conference. We're down a writer and we need to put the February issue to bed tomorrow. It's only the middle of December, I know, but we always work at least two months ahead."

I'm not entirely sure what 'mucking in' means, but

I'm thrilled to begin today. I've already drained one vodka bottle back at Kirsty and Tim's, and I'm now making inroads on the gin. It's either start now or become an alcoholic. "No problem. I'm happy to help."

"Brilliant. Now, come meet the rest of the team quickly, then I'll give you the conference details." Hurrying me around the cubicles, Ryan introduces Phillipa, Henry, and Gareth. They all respond with friendly waves, then turn back to their computers and clack away.

"We're on a tight deadline," Ryan calls over his shoulder. He scurries inside a larger cubicle, grabs a glossy press pack with the elaborate Dermisin logo on the front, and hands it over to me.

"Here you are. The conference is at the Charlotte Street Hotel at eleven." He glances at his watch. "It's half nine now. Should give you plenty of time to get there. Come back afterwards and write up a few lines on it, then we'll go over your employment details."

Ryan throws himself into a swivel chair and swings away from me, hammering at the keyboard.

God, nothing like diving into the deep end. Still, I can do this. If anyone's an expert on cosmetic surgery, it's me – especially after everything I've witnessed. I just hope I can do the article justice.

I thread through the cubicles and head out to the lift, relief flooding into me. Finally, I have a job, a start at something solid. Maybe Mom's hippie quotes aren't as bad as I thought.

CHAPTER TWENTY-EIGHT

The coffin-sized lift deposits me back in the nineteen-seventies-style foyer. I push out the frosted glass doors, then hurry down the busy stretch of road toward Newbury Park Tube station.

Thank God the Central Line train is pretty much deserted. I drop into a seat and scan the Dermisin materials, pleased to see it's all pretty familiar stuff. At least the clinic came in handy for something.

I sigh, thinking about the months I spent there with Peter. We haven't talked since the day we broke up. It's so funny – we lived together, for goodness' sake – but I don't miss him. Guess it goes to show it never was right for either of us, if we could let go so easily.

I exit the Tube at Tottenham Court Road and hustle through the crowds, ducking behind Oxford Street and over to the Charlotte Street Hotel. Inside the foyer, a discrete sign shows that the Dermisin press conference is in Event Room 1, on the lower ground floor. I scurry into the lift and press the button, trying my best to catch my breath and tidy my hair. I look at my watch – ten to eleven.

The lift doors slide open, revealing a scene straight

from a film set. Giant palm trees arch toward the ceiling, and bright orange flowers pop up everywhere. Even the air feels hot and humid, as if I've been transported to the tropics. I pause for a second, wondering if I'm in the right place, before remembering that Dermisin's claim to fame is their use of ethically-sourced plants from the rainforest. Yeah, right.

Rows of chairs are scattered strategically about the room, but hardly anyone's sitting down. A tuxedo-clad waiter circulates with a tray full of champagne flutes, and another waiter serves up strawberries and something that's wrapped in a leaf. Nausea rises as I watch everyone around me gorge themselves, courtesy of a company that makes its profits off people like Jeremy. I breathe in again to try to stop the queasy feeling from spreading, then sink onto a chair. Thank God I'm working for a credible magazine now. Maybe I can finally write a balanced article; get an interview from a doctor who's objective about the whole thing.

"Fancy seeing you here." A familiar smug voice pierces my thoughts.

I turn in horror. There, towering over me in stiletto knee-high boots and another Teflon creation, is Mia. Or, at least, I *think* it's Mia – it's hard to get past her lips to the features behind them. I struggle to keep my expression neutral as I examine the two over-inflated caterpillars on her face, jutting out almost as far as her nose.

"Thought you'd been banished for good from the journalistic world." Mia laughs, biting into a strawberry. The sight of her bulging lips manoeuvring themselves around the small red sphere is oddly hypnotic.

"Hi, Mia," I say quietly, determined not to show her

the emotion that's exploding inside.

"So who are you working for now?" She tosses back her hair and sips her champagne.

"*The British Journal of Continuing Medical Education*," I say, trying to get it all out without stumbling.

"Sounds . . . interesting." Mia's lips stretch into a grin, their surface smooth and shiny. "I'm sure you heard I'm writing for the health and beauty section of *The Daily Planet*. The hard copy," she sneers. "None of that rubbish online stuff. That's not real reporting, anyway."

"That's not what you thought," I say, standing to face her. "Back when you were so desperate to steal *Build a Man*."

"Oh, *Build a Man*." Mia waves a hand in the air. "How is your little friend, anyway?" She raises her voice into a breathy falsetto. "Ooh, Jeremy, I'm so sorry I wasn't honest with you. I've stopped writing that column now – I just couldn't carry on. Please get in touch and let me know where you are." Mia smacks her oversized lips together in a kissing noise, then snorts into her drink. "God, how pathetic."

My mouth drops open as the familiar phrases swirl around me. Those words aren't just Mia making fun. They're *exactly* the same words as in my letter to Jeremy."Wait a second. How did you get that letter?"

"Wasn't exactly rocket science," Mia says, settling into her seat as the Dermisin people file into the room. "After Jeremy disappeared from the hospital, I popped by his house on the off chance he might be there – or someone might know where he was. Instead, all I found was your mushy letter. Straight to the bin." Her lips twist in something like a smile.

My eyes bulge and my mind races. I can't *believe* Jeremy never got my letter. He's lying somewhere thinking I'm still working for the tabloid – and that I'm the one who revealed his identity! I'm so furious even Mia's mammoth lips slide out of focus.

"It doesn't matter now, anyway," she says, removing her notebook from a Louis Vuitton bag. "He's probably still drooling and pissing into a bedpan. Really, you should be thanking me for saving you from a relationship with an invalid."

"Hello, and welcome to the Dermisin Revonuskin press conference."

I try to concentrate on the man at the front of the room, but Mia's words keep circling around my mind. Jeremy might still be 'drooling and pissing into a bedpan', as she so sympathetically put it. But I don't care, I really don't. Because . . . I jerk upright as it hits me. Because Kirsty was right.

What I'm feeling is more than guilt – *much* more. It's the intensity of emotion that was lacking with Peter; the glow that makes my internal organs feel like they're immersed in a warm bath. And now that I know Jeremy doesn't have all the facts, a small ray of hope is growing and growing, like a sun rising inside of me. He believes I revealed his identity, yet he still hasn't turned me in. Maybe, possibly, he can forgive me? I have to get in touch with him somehow.

". . . and that's how our new filler, Revonuskin, works," the Dermisin man finishes a few minutes later. "Thank you all for coming. Questions?" He scans the room, looking pleased with himself.

I grab the literature they've handed us and stand. Even with half my brain trying to figure out how I'm going to reach Jeremy, I've still got more than enough BS here to fill Buckingham Palace ten times over. I can't wait to ask an objective industry expert how an all-natural rainforest product could be manufactured in – I squint at the tiny samples they've handed out – Slough. If writing this article doesn't convince Jeremy I've changed, nothing will. *If* I manage to find him, that is.

"See you later," Mia sneers. "Oh wait, actually, I probably won't. I'll be working in Paris for the next few months as the fashion correspondent." She smirks, tongue darting out to moisten her lips.

I stare at the two glistening orbs, then shake my head. At one time, working in Paris as a fashion correspondent would have been the pinnacle of my dreams. Now, I don't even care.

"Goodbye, Mia. I hope you and your lips have a very nice life together." I turn on my heel, then wend my way through the forest of palms toward the lift.

On the Tube to the office in Newbury Park, I browse through the Dermisin literature, then start making notes for my article. When the train pulls into the station, I have almost all of it written, the final chunk waiting for an interview with an independent source. It's fantastic to be writing seriously – to be accurate, factual, and provide both sides of the story – rather than wondering how to twist the content for maximum impact. Why didn't I think *this* could be exciting, too?

At the journal's headquarters, I jab the lift button impatiently, then rush over to the managing editor's desk. "I'm back. I've got the piece almost done."

Ryan looks up from his computer. "What do you need to finish?"

"Do we have a list of experts on cosmetic surgery?" I ask.

"Yes." Ryan waves a hand in the direction of an empty cubicle. "Take a seat over there – your new home. There's a file on your desktop called 'Expert Sources'." He glances at his watch. "You've got an hour."

I gulp. "No problem." I walk over to the cubicle and settle into the battered chair. The desk in front of me is scarred and stained with ink spots, and the stapler and light look like they've been rescued from a dump. On the desktop, a grimy Mac hunches over like it's exhausted every last drop of energy. I switch on the computer, wait as it rattles to life, then click on the document called 'Experts'.

Thirty minutes later, I've got everything I need. The clacking of my keyboard joins the furious tapping coming from the cubicles around me, and I can't help feeling a sense of teamwork as we all strive to meet the deadline.

"Finished?" Ryan appears over the top of my cubicle.

I nod and motion toward the screen, where my article is displayed in all its glory. "Finished." Ryan bends forward to read it, and my heart starts beating fast as I recall the first time Leza saw my work. What if I haven't made this serious enough? What if it's not what he's looking for?

"Good job." Ryan raises his eyebrows, looking impressed. "Solid, objective, and you obviously know your stuff about fillers." I grin as relief whooshes through me. "Yeah. I do." More than I want to, actually.

"Well, look. It's been a long day. Why don't you head home and we'll go over your employment package tomorrow. Nice to have you on the team." He scurries off before I can respond.

I stare at the article again, proofing the text one final time. Peter would be proud of my scientific accuracy, I think wryly – except for the minor detail that the expert source has discredited all Dermisin's claims.

But it's Jeremy I really want to see this. I don't know

how I'm going to hunt him down. But I know one thing: I'm not going to stop until I find him.

"Let's think about this, then." Kirsty, Tim and I are sitting in the Prince Regent later that night, celebrating my new job and holding a pow-wow on how to locate Jeremy. After crowing for ages how she *knew* there was more to my feelings than guilt, Kirsty got down to business to discuss a 'Finding Jeremy' strategy. Not even my long day can put a damper on the nervous energy sweeping through me whenever I think of seeing him again.

Kirsty pushes back her hair and takes a sip of sparkling water. "Think hard. He must have said something about where his family's from."

I press my hands to my temples, forcing myself to concentrate. "He mentioned his grandmother was from Wales. That doesn't mean *he's* from there, though." But something twigs in my mind when I think of Wales. I'm sure Jeremy said something else about it. I strain my brain, but whatever it is stays hidden, just out of reach. I take another sip of wine to try to dislodge it.

"If his grandmother's from Wales, at least it gives us a place to start. We can look for all the – what did you say his last name was?"

"Ritchie," I say absently, just as the bit of information I was looking for floats into my head. "Wait. He talked about a place in Wales called the Rye Valley. No, the Wye Valley. He owns a converted barn up there. Said it's like heaven or something." I look at Kirsty and Tim excitedly. "Do you think he could be there?"

Tim shrugs. "Well, it's possible. At least we have a region to start with." He glances over at the door and his expression changes. "Um, ladies . . ."

My heart stops as I follow his stare. Peter's coming through the entrance of the pub, and he's not alone. Holding onto his arm and staring up at him like he's a demigod is a woman with long, glossy blonde hair and the perfectly smooth skin of someone who's been Botoxed to within an inch of her life. As she shrugs off her coat, I notice she's wearing a beautifully cut dress that manages to be both sexy and professional at the same time. Together, the two of them look like they've stepped off the pages of a John Lewis catalogue. I try to lower myself in my seat, but it's too late – Peter's eyes meet mine. A look of unease flits across his face before his features relax into their usual placid expression. I raise my hand in a limp wave, and the couple starts to make their way toward our table.

"Hello, Serenity," Peter says stiffly when they're beside us. He nods to Kirsty and Tim, who bob their heads back.

"Hi, Peter. Good to see you." I smile, feeling surprisingly calm. Strangely, despite our acrimonious parting, it *is* good to see him, in the same bland way it's good to see a former classmate from a completely different phase of your life.

The woman by his side taps Peter's arm playfully. "Aren't you going to introduce us?"

The tips of Peter's ears go red, the only sign of his discomfort. "Oh yes. Serenity, this is Christina. Christina, Serenity."

"Pleasure, Serenity." Christina's face strains to smile.

I nod, struggling to find words.

"Christina is the clinic's new Botox sales rep," Peter says, to fill the empty air.

"Great." I toy with the stem of my wine glass, unsure what else to say. I feel so distant from him, the clinic, and that whole crazy world. It's almost difficult to imagine the two of us . . . I shake my head to dispel the image.

"Yes. Well." Peter glances at his watch, then slides an arm around Christina's non-existent waist. "We'd better sit down. Goodbye, Serenity."

"Bye." The three of us watch in silence as the couple glides around the corner out of sight.

"Well, that was awkward." Kirsty puts a hand on my arm. "You okay?"

"Yeah. Yeah, I am." I don't feel upset that Peter's with someone else. And Christina is exactly the kind of woman he should be with – polished, groomed, and gorgeous. Together with a bit of Botox, they can take over the world, one injection at a time.

"Good. Now all we need to do is find *your* man." With the look of determination on Kirsty's face, I'm sure she could have uncovered Osama Bin Laden in record time.

Two hours later, though, we're no closer. Despite poring over Google Earth back at the house – and spotting plenty of sheep engaged in rather risqué activities – we've yet to track down Jeremy.

"If he said it's within view of an abbey in the Wye Valley, he must mean Tintern Abbey." Tim points at a tiny dot on the computer screen. "Right here."

Kirsty chews her lip. "But what if there's more than one abbey in the Wye Valley? By the looks of things, it's a pretty big area."

Tim shrugs. "We've got nothing else to go by. Worth giving it a shot. Let's zoom in more. Maybe we'll see some barns around there." He clicks the mouse, and green blobs give way to fields and trees.

"Go left a bit." I hold my breath, waiting for the satellite image to come into focus. I could be looking at Jeremy's house in a second!

"There it is. That's Tintern." Tim squints at the screen. Stone columns and peaks rise up from a grassy field. Nearby, we can make out a few houses and settlements scattered here and there within view of the ruins. Any one of them might be Jeremy's. My heart drops. I don't know what I was expecting – a big sign with a flashing arrow saying 'Jeremy's house'?

"I'll do a search around the area to see if there are any hospitals or rehabilitation centres nearby. Jeremy might still be there." I gulp, wondering what condition he's in now.

"That's probably the most practical place to start," Tim agrees.

"I'll help you when we're home from work tomorrow." Pushing back from the computer, Kirsty lets out a giant yawn. "Right, I'm off to bed. Coming, Tim?"

He nods. "Night, Serenity."

"Night." I watch them go up the stairs together, then turn back to the screen, staring at the houses nestled against the countryside. In one of them, Jeremy might be puttering around the kitchen, plating up that yummy spaghetti . . . or kicking back in the living room, watching TV. On a whim, I pick up my phone, find his name in my contacts, and hit 'Call'. But it disconnects again.

Maybe he's blocked my number. I just hope that when I finally reach him, he won't block me.

CHAPTER TWENTY-NINE

"Got something to show you." Ryan sticks his head over the top of my cubicle, and I can't help smiling at the alfalfa sprouts his hair has formed. If possible, he looks even more like a hedgehog than, well, a hedgehog.

I push my chair back from the desk – quite a feat, really, since one of its wheels is broken.

"What is it? Not more wonderful photos of a digital rectal examination, I hope." I've recently undergone the office initiation of having to log the most cringe-worthy set of photos known to humankind. I shudder again, just thinking about the location of the doctor's fingers.

"Plenty more where those came from," Ryan jokes. "But no." He scoots around the side of the cubicle and hands me a shiny, glossy copy of the February issue. "Here – your first issue. Well, the proof copy, anyway. Your article is toward the front, if memory serves. Have a look through and let me know if you spot any errors."

I glance down at the thick magazine in my hands, pride growing inside of me. It's only been a week, but I'm really liking it here and starting to settle in, despite knowing *way* more now than I ever needed to about rectal exams. This job isn't where I want to be forever, but it's a start.

"Up for a bevvy?" Ryan interrupts my thoughts. "It's a tradition here. Every Friday, we all head out for a drink down the pub across the street. And it's the last Friday night before Christmas, so even more reason to join us."

"Um, sure. You guys go on, though. I want to do a bit more on this article." I gesture toward the screen.

Ryan nods and disappears around the side of the cubicle. I type a few more words into my feature on old-age dementia then rub my eyes, fatigue weighing down every muscle. I've spent the past few nights on a desperate mission to find Jeremy, but phone call after phone call to almost every hospital and rehabilitation centre in Wales has been fruitless. I've tried Jeremy's mobile at least fifty times each night, and I've walked by his house on Welbeck Street every day on my way home from work. But . . . nothing.

I shut down the computer as the office empties around me and silence descends. Then, slowly, I open the cover of the magazine and flip through the pages until my article appears.

Independent Scientist Refutes Dermisin Claims, the headline reads in stark black and white. There aren't any graphics, polls, or pretty pictures. The words are written in small font, crammed in on themselves so you almost need to squint. But they're serious, solid, and all mine. Ryan's made a few minor punctuation changes here and there, but the article is almost exactly as I'd written it.

Reading through the rest of my words, the feelings of pride and accomplishment grow stronger. This is me – *this* is the kind of journalism I want to be doing. It seems so clear now that I wonder how I ever desired anything different.

If only . . . if only I could find Jeremy and tell him I know what I want now. Not tabloids. Not Peter, but something real, something solid. *Him.*

Determination floods through me and I get to my feet. I'm done trying to track down Jeremy from afar. This mountain's going to Mohammed – even if the mountain doesn't exactly know where Mohammed is. George Bush isn't the only one who can smoke people out. I'll smoke out Jeremy from the Welsh wilds if it's the last thing I do.

I tear out of the building and down the street past the pub, smiling to myself at the group's stunned faces as I fly by them.

"See you Monday," I shout, not even caring they won't be able to hear me through the glass. I'm going to that abbey and finding Jeremy's barn. Somehow. And hopefully he'll be in it!

On the Tube back to Kirsty's, I formulate a plan: I'll rent a car and drive to Wales. My license from back home is still valid, and Kirsty might be able to lend me some money until I get paid. I gulp just thinking about navigating my way across England on the wrong side of the road, but it's the most practical thing. Now that I've made up my mind, I want to get to Wales as quickly as possible. A smile spreads across my face and my heart starts beating faster as I picture Jeremy's surprised expression when he sees me. I bite my lip, remembering he still thinks I revealed his identity. Fingers crossed he's surprised in a *good* way.

Out of breath, I burst into Kirsty's. Thankfully Kirsty and Tim are home, puttering around in the kitchen.

"Kirst! Need a favour." I collapse onto the kitchen chair, kicking off my flats.

"Are you all right?" Kirsty glances over at me, eyebrows raised. "What, have you just run a marathon?"

"Pretty much." I peel the sweaty blouse from my skin, flapping the fabric to get some air. "Can I borrow some cash? I'm going to rent a car and drive to Wales."

"What? Tonight?"

"Yes. I can't wait any longer." I try to make my breathing even and regular. "I'm tired of sitting around, waiting for Jeremy to get in touch."

"So you managed to find out where he is?" Kirsty asks.

"Um . . . well, that's the thing. I haven't exactly found him yet. I figure I'll go up, drive around, and get the lay of the land."

Kirsty hands a spoon to Tim and pulls out the chair beside me. "I know you want to tell Jeremy how you feel and make sure he's okay," she says. "But that sounds like a recipe for disaster. You could get all the way up there and find nothing. Or" – she touches my arm – "he could still be really sick. Remember my grandpa after his stroke? It took him ages to get better again. And even when he was fully recovered, he wasn't the same."

I shift in the wooden chair. When we were growing up, Kirsty's grandpa was the neighbourhood kids' favourite. He always had sweets, a big grin, and a belting belly laugh – kind of like Santa. He'd take us on treasure hunts through the fields, and he always listened. But after his stroke, he seemed sad and distant. He never returned to the man we loved.

A small flash of fear goes through me. What if Jeremy's not the same man? What if he hasn't recovered, if he's distant and bitter now, too?

"I need to see him, Kirsty," I say, holding her gaze.

"That's all. However he responds, I can deal with it."
My voice is strong, but inside I'm not so sure. *Is* it
enough for me to see him, to tell him how I feel? What
if he just blanks me?

I shake my head. I have to try, whatever the
outcome.

Kirsty nods. "Okay, then. Do you want me to go
with you?"

I turn the idea over in my mind. It would be good to
have company, but this is something I need to do on
my own. "Thanks, but no. I'll be fine."

She reaches over and gives me a quick hug. "I hope
you find him. And I hope you get what you want."

I give a short laugh. "Me too, Kirst. Me too."

A few hours later, I'm on the M4 highway in my little
rental car on the way to Wales. Darkness has closed in,
and all I can see for miles ahead are the red tail lights of
thousands of people fleeing London. I had a few hairy
moments getting through some roundabouts (has this
country never heard of traffic lights?) onto the
motorway, but thanks to the car's SatNav, it's been
smooth sailing ever since. I've been driving for almost
two hours, and the rhythm of the road is hypnotic.

In the distance, the lights of a bridge rear up in front
of me. Glancing at the SatNav, I see it's the bridge
spanning the River Severn, dividing England from
Wales. My palms grow clammy and cold on the
steering wheel. I'm getting close to Jeremy – once I
cross the river, it looks like it's only about ten miles to
Tintern Abbey. And then . . .

I shove away my nervousness, slowing to pay the
bridge toll. I'll find him. I will. I can't imagine going
back to London without seeing him, without
expressing how I feel.

Even if – I take a breath – even if he doesn't want me.

The bridge arches over the dark water, and I steer the car across the river and down into Wales. *Croeso i Gymru*, a sign spells out in what I guess is Welsh – the jumble of letters is unlike any other language I've seen. I pull over onto the shoulder of the road, pondering my next step. Maybe I should have planned this better, but all I could think about was getting here.

It's past ten now, and the roads are quiet. I roll down my window and breathe in the cold, fresh air scented with dead leaves and earth, so different from the gritty air of the metropolis. The only sound is the quiet whoosh of cars in the distance, and the stars above shine brightly. I forgot stars could be so dazzling – in London, you're lucky if you can catch sight of the moon. For the first time since leaving Maine, it feels kind of nice to be free from the grip of the city.

As much as I want to hunt down Jeremy, it's a bit too late to go investigating country barns. I shiver, roll the window back up, then dig out the guidebook on Wales that Kirsty packed in my bag. I'll just call a B&B in – I glance up at a road sign – Chepstow. Book in for the night, then start out tomorrow. I scrounge blindly in my black hole of a bag for my mobile, but none of the objects I grip are phone-shaped.

God. Cursing myself for being so disorganised, I dump the bag's contents onto the front seat and rummage through them. I couldn't have forgotten my phone. I couldn't have! No one sets out on a cross-country journey without a phone, right?

Wrong. Apparently I do. I shake my head, remembering Kirsty telling me to make sure to charge my mobile. I'd put it on the charger in the lounge . . . and left it there. I thump the steering wheel, then take a deep breath. Okay. Not a big deal. I'll just drive into Chepstow and find the tourist information centre or something; maybe spot a hotel on the way.

I key in my destination then start up the car engine, following the calm voice of my SatNav as it guides me through yet another roundabout and toward the town. The land slopes downwards, and I navigate between white-stoned buildings and under a narrow archway. Lights shine from pubs, and the streets are dotted with people here and there, wrapped up warmly. Christmas lights twinkle from boughs in shop windows, and I can't help being charmed.

Ah, there's the tourist information centre. And it's – my heart sinks as I take in the dark, deserted building – closed, of course. Inching down the empty street, I scan the white-washed houses, sagging in relief when I spot a building with a sign reading 'Chepstow Inn'. Yellow light streams from its windows, and inside I can see someone behind a desk. Thank God. After parking the car, I grab my bag and duck into the cosy interior.

"I'd like a room for the night, please." I hold my breath there's space at the inn.

"Of course. Just fill this out." The white-haired man at reception slides over some paperwork. His accent is lilting and soft, like Jeremy's but stronger. "Would you prefer a castle view or river view?"

There's a castle? I didn't even see it. "Um, castle, please." I love the thought of waking up to a castle.

He hands me an old-fashioned heavy metal key. I make my way to the room, suddenly exhausted. Once inside, I sink down on the soft white duvet, and before I can even kick off my boots, I'm asleep.

CHAPTER THIRTY

I awake the next morning to a strange white light seeping through the thin net curtains. I sit up slowly and yawn, trying to get my bearings. Gazing out the large window in front of me, I notice a stone castle sitting proudly on the side of a snow-covered hill. Something about the white blanket makes the castle seem otherworldly.

I stand and stretch, every muscle in my body protesting. My head is fuzzy and my neck sore, but even that can't stop the excitement building inside me. Today is the day. I'm going to find Jeremy.

One glimpse in the mirror brings me back down with a thud. Looking like this, I'd probably scare Jeremy back into a coma. My hair wings up over one ear like some kind of alien appendage, and mascara has trickled down my face to create a look even a raccoon would shun. I take a quick shower, carefully dry my hair, and ensure my mascara is clump-free. For good luck, I even slick on some lipstick before my customary gloss, then pinch my cheeks like they do in the movies. There, I think as I smack my lips. Ready to face the world. And Jeremy.

After gathering up my things, I head down to the reception and hand over the remaining notes that Kirsty's lent me. Thank God I'll get paid soon.

"You'll want to be careful driving out there," the man says as he checks me out. "They haven't got 'round to gritting the roads yet."

"Oh, I'll be fine." I look out the window at the small coating of snow. I don't know what all the fuss is about – back home, this wouldn't even qualify as a flurry.

I find out when I try to get my little car back up the hill. It goes a few feet, then slides sideways. Goes a few feet, then slides sideways – and repeat, a few hundred times. Thank God it's still early and the roads are empty. Finally, heart in my throat, I make it to the top of the hill and ease the car down the road, following the brown heritage signs and my trusty SatNav toward Tintern Abbey.

Despite my shaking hands and the car's slippery tires, I can't help noticing the beauty of the countryside. Trees gilded in white arch over the road, and hills swell in the distance. I gulp at the sheer drop on one side and the sign for falling rocks on the other, trying not to think what would happen if I lost control.

The road twists and turns, and finally I descend into a valley. To my right, I catch a glimpse of majestic stone ruins rising up from the land like a skeleton. Tintern Abbey, a sign says, and I pull off into the large car park and get out of the car. The graceful arches of the ruins are mesmerising, merging with the hills around it like something from a fairytale. I swivel in the early morning silence, taking in the valley's panorama. I can see why Jeremy loves it here so much. It *is* a piece of heaven.

'Follow your bliss and the universe will open doors where there were only walls.' Mom's quote pops unbidden into my head. A smile tugs at my lips as I run my eyes over the abbey's crumbling stone walls, that strange grey light streaming in through large gaps where doors once stood. This must be a good omen, right? I've followed my bliss, straight to the abbey. And here, there aren't even doors. I scan the valley again, sure Jeremy's nearby. I'm almost tempted to bellow out his name *à la* Rocky (Ad-ri-an! Jer-e-my! They even have the same number of syllables) but cars pulling into the car park stop me from recreating my favourite movie scene.

Two women get out, and I hear the chatter of their voices as they unlock the visitor centre, a small building a few yards from the gateway to the ruins. I hurry toward it, my breath making white puffs in the frosty air.

"Excuse me," I say when I finally reach them, just as they push open the doors.

"We're not open yet, love," a ruddy-cheeked, rounded woman responds. "Give us a half-hour, all right?" Her accent is even stronger than the man's back at the hotel, and its down-home warmth makes me feel cosy despite the cold.

"I'm looking for someone. Someone who lives around here," I blurt out before they can shut the door on me.

"Oh? Well, it's a small place, here. We might be able to help. What's the name?" The woman peers at me.

"For goodness' sake, Bronwyn," the other woman says. "Let her in. It's freezing."

I'm ushered inside and before I know it, Bronwyn's poured me a cup of tea from a Thermos. "So who are you looking for, dear?"

I take a sip of hot liquid, warming my hands around the mug. "His name's Jeremy. Jeremy Ritchie. I think he converted an old barn around here."

"Ah." Bronwyn taps the side of her head with a finger. "Jeremy Ritchie. The name does ring a bell."

I stare, my insides about to explode.

"Mary," she calls to the other woman bustling behind the counter. "Do you know someone called Jeremy Ritchie?"

Mary nods. "Isn't he the one who took over the Jones's barn? Just up the hill there?" She waves a hand behind us.

"Yes, I think that might be him. Fastest way to get there is to leave your car here. Go across the river on the footbridge, then follow the track up the side of the hill. You'll come to an old farmstead. Your man's in the barn, not the big house. Mind you don't disturb Mrs Jones."

"Great. Thank you so much." My heart's pounding and I don't even look back as I race out the door and along a small river track until I come to a narrow bridge. I thump across it, ignoring the curious looks from locals with walking sticks out with their dogs. My breath's coming fast and my chest burns, but I can't stop. Not until I find Jeremy.

I push between trees clogging the narrow path, not even flinching as snowy branches slap my face. Up ahead, the track merges with a gravel road, leading to a wooden gate. I unlatch the gate and gulp in some air, crunching across loose stones toward a clearing. A large wooden barn nestles under snow-covered trees. Further down, there's an old farmhouse, smoke curling from its chimney.

I take a few steps toward the barn, then stop stock-still in the middle of the clearing. Just there, behind those walls, is the man I've been searching for. Now that I'm so close, I almost want to stay in this limbo state between happy reunion and rejection.

But I didn't come all the way to Wales to chicken out now. Moving toward the barn, my legs churn faster and faster as I get closer, so that I'm almost running by the time I reach the door. I grab the iron knocker and rap it hard. Silence. I knock again, even louder. It's a big barn. Maybe Jeremy's in another part of it. Or maybe he's sleeping.

Still silence.

Right, well, he could be having mobility issues. The doctors did say it might take time to fully recover. I'll just wait, be patient. The last thing I want is to annoy him by rapping again if he's on his way. I sag against the door, breathing in the fresh scent of the wood.

Five minutes later, I've had my fill of pine, and there's neither sight nor sound of Jeremy. But I will not be defeated. He *must* be here. Pushing away from the door, I round the corner of the barn and peer through a window. I can't see anything in the dim light inside. Maybe he's popped out for a second, to get some . . . coffee or something. Although God knows where you'd pop out to get coffee in these parts.

I tramp around to the back of the barn, where a small stream tinkles through ice-covered tree roots. Sinking down onto a bench, my shoulders lift in a sigh. I'll just hang out here for a while. Jeremy will have to come home sooner or later.

"Hey! You!"

My head snaps up. An angry woman in rubber boots is dragging a large German Shepherd toward me.

"What are you doing here?" she asks. "This is private property."

"Oh!" I scramble to my feet. "Sorry. I was just waiting for Jeremy Ritchie. I'm a friend of his." I hope.

Her face softens slightly. "Ah. Well, you've a long

wait. He's gone. Left early this morning."

My heart drops. "Gone? Do you know where?"

The woman shakes her head, yanking the chain as the German Shepherd tugs on it. "Sit *down*, Judas." The dog whines. "No idea. Just packed up the car with his things and left. Poor lad. Been through so much lately."

My ears perk up, and I scan her face for any sign of how Jeremy is now. "Is he all right?"

She gives me a suspicious look. "Thought you said you were a friend."

"I am, it's just . . ." My voice fades away.

"Go on, now," the woman says, advancing on me. "Before I call the police." As if on cue, Judas gives a low growl, baring his teeth.

I hold up my hands and back away, eying the fierce dog and the even fiercer woman. "Okay, okay. If you do see him, can you tell him Serenity stopped by?"

The woman snorts, and Judas starts barking.

"Guess that's a no," I mutter, quickening my steps around the side of the barn and back onto the track. It's raining now, and clumps of sodden snow plop off the trees. One lands with a giant splodge right on my head, dripping down the side of my face. I don't even bother wiping it away, and the liquid mingles with the tears spilling from my eyes.

That's it, then. Jeremy's not here. And by the sound of things, he won't be back for a while – there's no point waiting. I pull my sodden coat around me and squish back across the footbridge, cold seeping into my boots with every step I take.

"Find your man?" Bronwyn sticks her head out the door of the still-deserted visitor centre as I pass.

I try to return her friendly smile, but the corners of my mouth refuse to budge. "No."

I'm beginning to think I never will.

CHAPTER THIRTY-ONE

The drive back to London is endless. I sit in the car for hours, caught in traffic jams as far as the eye can see. My damp clothes cling to me, and even though I have the heating on high, I still feel cold and shivery. Nothing can reach the pit of ice forming inside – the little knot of fear that I'll never find Jeremy; never be able to tell him how I feel. Several times I reach for the phone to call Kirsty before remembering it's still in the lounge, on the charger. Being cut off gives me a strange feeling, like I'm in my own little cocoon of time and space.

It's dark when I finally head out of the Baker Street Tube after dropping off the rental car. The rain has stopped, but everything is damp and frigid. Christmas lights on the houses lining the street reflect on the wet pavement. All around me, people hurry home, carrying shopping bags and packages. Despite the rain, the air is festive – making me feel even more isolated.

Tiredness seeps through my bones with every step as I drag my aching body down the street and open the door to Kirsty's. Kirsty and Tim's voices drift down from the bedroom upstairs.

"I'm back!" I shout, dropping my bag in the hall and rounding the corner to the lounge.

I freeze.

There, on the sofa in front of me, is the man I've been waiting – longing – to hear from.

"Jeremy?" I breathe, unable to believe my eyes. His cheeks are hollow and he's lost some weight, but it's *him*.

He smiles, and my heart leaps when I see that his face is back to normal. "Yes."

I take a small step toward him, almost afraid he's a mirage that will disappear. "What are you doing here?" My brain spins frantically, trying to work it out.

Jeremy fixes me with those green eyes and my heart starts galloping. "I didn't think I'd ever want to see you again, you know."

A stab of pain hits me, so intense I can barely stay standing.

"When the hospital told me about the column and I figured out what you'd been up to . . ." His voice trails off. "Well, I wanted to put as much time and distance between us as possible."

"I'm so sorry, Jeremy." My mouth is dry with fear and my voice cracks. "I'm sorry I lied. I never thought it would hurt you – it was all supposed to be anonymous. But then my editor revealed who you were, and, well . . ." I wince as my stomach twists with guilt and regret.

"I know you tried to protect me," Jeremy says, eyes softening. "Kirsty told me everything."

"But how–"

"I was at a rehab unit for a few weeks in Newport. They released me as an outpatient once I was well enough to get by without help. I couldn't face going back to London, with everything that happened here. So I went to my place in Tintern."

Tears fill my eyes as I imagine him there alone. "I'm

sorry I pushed you to have that surgery."

"I wanted to be angry with you, Serenity; to blame someone for what happened to me. When I found out you lied, it gave me the perfect excuse. I didn't want to hear any explanation. I didn't think there could be anything to justify what you'd done, so I blocked your number."

He sighs. "The truth is, I was mainly angry at *me* – that's why I couldn't bring myself to report you to the hospital. You weren't honest, sure, and you encouraged me to go through with the operation. But none of this would have happened if I hadn't been on-board with the makeover. I was the one who made the decision. Not you."

We hold each other's gaze, tears dripping down my cheeks as the icy coldness inside me begins to thaw.

"But I realised that I missed you, despite everything." Jeremy drops his head, then meets my eyes again. "No, more than just missing you."

I nod, unable to push any words past the lump in my throat as a volcano of happiness erupts in my belly.

Jeremy smiles gently at me. "So I called the clinic yesterday. I had a whole story made up about aftercare treatment, but I just wanted to talk to you. See how you were." His cheeks flush. "And then when the woman who answered told me you were no longer working there, I tried your mobile." He gestures to the corner, where it's still plugged in. "I called and called, but you didn't answer. So I came down to London."

A slow smile tugs at my lips as the heat within me rises.

"Kirsty finally answered your phone and told me everything – about you and Doctor Lycett, the tabloid, your new job. She said you'd gone to Wales to find me, and I came here to wait for you."

I take another step closer, my smile growing wider. "I've been trying to find you, to get in touch for ages. Because" – I swallow hard – "because, I really need to tell you . . ." My voice fades as I try to get the words out, to let him know how I feel. Now that Jeremy's here in front of me, everything seems to be stuck inside. Everything except for the bright flame burning in my chest, happiness streaming from my every pore.

Jeremy lifts a hand in the air to stop my halting explanation and struggles to his feet. My eyes widen as I notice the metal cane he's leaning on. I almost move to help him before I see the determination in his eyes. He takes a few shaky steps then I practically fly toward him, closing the gap between us until we're face to face.

I lift a hand to his stubbly cheek and trace those little lines by the side of his eye, and all of a sudden, we're kissing. Jeremy's cane clanks onto the floor as he slides his arms around me, pulling me tightly against him. His lips are just as soft as I imagined, and his heart thuds away against mine.

I wind my arms around his neck and breathe in the spicy scent, then pull back to look at his face again.

"What?" he asks, brow crinkling.

I shake my head, grinning so hard my face aches. I know things won't be easy, that the road ahead will be full of twists and turns. That Jeremy still has a long way to recovery; that I'll need to work hard at my new job to be successful.

In my future, there won't be any glitz, and there definitely won't be glamour.

Nothing will be perfect – not by a long shot.

But you know what?

That's just the way I want it.

THE END

COMING SOON:
Construct A Couple

With a great job at a reputable magazine and a man who's the perfect match, Serenity Holland thinks she's laid the foundation for an ideal London life. When a routine assignment uncovers a shocking secret threatening her boyfriend's livelihood, Serenity decides to leave nothing to chance, taking matters into her own hands. Soon, though, she realises keeping secrets isn't as easy as she thought . . . and the consequences are far worse than she ever imagined.

ABOUT THE AUTHOR

Talli Roland writes fun, romantic fiction with a touch of snark. Born and raised in Canada, Talli now lives in London, where she savours the great cultural life (coffee and wine). Despite training as a journalist, Talli soon found she preferred making up her own stories — complete with happy endings.

Talli's debut novel *The Hating Game* was short-listed for Best Romantic Read at the UK's Festival of Romance, while her second, *Watching Willow Watts*, was selected as an Amazon Customer Favourite. Her novels have also been chosen as top books of the year by industry review websites and have been bestsellers in Britain and the United States.

To learn more Talli, go to www.talliroland.com.

ALSO BY TALLI ROLAND

The Hating Game

When Mattie Johns agrees to star on a dating game show to save her ailing recruitment business, she's confident she'll sail through to the end without letting down the perma-guard she's perfected from years of her love 'em and leave 'em dating strategy. After all, what can go wrong with dating a few losers and hanging out long enough to pick up a juicy £200,000 prize? Plenty, Mattie discovers, when it's revealed that the contestants are four of her very unhappy exes. Can Mattie confront her past to get the prize money she so desperately needs, or will her exes finally wreak their long-awaited revenge? And what about the ambitious TV producer whose career depends on stopping her from making it to the end?

I thought THE HATING GAME was incredibly well written . . . I really found myself blown away with Talli's debut novel. She's a fantastic story-teller and I really can't wait to see what's next from Talli. She could become a huge Chick Lit star, there's no denying it.
Chick Lit Reviews

THE HATING GAME is a wryly observed take on reality TV and the numerous twists and manipulations that take place had me gripped but there is also a wonderfully romantic story running underneath which had me rooting for Mattie to come out as a winner. This is chick lit with attitude and I loved it!
One More Page

Watching Willow Watts

For Willow Watts, life has settled into a predictably dull routine: days behind the counter at her father's antique shop and nights watching TV, as the pension-aged residents of Britain's Ugliest Village bed down for yet another early night. But everything changes when a YouTube video of Willow's epically embarrassing Marilyn Monroe impersonation gets millions of hits after a viewer spots Marilyn's ghostly image in a frame. Instantly, Willow's town is overrun with fans flocking to see the 'new Marilyn'. Egged on by the villagers – whose shops and businesses are cashing in – Willow embraces her new identity, dying her hair platinum and ramming herself full of cakes to achieve Marilyn's legendary curves. But when a former flame returns seeking the old Willow, Willow must decide: can she risk her stardom and her village's newfound fortune on love, or is being Marilyn her ticket to happiness?

WATCHING WILLOW WATTS is made up of a bevy of fun and interesting characters, which made this book interesting to read throughout. Light-hearted, humorous, and a sweet happy ending made me a happy reader!
Chick Lit Plus

A fresh and well-thought-out narrative, likeable characters, dry wit and an interesting perspective on overnight fame.
Chick Lit Club

AVAILABLE NOW
AS E-BOOKS AND PAPERBACKS.

Printed in Great Britain
by Amazon.co.uk, Ltd.,
Marston Gate.